Drinking Coffee

Elsewhere

⟳

Drinking Coffee Elsewhere

ZZ PACKER

RIVERHEAD BOOKS

a member of Penguin Putnam Inc.

New York

2003

This is a work of fiction. Names, characters, places, and incidents either are the product of the author's imagination or are used fictitiously, and any resemblance to actual persons, living or dead, business establishments, events, or locales is entirely coincidental.

Riverhead Books
a member of
Penguin Putnam Inc.
375 Hudson Street
New York, NY 10014

ISBN 1-57322-234-8

Printed in the United States of America

Book design by Stephanie Huntwork

To my mother,
Rose Northington Packer,
who "made a way out of no way"

Acknowledgments

This collection would not have been possible without support from the Rona Jaffe Foundation, the Mrs. Giles Whiting Foundation, the Wallace Stegner/Truman Capote Fellowship program, and the MacDowell Colony. Much love to my two families, the Northingtons and the Packers, both of whom raise storytelling to an art.

Many thanks to my mentors at the Iowa Writers' Workshop: Frank Conroy for his ever-vigilant eye; Marilynne Robinson for her infinite wisdom; Stuart Dybek for his unflagging support and friendship; and James Alan McPherson, who is an example to us all.

I am forever in the debt of Connie Brothers, Deb West, and Paul Mcintel, all of whom preserved my sanity and made Iowa a happier, brighter place. John Barth, Stephen Dixon, and Allen Grossman at Johns Hopkins University were incredible models of how to live a "writer's life." Special thanks to Francine Prose for her sharp wit and constant support.

John L'Heureux, Tobias Wolff, and Elizabeth Tallent at Stanford were invaluable to me in revising this manuscript. Thanks also to Gay Pierce, who kept the Stegner program running smoothly.

My thanks to friends and peers who have read these stories in their numerous incarnations: Julie Orringer, Edward Schwartz-child, Adam Johnson, Bridget Garrity, Doug Dorst, Ron Nyren, Malinda McCollum, Katherine Noel, Lysley Tenorio, Jack Livings, Otis Haschenmeyer, Rick Barot, Jane Rosenzweig, Carrie Messenger, Brian Teare, and the glorious Salvatore Scibona.

Thanks to Mara Folz for being my first reader and fan; to Felicia Ward for those many "writing dates." Faith Adiele, LJ Jesse, Angela Pneuman, Cate Marvin, and my sister Jamila are the best friends a girl can have.

Special thanks to the fine editors at *The New Yorker,* Cressida Leyshon and Bill Buford, who took a chance on a young unknown; to Colin Harrison and Barbara Jones at *Harper's;* and last but not least, to the wise and intrepid Lois Rosenthal at *Story.*

Finally, heartfelt thanks to the wonderful Eric Simonoff, who does triple duty as agent, reader, and friend; to Venetia van Kuffeler, the fab assistant to my editor at Riverhead, Cindy Spiegel, whose time, patience, and skill made this book what it is; and to Michael Boros, without whose love I wouldn't be.

Grateful acknowledgment is made to the following magazines, where these stories first appeared, some in a slightly different form: *Harper's*: "Brownies"; *Ploughshares*: "Every Tongue Shall Confess";

Acknowledgments

Story: "Our Lady of Peace"; *The New Yorker*: "The Ant of the Self," "Drinking Coffee Elsewhere"; *Zoetrope All-Story*: "Doris Is Coming."

"Brownies" also appeared in *The Best American Short Stories 2000*; "Our Lady of Peace" in *Symphony Space's Selected Shorts*; "Drinking Coffee Elsewhere" in *Here Lies*, edited by David Gilbert; "Speaking in Tongues" in *The Workshop: Seven Decades of the Iowa Writers' Workshop*, edited by Tom Grimes. "Geese" originally appeared in *Twenty-five and Under*.

Contents

⁓

Join me in the hope that this story of our people can help
to alleviate the legacies of the fact that preponderantly
the histories have been written by the winners.

—ALEX HALEY, *ROOTS*

Drinking Coffee
Elsewhere

Brownies

༄

 Y OUR SECOND DAY at Camp Crescendo, the girls in my
B Brownie troop had decided to kick the asses of each and every
girl in Brownie Troop 909. Troop 909 was doomed from the first
day of camp; they were white girls, their complexions a blend of
ice cream: strawberry, vanilla. They turtled out from their bus in
pairs, their rolled-up sleeping bags chromatized with Disney characters: Sleeping Beauty, Snow White, Mickey Mouse; or the generic
ones cheap parents bought: washed-out rainbows, unicorns, curly-
eyelashed frogs. Some clutched Igloo coolers and still others held on
to stuffed toys like pacifiers, looking all around them like tourists
determined to be dazzled.

 Our troop was wending its way past their bus, past the ranger station, past the colorful trail guide drawn like a treasure map, locked behind glass.

"Man, did you smell them?" Arnetta said, giving the girls a slow once-over, "They smell like Chihuahuas. *Wet* Chihuahuas." Their troop was still at the entrance, and though we had passed them by yards, Arnetta raised her nose in the air and grimaced.

Arnetta said this from the very rear of the line, far away from Mrs. Margolin, who always strung our troop behind her like a brood of obedient ducklings. Mrs. Margolin even looked like a mother duck—she had hair cropped close to a small ball of a head, almost no neck, and huge, miraculous breasts. She wore enormous belts that looked like the kind that weightlifters wear, except hers would be cheap metallic gold or rabbit fur or covered with gigantic fake sunflowers, and often these belts would become nature lessons in and of themselves. "See," Mrs. Margolin once said to us, pointing to her belt, "this one's made entirely from the feathers of baby pigeons."

The belt layered with feathers was uncanny enough, but I was more disturbed by the realization that I had never actually *seen* a baby pigeon. I searched weeks for one, in vain—scampering after pigeons whenever I was downtown with my father.

But nature lessons were not Mrs. Margolin's top priority. She saw the position of troop leader as an evangelical post. Back at the A.M.E. church where our Brownie meetings were held, Mrs. Margolin was especially fond of imparting religious aphorisms by means of acrostics—"Satan" was the "Serpent Always Tempting and Noisome"; she'd refer to the "Bible" as "Basic Instructions Before Leaving Earth." Whenever she quizzed us on these, expecting to hear the acrostics parroted back to her, only Arnetta's correct replies soared over our vague mumblings. "Jesus?" Mrs. Margolin might ask expectantly, and Arnetta alone would dutifully answer, "Jehovah's Example, Saving Us Sinners."

Arnetta always made a point of listening to Mrs. Margolin's religious talk and giving her what she wanted to hear. Because of this, Arnetta could have blared through a megaphone that the white girls of Troop 909 were "wet Chihuahuas" without so much as a blink from Mrs. Margolin. Once, Arnetta killed the troop goldfish by feeding it a french fry covered in ketchup, and when Mrs. Margolin demanded that she explain what had happened, claimed the goldfish had been eyeing her meal for *hours,* then the fish—giving in to temptation—had leapt up and snatched a whole golden fry from her fingertips.

"*Serious* Chihuahua," Octavia added, and though neither Arnetta nor Octavia could *spell* "Chihuahua," had ever *seen* a Chihuahua, trisyllabic words had gained a sort of exoticism within our fourth-grade set at Woodrow Wilson Elementary. Arnetta and Octavia would flip through the dictionary, determined to work the vulgar-sounding ones like "Djibouti" and "asinine" into conversation.

"*Caucasian* Chihuahuas," Arnetta said.

That did it. The girls in my troop turned elastic: Drema and Elise doubled up on one another like inextricably entwined kites; Octavia slapped her belly; Janice jumped straight up in the air, then did it again, as if to slam-dunk her own head. They could not stop laughing. No one had laughed so hard since a boy named Martez had stuck a pencil in the electric socket and spent the whole day with a strange grin on his face.

"Girls, girls," said our parent helper, Mrs. Hedy. Mrs. Hedy was Octavia's mother, and she wagged her index finger perfunctorily, like a windshield wiper. "Stop it, now. Be good." She said this loud enough to be heard, but lazily, bereft of any feeling or indication that she meant to be obeyed, as though she could say these words again at the exact same pitch if a button somewhere on her were pressed.

But the rest of the girls didn't stop; they only laughed louder. It was the word "Caucasian" that got them all going. One day at school, about a month before the Brownie camping trip, Arnetta turned to a boy wearing impossibly high-ankled floodwater jeans and said, "What are you? *Caucasian?*" The word took off from there, and soon everything was Caucasian. If you ate too fast you ate like a Caucasian, if you ate too slow you ate like a Caucasian. The biggest feat anyone at Woodrow Wilson could do was to jump off the swing in midair, at the highest point in its arc, and if you fell (as I had, more than once) instead of landing on your feet, knees bent Olympic gymnast–style, Arnetta and Octavia were prepared to comment. They'd look at each other with the silence of passengers who'd narrowly escaped an accident, then nod their heads, whispering with solemn horror, *"Caucasian."*

Even the only white kid in our school, Dennis, got in on the Caucasian act. That time when Martez stuck a pencil in the socket, Dennis had pointed and yelled, "That was *so* Caucasian!"

W H E N   Y O U lived in the south suburbs of Atlanta, it was easy to forget about whites. Whites were like those baby pigeons: real and existing, but rarely seen or thought about. Everyone had been to Rich's to go clothes shopping, everyone had seen white girls and their mothers coo-cooing over dresses; everyone had gone to the downtown library and seen white businessmen swish by importantly, wrists flexed in front of them to check the time as though they would change from Clark Kent into Superman at any second. But those images were as fleeting as cards shuffled in a deck, whereas the ten white girls behind us—*invaders,* Arnetta would later call them—were instantly real and memorable, with their long, shampoo-commercial hair, straight as spaghetti from the box. This alone was reason for envy and hatred. The only black girl most of us had ever seen with hair that long was Octavia, whose hair hung past her butt like a Hawaiian hula dancer's. The sight of Octavia's mane prompted other girls to listen to her reverentially, as though whatever she had to say would somehow activate their own follicles. For example, when, on the first day of camp, Octavia made as if to speak, and everyone fell silent. "Nobody," Octavia said, "calls us niggers."

At the end of that first day, when half of our troop made their way back to the cabin after tag-team restroom visits, Arnetta said she'd heard one of the Troop 909 girls call Daphne a nigger. The other half of the girls and I were helping Mrs. Margolin clean up the pots and pans from the campfire ravioli dinner. When we made our way to the restrooms to wash up and brush our teeth, we met up with Arnetta midway.

"Man, I completely heard the girl," Arnetta reported. "Right, Daphne?"

Daphne hardly ever spoke, but when she did, her voice was petite and tinkly, the voice one might expect from a shiny new earring. She'd written a poem once, for Langston Hughes Day, a poem brimming with all the teacher-winning ingredients—trees and oceans, sunsets and moons—but what cinched the poem for the grown-ups, snatching the win from Octavia's musical ode to Grandmaster Flash and the Furious Five, were Daphne's last lines:

You are my father, the veteran
When you cry in the dark
It rains and rains and rains in my heart

She'd always worn clean, though faded, jumpers and dresses when Chic jeans were the fashion, but when she went up to the dais to receive her prize journal, pages trimmed in gold, she wore a new dress with a velveteen bodice and a taffeta skirt as wide as an umbrella. All the kids clapped, though none of them understood the poem. I'd read encyclopedias the way others read comics, and I didn't get it. But those last lines pricked me, they were so eerie, and as my father and I ate cereal, I'd whisper over my Froot Loops, like a mantra, *"You are my father, the veteran. You are my father, the veteran, the veteran, the veteran,"* until my father, who acted in plays as Caliban and Othello and was not a veteran, marched me up to my teacher one morning and said, "Can you tell me what's wrong with this kid?"

I thought Daphne and I might become friends, but I think she grew spooked by me whispering those lines to her, begging her to tell me what they meant, and I soon understood that two quiet people like us were better off quiet alone.

"Daphne? Didn't you hear them call you a nigger?" Arnetta asked, giving Daphne a nudge.

The sun was setting behind the trees, and their leafy tops formed a canopy of black lace for the flame of the sun to pass through. Daphne shrugged her shoulders at first, then slowly nodded her head when Arnetta gave her a hard look.

Twenty minutes later, when my restroom group returned to the cabin, Arnetta was still talking about Troop 909. My restroom group had passed by some of the 909 girls. For the most part, they deferred to us, waving us into the restrooms, letting us go even though they'd gotten there first.

We'd seen them, but from afar, never within their orbit enough to see whether their faces were the way all white girls appeared on TV—ponytailed and full of energy, bubbling over with love and money. All I could see was that some of them rapidly fanned their faces with their hands, though the heat of the day had long passed. A few seemed to be lolling their heads in slow circles, half purpose-fully, as if exercising the muscles of their necks, half ecstactically, like Stevie Wonder.

"We can't let them get away with that," Arnetta said, dropping her voice to a laryngitic whisper. "We can't let them get away with calling us niggers. I say we teach them a lesson." She sat down cross-legged on a sleeping bag, an embittered Buddha, eyes glimmering acrylic-black. "We can't go telling Mrs. Margolin, either. Mrs. Mar-golin'll say something about doing unto others and the path of right-eousness and all. Forget that shit." She let her eyes flutter irreverently till they half closed, as though ignoring an insult not worth return-ing. We could all hear Mrs. Margolin outside, gathering the last of the metal campware.

Nobody said anything for a while. Usually people were quiet after Arnetta spoke. Her tone had an upholstered confidence that was somehow both regal and vulgar at once. It demanded a few moments of silence in its wake, like the ringing of a church bell or the playing of taps. Sometimes Octavia would ditto or dissent to whatever Arnetta had said, and this was the signal that others could speak. But this time Octavia just swirled a long cord of hair into pretzel shapes.

"Well?" Arnetta said. She looked as if she had discerned the hid-den severity of the situation and was waiting for the rest of us to catch up. Everyone looked from Arnetta to Daphne. It was, after all,

Daphne who had supposedly been called the name, but Daphne sat on the bare cabin floor, flipping through the pages of the Girl Scout handbook, eyebrows arched in mock wonder, as if the handbook were a catalogue full of bright and startling foreign costumes. Janice broke the silence. She clapped her hands to broach her idea of a plan.

"They gone be sleeping," she whispered conspiratorially, "then we gone sneak into they cabin, then we'll put daddy longlegs in they sleeping bags. Then they'll wake up. Then we gone beat 'em up till they're as flat as frying pans!" She jammed her fist into the palm of her hand, then made a sizzling sound.

Janice's country accent was laughable, her looks homely, her jumpy acrobatics embarrassing to behold. Arnetta and Octavia volleyed amused, arrogant smiles whenever Janice opened her mouth, but Janice never caught the hint, spoke whenever she wanted, fluttered around Arnetta and Octavia futilely offering her opinions to their departing backs. Whenever Arnetta and Octavia shooed her away, Janice loitered until the two would finally sigh and ask, "What *is* it, Miss Caucausoid? What do you *want*?"

"Shut up, Janice," Octavia said, letting a fingered loop of hair fall to her waist as though just the sound of Janice's voice had ruined the fun of her hair twisting.

Janice obeyed, her mouth hung open in a loose grin, unflappable, unhurt.

"All right," Arnetta said, standing up. "We're going to have a se-cret meeting and talk about what we're going to do."

Everyone gravely nodded her head. The word "secret" had a built-in importance, the modifier form of the word carried more clout than the noun. A secret meant nothing; it was like gossip: just a bit of unpleasant knowledge about someone who happened to be someone other than yourself. A secret *meeting,* or a secret *club* was entirely different.

That was when Arnetta turned to me as though she knew that doing so was both a compliment and a charity.

"Snot, you're not going to be a bitch and tell Mrs. Margolin, are you?"

I had been called "Snot" ever since first grade, when I'd sneezed in class and two long ropes of mucus had splattered a nearby girl.

"Hey," I said. "Maybe you didn't hear them right—I mean—"

"Are you gonna tell on us or not?" was all Arnetta wanted to know, and by the time the question was asked, the rest of our Brownie troop looked at me as though they'd already decided their course of action, me being the only impediment.

CAMP CRESCENDO used to double as a high-school-band and field hockey camp until an arcing field hockey ball landed on the clasp of a girl's metal barrette, knifing a skull nerve and paralyzing the right side of her body. The camp closed down for a few years and the girl's teammates built a memorial, filling the spot on which the girl fell with hockey balls, on which they had painted—all in nail polish—get-well tidings, flowers, and hearts. The balls were still stacked there, like a shrine of ostrich eggs embedded in the ground.

On the second day of camp, Troop 909 was dancing around the mound of hockey balls, their limbs jangling awkwardly, their cries like the constant summer squeal of an amusement park. There was a stream that bordered the field hockey lawn, and the girls from my troop settled next to it, scarfing down the last of lunch: sandwiches made from salami and slices of tomato that had gotten waterlogged from the melting ice in the cooler. From the stream bank, Arnetta eyed the Troop 909 girls, scrutinizing their movements to glean inspiration for battle.

"Man," Arnetta said, "we could bumrush them right now if that damn lady would *leave*."

The 909 troop leader was a white woman with the severe pageboy hairdo of an ancient Egyptian. She lay on a picnic blanket, sphinx-like, eating a banana, sometimes holding it out in front of her like a microphone. Beside her sat a girl slowly flapping one hand like a bird with a broken wing. Occasionally, the leader would call out the names of girls who'd attempted leapfrogs and flips, or of girls who yelled too loudly or strayed far from the circle.

"I'm just glad Big Fat Mama's not following us here," Octavia said. "At least we don't have to worry about her." Mrs. Margolin, Octavia assured us, was having her Afternoon Devotional, shrouded in mosquito netting, in a clearing she'd found. Mrs. Hedy was cleaning mud from her espadrilles in the cabin.

"I handled them." Arnetta sucked on her teeth and proudly grinned. "I told her we was going to gather leaves."

"Gather leaves," Octavia said, nodding respectfully. "That's a good one. Especially since they're so mad-crazy about this camping thing." She looked from ground to sky, sky to ground. Her hair hung down her back in two braids like a squaw's. "I mean, I really don't know why it's even called *camping*—all we ever do with Nature is find some twigs and say something like, 'Wow, this fell from a tree.'" She then studied her sandwich. With two disdainful fingers, she picked out a slice of dripping tomato, the sections congealed with red slime. She pitched it into the stream embrowned with dead leaves and the murky effigies of other dead things, but in the opaque water, a group of small silver-brown fish appeared. They surrounded the tomato and nibbled.

"Look!" Janice cried. "Fishes! Fishes!" As she scrambled to the edge of the stream to watch, a covey of insects threw up tantrums from the wheatgrass and nettle, a throng of tiny electric machines, all going at once. Octavia sneaked up behind Janice as if to push her in. Daphne and I exchanged terrified looks. It seemed as though only we knew that Octavia was close enough—and bold enough—to actually push Janice into the stream. Janice turned around quickly, but Octavia was already staring serenely into the still water as though she was gathering some sort of courage from it. "What's so funny?" Janice said, eyeing them all suspiciously.

Elise began humming the tune to "Karma Chameleon," all the girls joining in, their hums light and facile. Janice also began to hum, against everyone else, the high-octane opening chords of "Beat It."

"I love me some Michael Jackson," Janice said when she'd finished humming, smacking her lips as though Michael Jackson were a favorite meal. "I *will* marry Michael Jackson."

Before anyone had a chance to impress upon Janice the impossibility of this, Arnetta suddenly rose, made a sun visor of her hand, and watched Troop 909 leave the field hockey lawn.

"Dammit!" she said. "We've got to get them *alone*."

"They won't ever be alone," I said. All the rest of the girls looked at me, for I usually kept quiet. If I spoke even a word, I could count on someone calling me Snot. Everyone seemed to think that we could beat up these girls; no one entertained the thought that they might fight *back*. "The only time they'll be unsupervised is in the bathroom."

"Oh shut up, Snot," Octavia said.

But Arnetta slowly nodded her head. "The bathroom," she said.

"The bathroom," she said, again and again. "The bathroom! The bathroom!"

A C C O R D I N G   T O Octavia's watch, it took us five minutes to hike to the restrooms, which were midway between our cabin and Troop 909's. Inside, the mirrors above the sinks returned only the vaguest of reflections, as though someone had taken a scouring pad to their surfaces to obscure the shine. Pine needles, leaves, and dirty, flattened wads of chewing gum covered the floor like a mosaic. Webs of hair matted the drain in the middle of the floor. Above the sinks and below the mirrors, stacks of folded white paper towels lay on a long metal counter. Shaggy white balls of paper towels sat on the sinktops in a line like corsages on display. A thread of floss snaked from a wad of tissues dotted with the faint red-pink of blood. One of those white girls, I thought, had just lost a tooth.

Though the restroom looked almost the same as it had the night before, it somehow seemed stranger now. We hadn't noticed the wooden rafters coming together in great V's. We were, it seemed, inside a whale, viewing the ribs of the roof of its mouth.

"Wow. It's a mess," Elise said.

"You can say that again."

Arnetta leaned against the doorjamb of a restroom stall. "This is where they'll be again," she said. Just seeing the place, just having a plan seemed to satisfy her. "We'll go in and talk to them. You know, 'How you doing? How long'll you be here?' That sort of thing. Then Octavia and I are gonna tell them what happens when they call any one of us a nigger."

"I'm going to say something, too," Janice said.

Arnetta considered this. "Sure," she said. "Of course. Whatever you want."

Janice pointed her finger like a gun at Octavia and rehearsed the line she'd thought up, "'We're gonna teach you a *lesson*!' That's what I'm going to say." She narrowed her eyes like a TV mobster. "'We're gonna teach you little girls a lesson!'"

With the back of her hand, Octavia brushed Janice's finger away. "You couldn't teach me to shit in a toilet."

"But," I said, "what if they say, 'We didn't say that? We didn't call anyone an N-I-G-G-E-R.'"

"Snot," Arnetta said, and then sighed. "Don't think. Just fight. If you even know how."

Everyone laughed except Daphne. Arnetta gently laid her hand on Daphne's shoulder. "Daphne. You don't have to fight. We're doing this for you."

Daphne walked to the counter, took a clean paper towel, and carefully unfolded it like a map. With it, she began to pick up the trash all around. Everyone watched.

"C'mon," Arnetta said to everyone. "Let's beat it." We all ambled toward the doorway, where the sunshine made one large white rectangle of light. We were immediately blinded, and we shielded our eyes with our hands and our forearms.

"Daphne?" Arnetta asked. "Are you coming?"

We all looked back at the bending girl, the thin of her back hunched like the back of a custodian sweeping a stage, caught in limelight. Stray strands of her hair were lit near-transparent, thin fiber-optic threads. She did not nod yes to the question, nor did she shake her head no. She abided, bent. Then she began again, picking up leaves, wads of paper, the cotton fluff innards from a torn stuffed toy. She did it so methodically, so exquisitely, so humbly, she must have been trained. I thought of those dresses she wore, faded and old, yet so pressed and clean. I then saw the poverty in them; I then could imagine her mother, cleaning the houses of others, returning home, weary.

"I guess she's not coming."

We left her and headed back to our cabin, over pine needles and leaves, taking the path full of shade.

"What about our secret meeting?" Elise asked.

Arnetta enunciated her words in a way that defied contradiction: "We just had it."

I T W A S nearing our bedtime, but the sun had not yet set.

"Hey, your mama's coming," Arnetta said to Octavia when she saw Mrs. Hedy walk toward the cabin, sniffling. When Octavia's mother wasn't giving bored, parochial orders, she sniffled continuously, mourning an imminent divorce from her husband. She might begin a sentence, "I don't know what Robert will do when Octavia and I are gone. Who'll buy him cigarettes?" and Octavia would hotly whisper, *"Mama,"* in a way that meant: Please don't talk about our problems in front of everyone. Please shut up.

But when Mrs. Hedy began talking about her husband, thinking about her husband, seeing clouds shaped like the head of her husband, she couldn't be quiet, and no one could dislodge her from the comfort of her own woe. Only one thing could perk her up— Brownie songs. If the girls were quiet, and Mrs. Hedy was in her dopey, sorrowful mood, she would say, "Y'all know I like those songs, girls. Why don't you sing one?" Everyone would groan, except me and Daphne. I, for one, liked some of the songs.

"C'mon, everybody," Octavia said drearily. "She likes the Brownie song best."

We sang, loud enough to reach Mrs. Hedy:

"I've got something in my pocket;
It belongs across my face.
And I keep it very close at hand
in a most convenient place.
I'm sure you couldn't guess it
If you guessed a long, long while.
So I'll take it out and put it on—
It's a great big Brownie smile!"

The Brownie song was supposed to be sung cheerfully, as though we were elves in a workshop, singing as we merrily cobbled shoes, but everyone except me hated the song so much that they sang it like a maudlin record, played on the most sluggish of rpms.

"That was good," Mrs. Hedy said, closing the cabin door behind her. "Wasn't that nice, Linda?"

"Praise God," Mrs. Margolin answered without raising her head from the chore of counting out Popsicle sticks for the next day's craft session.

"Sing another one," Mrs. Hedy said. She said it with a sort of joyful aggression, like a drunk I'd once seen who'd refused to leave a Korean grocery.

"God, Mama, get over it," Octavia whispered in a voice meant only for Arnetta, but Mrs. Hedy heard it and started to leave the cabin.

"Don't go," Arnetta said. She ran after Mrs. Hedy and held her by the arm. "We haven't finished singing." She nudged us with a single look. "Let's sing the 'Friends Song.' For Mrs. Hedy."

Although I liked some of the songs, I hated this one:

> Make new friends
> But keep the o-old,
> One is silver
> And the other gold.

If most of the girls in the troop could be any type of metal, they'd be bunched-up wads of tinfoil, maybe, or rusty iron nails you had to get tetanus shots for.

"No, no, no," Mrs. Margolin said before anyone could start in on the "Friends Song." "An uplifting song. Something to lift her up and take her mind off all these earthly burdens."

Arnetta and Octavia rolled their eyes. Everyone knew what song Mrs. Margolin was talking about, and no one, no one, wanted to sing it.

"Please, no," a voice called out. "Not 'The Doughnut Song.'"

"Please not 'The Doughnut Song,'" Octavia pleaded.

"I'll brush my teeth two times if I don't have to sing 'The Doughnut—'"

"Sing!" Mrs. Margolin demanded.

We sang:

> "Life without Jesus is like a do-ough-nut!
> Like a do-ooough-nut!
> Like a do-ooough-nut!
> Life without Jesus is like a do-ough-nut!
> There's a hole in the middle of my soul!"

There were other verses, involving other pastries, but we stopped after the first one and cast glances toward Mrs. Margolin to see if we could gain a reprieve. Mrs. Margolin's eyes fluttered blissfully. She was half asleep.

"Awww," Mrs. Hedy said, as though giant Mrs. Margolin were a cute baby, "Mrs. Margolin's had a long day."

"Yes indeed," Mrs. Margolin answered. "If you don't mind, I might just go to the lodge where the beds are. I haven't been the same since the operation."

I had not heard of this operation, or when it had occurred, since Mrs. Margolin had never missed the once-a-week Brownie meetings, but I could see from Daphne's face that she was concerned, and I could see that the other girls had decided that Mrs. Margolin's operation must have happened long ago in some remote time unconnected to our own. Nevertheless, they put on sad faces. We had all been taught that adulthood was full of sorrow and pain, taxes and bills, dreaded work and dealings with whites, sickness and death. I tried to do what the others did. I tried to look silent.

"Go right ahead, Linda," Mrs. Hedy said. "I'll watch the girls." Mrs. Hedy seemed to forget about divorce for a moment; she looked at us with dewy eyes, as if we were mysterious, furry creatures. Meanwhile, Mrs. Margolin walked through the maze of sleeping bags until she found her own. She gathered a neat stack of clothes and pajamas slowly, as though doing so was almost painful. She took her toothbrush, her toothpaste, her pillow. "All right!" Mrs. Margolin said, addressing us all from the threshold of the cabin. "Be in bed by nine." She said it with a twinkle in her voice, letting us know she was allowing us to be naughty and stay up till nine-fifteen.

"C'mon everybody," Arnetta said after Mrs. Margolin left. "Time for us to wash up."

Everyone watched Mrs. Hedy closely, wondering whether she would insist on coming with us since it was night, making a fight with Troop 909 nearly impossible. Troop 909 would soon be in the bathroom, washing their faces, brushing their teeth—completely unsuspecting of our ambush.

"We won't be long," Arnetta said. "We're old enough to go to the restrooms by ourselves."

Ms. Hedy pursed her lips at this dilemma. "Well, I guess you Brownies are almost Girl Scouts, right?"

"Right!"

"Just one more badge," Drema said.

"And about," Octavia droned, "a million more cookies to sell." Octavia looked at all of us, *Now's our chance,* her face seemed to say, but our chance to do *what,* I didn't exactly know.

Finally, Mrs. Hedy walked to the doorway where Octavia stood dutifully waiting to say goodbye but looking bored doing it. Mrs. Hedy held Octavia's chin. "You'll be good?"

"Yes, Mama."

"And remember to pray for me and your father? If I'm asleep when you get back?"

"Yes, Mama."

WHEN THE other girls had finished getting their toothbrushes and washcloths and flashlights for the group restroom trip, I was drawing pictures of tiny birds with too many feathers. Daphne was sitting on her sleeping bag, reading.

"You're not going to come?" Octavia asked.

Daphne shook her head.

"I'm gonna stay, too," I said. "I'll go to the restroom when Daphne and Mrs. Hedy go."

Arnetta leaned down toward me and whispered so that Mrs. Hedy, who'd taken over Mrs. Margolin's task of counting Popsicle sticks, couldn't hear. "No, Snot. If we get in trouble, you're going to get in trouble with the rest of us."

W E   M A D E   our way through the darkness by flashlight. The tree branches that had shaded us just hours earlier, along the same path, now looked like arms sprouting menacing hands. The stars sprinkled the sky like spilled salt. They seemed fastened to the darkness, high up and holy, their places fixed and definite as we stirred beneath them.

Some, like me, were quiet because we were afraid of the dark; others were talking like crazy for the same reason.

"Wow!" Drema said, looking up. "Why are all the stars out here? I never see stars back on Oneida Street."

"It's a camping trip, that's why," Octavia said. "You're supposed to see stars on camping trips."

Janice said, "This place smells like my mother's air freshener."

"These woods are *pine,*" Elise said. "Your mother probably uses *pine* air freshener."

Janice mouthed an exaggerated "Oh," nodding her head as though she just then understood one of the world's great secrets.

No one talked about fighting. Everyone was afraid enough just walking through the infinite deep of the woods. Even though I didn't fight to fight, was afraid of fighting, I felt I was part of the rest of the troop; like I was defending something. We trudged against the slight incline of the path, Arnetta leading the way.

"You know," I said, "their leader will be there. Or they won't even be there. It's dark already. Last night the sun was still in the sky. I'm sure they're already finished."

Arnetta acted as if she hadn't heard me. I followed her gaze with my flashlight, and that's when I saw the squares of light in the darkness. The bathroom was just ahead.

B U T   T H E girls were there. We could hear them before we could see them.

"Octavia and I will go in first so they'll think there's just two of us, then wait till I say, 'We're gonna teach you a lesson,'" Arnetta said. "Then, bust in. That'll surprise them."

"That's what I was supposed to say," Janice said.

Arnetta went inside, Octavia next to her. Janice followed, and the rest of us waited outside.

They were in there for what seemed like whole minutes, but something was wrong. Arnetta hadn't given the signal yet. I was with the girls outside when I heard one of the Troop 909 girls say, "NO. That did NOT happen!"

That was to be expected, that they'd deny the whole thing. What I hadn't expected was *the voice* in which the denial was said. The girl sounded as though her tongue were caught in her mouth. "That's a BAD word!" the girl continued. "We don't say BAD words!"

"Let's go in," Elise said.

"No, " Drema said, "I don't want to. What if we get beat up?"

"Snot?" Elise turned to me, her flashlight blinding. It was the first time anyone had asked my opinion, though I knew they were just asking because they were afraid.

"I say we go inside, just to see what's going on."

"But Arnetta didn't give us the signal," Drema said. "She's supposed to say, 'We're gonna teach you a lesson,' and I didn't hear her say it."

"C'mon," I said. "Let's just go in."

We went inside. There we found the white girls—about five girls huddled up next to one big girl. I instantly knew she was the owner of the voice we'd heard. Arnetta and Octavia inched toward us as soon as we entered.

"Where's Janice?" Elise asked, then we heard a flush. "Oh."

"I think," Octavia said, whispering to Elise, "they're retarded."

"We ARE NOT retarded!" the big girl said, though it was obvious that she was. That they all were. The girls around her began to whimper.

"They're just pretending," Arnetta said, trying to convince herself. "I know they are."

Octavia turned to Arnetta. "Arnetta. Let's just leave."

Janice came out of a stall, happy and relieved, then she suddenly remembered her line, pointed to the big girl, and said, "We're gonna teach you a lesson."

"Shut up, Janice," Octavia said, but her heart was not in it. Arnetta's face was set in a lost, deep scowl. Octavia turned to the big girl and said loudly, slowly, as if they were all deaf, "We're going to leave. It was nice meeting you, O.K.? You don't have to tell anyone that we were here. O.K.?"

"Why not?" said the big girl, like a taunt. When she spoke, her lips did not meet, her mouth did not close. Her tongue grazed the roof of her mouth, like a little pink fish. "You'll get in trouble. I know. *I* know."

Arnetta got back her old cunning. "If you said anything, then you'd be a tattletale."

The girl looked sad for a moment, then perked up quickly. A flash of genius crossed her face. "I *like* tattletale."

"I t ' s a l l right, girls. It's gonna be all right!" the 909 troop leader said. All of Troop 909 burst into tears. It was as though someone had instructed them all to cry at once. The troop leader had girls under her arm, and all the rest of the girls crowded about her. It reminded me of a hog I'd seen on a field trip, where all the little hogs gathered about the mother at feeding time, latching onto her teats. The 909 troop leader had come into the bathroom, shortly after the big girl had threatened to tell. Then the ranger came, then, once the ranger had radioed the station, Mrs. Margolin arrived with Daphne in tow.

The ranger had left the restroom area, but everyone else was huddled just outside, swatting mosquitoes.

"Oh. They *will* apologize," Mrs. Margolin said to the 909 troop leader, but she said this so angrily, I knew she was speaking more to us than to the other troop leader. "When their parents find out, every one a them will be on punishment."

"It's all right, it's all right," the 909 troop leader reassured Mrs. Margolin. Her voice lilted in the same way it had when addressing the girls. She smiled the whole time she talked. She was like one of those TV-cooking-show women who talk and dice onions and smile all at the same time.

"See. It could have happened. I'm not calling your girls fibbers or anything." She shook her head ferociously from side to side, her Egyptian-style pageboy flapping against her cheeks like heavy drapes. "It *could* have happened. See. Our girls are *not* retarded. They are *delayed* learners." She said this in a syrupy instructional voice, as though our troop might be delayed learners as well. "We're from the Decatur Children's Academy. Many of them just have special needs."

"Now we won't be able to walk to the bathroom by ourselves!" the big girl said.

"Yes you will," the troop leader said, "but maybe we'll wait till we get back to Decatur—"

"I don't want to wait!" the girl said. "I want my Independence badge!"

The girls in my troop were entirely speechless. Arnetta looked stoic, as though she were soon to be tortured but was determined not to appear weak. Mrs. Margolin pursed her lips solemnly and said, "Bless them, Lord. Bless them."

In contrast, the Troop 909 leader was full of words and energy. "Some of our girls are echolalic—" She smiled and happily presented one of the girls hanging onto her, but the girl widened her eyes in horror, and violently withdrew herself from the center of attention, sensing she was being sacrificed for the village sins. "Echolalic," the troop leader continued. "That means they will say whatever they hear, like an echo—that's where the word comes from. It comes from 'echo.'" She ducked her head apologetically, "I mean, not all of them have the most *progressive* of parents, so if they heard a bad word, they might have repeated it. But I guarantee it would not have been *intentional*."

Arnetta spoke. "I saw her say the word. I heard her." She pointed to a small girl, smaller than any of us, wearing an oversized T-shirt that read: "Eat Bertha's Mussels."

The troop leader shook her head and smiled, "That's impossible. She doesn't speak. She can, but she doesn't."

Arnetta furrowed her brow. "No. It wasn't her. That's right. It was *her*."

The girl Arnetta pointed to grinned as though she'd been paid a compliment. She was the only one from either troop actually wearing a full uniform: the mocha-colored A-line shift, the orange ascot, the sash covered with badges, though all the same one—the Try-It patch. She took a few steps toward Arnetta and made a grand sweeping gesture toward the sash. "See," she said, full of self-importance, "I'm a Brownie." I had a hard time imagining this girl calling anyone a "nigger"; the girl looked perpetually delighted, as though she would have cuddled up with a grizzly if someone had let her.

ON THE fourth morning, we boarded the bus to go home.

The previous day had been spent building miniature churches from Popsicle sticks. We hardly left the cabin. Mrs. Margolin and Mrs. Hedy guarded us so closely, almost no one talked for the entire day.

Even on the day of departure from Camp Crescendo, all was serious and silent. The bus ride began quietly enough. Arnetta had to sit beside Mrs. Margolin; Octavia had to sit beside her mother. I sat beside Daphne, who gave me her prize journal without a word of explanation.

"You don't want it?"

She shook her head no. It was empty.

Then Mrs. Hedy began to weep. "Octavia," Mrs. Hedy said to her daughter without looking at her, "I'm going to sit with Mrs. Margolin. All right?"

Arnetta exchanged seats with Mrs. Hedy. With the two women up front, Elise felt it safe to speak. "Hey," she said, then she set her face into a placid, vacant stare, trying to imitate that of a Troop 909 girl. Emboldened, Arnetta made a gesture of mock pride toward an imaginary sash, the way the girl in full uniform had done. Then they all made a game of it, trying to do the most exaggerated imitations of the Troop 909 girls, all without speaking, all without laughing loud enough to catch the women's attention.

Daphne looked down at her shoes, white with sneaker polish. I opened the journal she'd given me. I looked out the window, trying to decide what to write, searching for lines, but nothing could compare with what Daphne had written, *"My father, the veteran,"* my favorite line of all time. It replayed itself in my head, and I gave up trying to write.

By then, it seemed that the rest of the troop had given up making fun of the girls in Troop 909. They were now quietly gossiping about who had passed notes to whom in school. For a moment the gossiping fell off, and all I heard was the hum of the bus as we sped down the road and the muffled sounds of Mrs. Hedy and Mrs. Margolin talking about serious things.

"You know," Octavia whispered, "why did *we* have to be stuck at a camp with retarded girls? You know?"

"*You* know why," Arnetta answered. She narrowed her eyes like a cat. "My mama and I were in the mall in Buckhead, and this white lady just kept looking at us. I mean, like we were foreign or something. Like we were from China."

"What did the woman say?" Elise asked.

"Nothing," Arnetta said. "She didn't say nothing."

A few girls quietly nodded their heads.

"There was this time," I said, "when my father and I were in the mall and—"

"Oh shut up, Snot," Octavia said.

I stared at Octavia, then rolled my eyes from her to the window. As I watched the trees blur, I wanted nothing more than to be through with it all: the bus ride, the troop, school—all of it. But we were going home. I'd see the same girls in school the next day. We were on a bus, and there was nowhere else to go.

"Go on, Laurel," Daphne said to me. It seemed like the first time she'd spoken the whole trip, and she'd said my name. I turned to her and smiled weakly so as not to cry, hoping she'd remember when I'd tried to be her friend, thinking maybe that her gift of the journal was an invitation of friendship. But she didn't smile back. All she said was, "What happened?"

I studied the girls, waiting for Octavia to tell me to shut up again before I even had a chance to utter another word, but everyone was amazed that Daphne had spoken. The bus was silent. I gathered my voice. "Well," I said. "My father and I were in this mall, but *I* was the one doing the staring." I stopped and glanced from face to face. I continued. "There were these white people dressed like Puritans or something, but they weren't Puritans. They were Mennonites. They're these people who, if you ask them to do a favor, like paint your porch or something, they have to do it. It's in their rules."

"That sucks," someone said.

"C'mon," Arnetta said. "You're lying."

"I am not."

"How do you know that's not just some story someone made up?" Elise asked, her head cocked full of daring. "I mean, who's gonna do whatever you ask?"

"It's not made up. I know because when I was looking at them, my father said, 'See those people? If you ask them to do something, they'll do it. Anything you want.'"

No one would call anyone's father a liar—then they'd have to fight the person. But Drema parsed her words carefully. "How does your *father* know that's not just some story? Huh?"

"Because," I said, "he went up to the man and asked him would he paint our porch, and the man said yes. It's their religion."

"Man, I'm glad I'm a Baptist," Elise said, shaking her head in sympathy for the Mennonites.

"So did the guy do it?" Drema asked, scooting closer to hear if the story got juicy.

"Yeah," I said. "His whole family was with him. My dad drove them to our house. They all painted our porch. The woman and girl were in bonnets and long, long skirts with buttons up to their necks. The guy wore this weird hat and these huge suspenders."

"Why," Arnetta asked archly, as though she didn't believe a word, "would someone pick a *porch*? If they'll do anything, why not make them paint the whole *house*? Why not ask for a hundred bucks?"

I thought about it, and then remembered the words my father had said about them painting our porch, though I had never seemed to think about his words after he'd said them.

"He said," I began, only then understanding the words as they uncoiled from my mouth, "it was the only time he'd have a white man on his knees doing something for a black man for free."

I now understood what he meant, and why he did it, though I didn't like it. When you've been made to feel bad for so long, you jump at the chance to do it to others. I remembered the Mennonites bending the way Daphne had bent when she was cleaning the restroom. I remembered the dark blue of their bonnets, the black of their shoes. They painted the porch as though scrubbing a floor. I was already trembling before Daphne asked quietly, "Did he thank them?"

I looked out the window. I could not tell which were the thoughts and which were the trees. "No," I said, and suddenly knew there was something mean in the world that I could not stop.

Arnetta laughed. "If I asked them to take off their long skirts and bonnets and put on some jeans, would they do it?"

And Daphne's voice, quiet, steady: "Maybe they would. Just to be nice."

Every Tongue Shall Confess

As PASTOR EVERETT MADE the announcements that began the service, Clareese Mitchell stood with her choir members, knowing that once again she had to Persevere, put on the Strong Armor of God, the Breastplate of Righteousness, but she was having her monthly womanly troubles and all she wanted to do was curse the Brothers' Church Council of Greater Christ Emmanuel Pentecostal Church of the Fire Baptized, who'd decided that the Sisters had to wear *white* every Missionary Sunday, which was, of course, the day of the month when her womanly troubles were always at their absolute worst! And to think that the Brothers' Church Council of Greater Christ Emmanuel Pentecostal Church of the Fire Baptized had been the first place she'd looked for guidance and companionship nearly ten years ago when her aunt Alma had fallen ill. And why not? They were God-fearing, churchgoing men; men like Deacon Julian Jeffers, now sitting in the first row of pews, closest to the altar, right under the leafy top of the corn plant she'd brought in to make the sanctuary more homey. Two months ago she'd been reading the book of Micah and posed the idea of a Book of Micah discussion group to the Deacon Jeffers and he'd said, "Oh, Sister Clareese! We should make *you* a deacon!" Which of course they didn't. Deacons, like pastors, were men—not that she was complaining. But it still rankled that Jeffers had said he'd get back to her about the Micah discussion group and he never had.

Clareese's cross-eyes roved to the back of the church where Sister Drusella and Sister Maxwell sat, resplendent in their identical wide-brimmed, purple-flowered hats, their unsaved guests sitting next to them. The guests wore frightened smiles, and Clareese tried to shoot them reassuring looks. The gold-lettered banner behind them read: "We Are More Than Conquerors in Christ Our Lord," and she tried to use this as a focal point. But her cross-eyes couldn't help it; they settled, at last, on Deacon McCreedy, making his way down the aisle for the second time. Oh, how she hated him!

She would never forget—never, never, never—the day he came to the hospital where she worked; she was still wearing her white nurse's uniform and he'd said he was concerned about her spiritual well-being—*Liar!*—then drove her to where she lived with her aunt Alma, whose room resounded with perpetual snores and hacking and wheezing—as if Clareese didn't have enough of this at the hospital—and while Alma slept, Clareese poured Deacon McCreedy some fruit punch, which he drank between forkfuls of chicken, plus half their pork roast. No sooner than he'd wiped his hands on the napkin—didn't bother using a fork—he stood and walked behind her, covering her cross-eyes as though she were a child, as though he were about to give her a gift—a Bible with her very own name engraved on it, perhaps—but he didn't give her anything, he'd just covered her wandering eyes and said, "Sing 'On Christ the Solid Rock I Stand.' Make sure to do the Waterfall." And she was happy to do it, happy to please Deacon McCreedy, so she began singing in her best, cleanest voice until she felt his hand slide up the scratchy white pantyhose of her nurse's uniform and up toward the control-top of her pantyhose. Before she could stop him, one finger was wriggling around inside, and by then it was too late to tell him she was having her monthly womanly troubles. He drew back in disgust—no, *hatred*—then rinsed his hand in the kitchen sink and left without saying a word, not a thanks for the chicken or the pork roast or her singing. Not a single word of apology for anything. But she could have forgiven him—if Sisters could even forgive Deacons—for she could have understood that an unmarried man might have *needs,* but what really bothered her was how he ignored her. How a few weeks later she and Aunt Alma had been waiting for the bus after Wednesday-night prayer meeting and he *drove past.* That's right. No offer of a ride, no slowing down, no nothing. Aunt Alma was nearly blind and couldn't even see it was him, but Clareese recognized his car at once.

Yes, she wanted to curse the Brothers' Church Council of Greater Christ Emmanuel Pentecostal Church of the Fire Baptized, but Sisters and Brothers could not curse, could not even swear or take an oath, for *neither shalt thou swear by thy head, because thou canst not make one hair white or black.* So no oath, no swearing, and of course no betting—an extension of swearing—which was why she'd told the other nurses at University Hospital that she would not join their betting pool to predict who would get married first, Patty or Edwina. She told them about the black and white hairs and all Nurse Holloway did was clomp her pumps—as if she was too good for the standard orthopedically correct shoes—down the green tiles of the hall and shout behind her back, "Somebody sure needs to get laid." Oh, how the other RNs tittered in their gossipy way.

Now everyone applauded when Pastor Everett announced that Sister Nina would be getting married to Harold, one of the Brothers from Broadway Tongues of Spirit Church. Then Pastor Everett said, "Sister Nina will be holding a Council so we can get husbands for the rest of you hardworking Sisters." Like Sister Clareese, is what he meant. The congregation laughed at the joke. Ha ha. And perhaps the joke *was* on her. If she'd been married, Deacon Mc-Creedy wouldn't have dared do what he did; if she'd been married perhaps she'd also be working fewer shifts at the hospital, perhaps she would have never met that patient—that man—who'd almost gotten her fired! And at exactly that moment, it hit her, right below the gut, a sharp pain, and she imagined her uterus, that Texas-shaped organ, the Rio Grande of her monthly womanly troubles flushing out to the Gulf.

Pastor Everett had finished the announcements. Now it was time for testimony service. She tried to distract herself by thinking of suitable testimonies. Usually she testified about work. Last week, she'd testified about the poor man with a platelet count of seven, meaning he was a goner, and how Nurse Holloway had told him, "We're bringing you more platelets," and how he'd said, "That's all right. God sent me more." No one at the nurses' station—to say nothing of those atheist doctors—believed him. But when Nurse Holloway checked, sure enough, Glory be to God, he had a count of sixteen. Clareese told the congregation how she knelt on the cold tiled floor of University Hospital's corridor, right then and there, arms outstretched to Glory. And what could the other nurses say to that? Nothing, that's what.

She remembered her testimony from a month ago, how she'd been working the hotline, and a mother had called to say that her son had eaten ants, and Sister Clareese had assured the woman that ants were God's creatures, and though disturbing, they wouldn't harm the boy. But the Lord told Clareese to stay on the line with the mother, not to rush the way other nurses often did, so Clareese stayed on the line. And Glory be to God that she did! Once the mother had calmed down she'd said, "Thank goodness. The insecticide I gave Kevin must have worked." Sister Clareese had stayed after her shift to make sure the woman brought her boy into Emergency. Afterward she told the woman to hold hands with Kevin and give God the Praise he deserved.

But she had told these stories already. As she fidgeted in her choirmistress's chair, she tried to think of new ones. The congregation wouldn't care about how she had to stay on top of codes, or how she had to triple-check patients' charts. The only patients who stuck in her mind were Mrs. Geneva Bosma, whose toe was rotting off, and Mr. Toomey, who had prostate cancer. And, of course, Mr. Cleophus Sanders, the cause of all her current problems. Cleophus was an amputee who liked to turn the volume of his television up so high that his channel-surfing sounded as if someone were being electrocuted, repeatedly. At the nurses' station she'd overheard that Cleophus Sanders was once a musician who in his heyday went by the nickname "Delta Sweetmeat." But he'd gone in and out of the music business, sometimes taking construction jobs. A crane had fallen on his leg and he'd been amputated from the below the knee. No, none of these cases was Edifying in God's sight. Her run-in with Cleophus had been downright un-Edifying.

When Mr. Sanders had been moved into Mr. Toomey's room last Monday, she'd told them both, "I hope everyone has a blessed day!" She'd made sure to say this only after she was safely inside with the door closed behind her. She had to make sure she didn't mention God until the door was closed *behind* her, because Nurse Holloway was always clomping about, trying to say that this was a *university* hospital, as well as a *research* hospital, one at the very *forefront* of medicine, and didn't Registered Nurse Clareese Mitchell recognize and *respect* that not everyone shared her beliefs? That the hospital catered not only to Christians, but to people of the Jewish faith? To Muslims, Hindus, and agnostics? Atheists, even?

This Clareese knew only too well, which was why it was all the more important for her to to Spread the Gospel. So she shut the door, and said to Mr. Toomey, louder this time, "I HOPE EVERY-ONE HAS A BLESSED DAY!"

Mr. Toomey grunted. Heavy and completely white, he reminded Sister Clareese of a walrus: everything about him drooped, his eyes like twin frowns, his nose, perhaps even his mouth, though it was hard to make out because of his frowning blond mustache. Well, Glory be to God, she expected something like a grunt from him, she couldn't say she was surprised: junkies who detox scream and writhe before turning clean; the man with a hangover does not like to wake to the sun. So it was with sinners exposed to the harsh, cur-ing Light of the Lord.

"Hey, sanctified lady!" Cleophus Sanders called from across the room. "He got cancer! Let the man alone."

"I *know* what he *has*," Sister Clareese said. "I'm his *nurse*." This wasn't how she wanted the patient–RN relationship to begin, but

Cleophus had gotten the better of her. Yes, that was the problem, wasn't it? *He'd* gotten the better of *her.* This was how Satan worked, throwing you off a little at a time. She would have to Persevere, put on the Strong Armor of God. She tried again.

"My name is Sister Clareese Mitchell, your assigned registered nurse. I can't exactly say that I'm pleased to meet you, because that would be a lie and 'lying lips are an abomination to the Lord.' I will say that I am pleased to do my duty and help you recover."

"Me oh my!" Cleophus Sanders said, and he laughed big and long, the kind of laughter that could go on and on, rising and rising, restarting itself if need be, like yeast. He slapped the knee of his amputated leg, the knee that would probably come off if his infection didn't stop eating away at it. But Cleophus Sanders didn't care. He just slapped that infected knee, hooting all the while in an ornery, backwoods kind of way that made Clareese want to hit him. But of course she would never, never do that.

She busied herself by changing Mr. Toomey's catheter, then remaking his bed, rolling the walrus of him this way and that, with little help on his part. As soon as she was done with Mr. Toomey, he turned on the Knicks game. The whole time she'd changed Mr. Toomey's catheter, however, Cleophus had watched her, laughing under his breath, then outright, a waxing and waning of hilarity as if her every gesture were laughably prim and proper.

"Look, Mr. *Cleophus Sanders,*" she said, glad for the chance to bite on the ridiculous name, "I am a professional. You may laugh at what I do, but in doing so you laugh at the Almighty who has given me the breath to do it!"

She'd steeled herself for a vulgar reply. But no. Mr. Toomey did the talking.

"I tell *you* what!" Mr. Toomey said, pointing his remote at Sister

Clareese. "I'm going to sue this hospital for lack of peace and quiet. All your 'Almighty this' and 'Oh Glory that' is keeping me from watching the game!"

So Sister Clareese murmured her apologies to Mr. Toomey, the whole while Cleophus Sanders put on an act of restraining his amusement, body and bed quaking in seizure-like fits.

Now sunlight filtered through the yellow-tinted windows of Greater Christ Emmanuel Pentecostal Church of the Fire Baptized, lighting Brother Hopkins, the organist, with a halo-like glow. The rest of the congregation had given their testimonies, and it was now time for the choir members to testify, starting with Clareese. Was there any way she could possibly turn her incident with Cleophus Sanders into an edifying testimony experience? Just then, another hit, and she felt a cramping so hard she thought she might double over. It was her turn. Cleophus's laughter and her cramping womb seemed one and the same; he'd inhabited her body like a demon, preventing her from thinking up a proper testimony. As she rose, unsteadily, to her feet, all she managed to say was, "Pray for me."

I t w a s almost time for Pastor Everett to preach his sermon. To introduce it, Sister Clareese had the choir sing "Every Knee Shall Bow, Every Tongue Shall Confess." It was an old-fashioned hymn, unlike the hopped-up gospel songs churches were given to nowadays. And she liked the slow unfolding of its message: how without people uttering a word, all their hearts would be made plain to the Lord; that He would know you not by what you said or did, but by what you'd hoped and intended. The teens, however, mumbled over the verses, and older choir members sang without vigor. The hymn ended up sounding like the national anthem at a school assembly: a stouthearted song rendered in monotone.

"Thank you, thank you, thank you, Sister Clareese," Pastor Everett said, looking back at her, "for that wonderful tune."

Tune? She knew that Pastor Everett thought she was not the kind of person a choirmistress should be; she was quiet, nervous, skinny in all the wrong places, and completely cross-eyed. She knew he thought of her as something worse than a spinster, because she wasn't yet old.

Pastor Everett hunched close to the microphone, as though about to begin a forlorn love song. From the corners of her vision she saw him smile—only for a second but with every single tooth in his mouth. He was yam-colored, and given to wearing epaulets on the shoulders of his robes and gold braiding all down the front. Sister Clareese felt no attraction to him, but she seemed to be the only one who didn't; even the Sisters going on eighty were charmed by Pastor Everett, who, though not entirely handsome, had handsome moments.

"Sister Clareese," he said, turning to where she stood with the choir. "Sister Clareese, I know y'all just sang for us, but I need some *more* help. Satan got these Brothers and Sisters putting m'Lord on hold!"

Sister Clareese knew that everyone expected her and her choir to begin singing again, but she had been alerted to what he was up to; he had called her yesterday. He had thought nothing of asking her to unplug her telephone—her *only* telephone, her *private* line—to bring it to church so that he could use it in some sermon about call-waiting. Hadn't even asked her how she was doing, hadn't bothered to pray over her aunt Alma's sickness. Nevertheless, she'd said, "Why certainly, Pastor Everett. Anything I can do to help."

Now Sister Clareese produced her Princess telephone from under her seat and handed it to the Pastor. Pastor Everett held the telephone aloft, shaking it as if to rid it of demons. "How many of y'all—Brothers and Sisters—got telephones?" the Pastor asked.

One by one, members of the congregation timidly raised their hands.

"All right," Pastor Everett said, as though this grieved him, "almost all of y'all." He flipped through his huge pulpit Bible. "How many of y'all—Brothers and Sisters—got call-waiting?" He turned pages quickly, then stopped, as though he didn't need to search the scripture after all. "Let me tell ya," the Pastor said, nearly kissing the microphone, "there is *Someone!* Who won't *accept* your call-waiting! There is *Someone!* Who won't *wait,* when you put Him on hold!" Sister Nancy Popwell and Sister Drusella Davies now had their eyes closed in concentration, their hands waving slowly in the air in front of them as though they were trying to make their way through a dark room.

The last phone call Sister Clareese had made was on Wednesday, to Mr. Toomey. She knew both he and Cleophus were likely to reject the Lord, but she had a policy of sorts, which was to call patients who'd been in her care for at least a week. She considered it her Christian duty to call—even on her day off—to let them know that Jesus cared, and that she cared. The other RNs resorted to callous catchphrases that they bandied about the nurses' station: "Just because I care *for* them doesn't mean I have to care *about* them," or, "I'm a nurse, not a nursery." Not Clareese. Perhaps she'd been curt with Cleophus Sanders, but she had been so in defense of God. Perhaps Mr. Toomey had been curt with her, but he was going into O.R. soon, and grouchiness was to be expected.

Nurse Patty had been switchboard operator that night and Clareese had had to endure her sighs before the girl finally connected her to Mr. Toomey.

"Praise the Lord, Mr. Toomey!"

"Who's this?"

"This is your nurse, Sister Clareese, and I'm calling to say that Jesus will be with you through your surgery."

"Who?"

"Jesus," she said.

She thought she heard the phone disconnect, then, a voice. Of course. Cleophus Sanders.

"Why ain't you called *me?*" Cleophus said.

Sister Clareese tried to explain her policy, the thing about the week.

"So you care more about some white dude than you care about good ol' Cleophus?"

"It's not that, Mr. Sanders. God cares for white and black alike. Acts 10:34 says, 'God is no respecter of persons.' Black or white. Red, purple, or green—he doesn't care, as long as you accept his salvation and live right." When he was silent on the other end she said, "It's that I've only known you for two days. I'll see you tomorrow."

She tried to hang up, but he said, "Let me play something for you. Something interesting, since all you probably listen to is monks chanting and such."

Before she could respond, there was a noise on the other end that sounded like juke music. Then he came back on the phone and said, "Like that, don't you?"

"I had the phone away from my ear."

"I thought you said 'lying is the abominable.' Do you like or do you don't?" When she said nothing he said, "Truth, now."

She answered yes.

She didn't want to answer yes. But she also didn't want to lie. And what was one to do in that circumstance? If God looked into your heart right then, what would He think? Or would He have to approve because He made your heart that way? Or were you obliged to train it against its wishes? She didn't know what to think, but on the other end Cleophus said, "What you just heard there was the blues. What you just heard there was me."

". . . L E T M E tell ya!" Pastor Everett shouted, his voice hitting its highest octave, "*Jeeeee-zus*—did not *tell* his *Daddy*—'I'm sorry, Pops, but my girlfriend is on the other line'; *Jeeeee-zus*—never *told* the Omnipotent One, 'Can you wait a sec, I think I got a call from the electric company!' *Jeeeeeeee-zus*—never told Matthew, Mark, Luke, or John, 'I'm *sorry*, but I got to put you on hold; I'm sorry, Brother Luke, but I got some mac and cheese in the oven; I'm *sorry*, but I got to eat this fried chicken'"—and at this, Pastor Everett paused, grinning in anticipation of his own punch line—"'cause it's finger-licking good!'"

Drops of sweat plunked onto his microphone.

Sister Clareese watched as the congregation cheered, the women flagging their Bibles in the air as though the Bibles were as light and yielding as handkerchiefs; their bosoms jouncing as though they were harboring sacks of potatoes in their blouses. They shook tambourines, scores of them all going at once, the sound of something sizzling and frying.

That was it? That was The Message? Of course, she'd only heard part of it, but still. Of course she believed that one's daily life shouldn't outstrip one's spiritual one, but there seemed no place for true belief at Greater Christ Emmanuel Pentecostal Church of the

Fire Baptized. Everyone wanted flash and props, no one wanted the Word itself, naked in its fiery glory.

Most of the Brothers and Sisters were up on their feet. "Tell it!" yelled some, while others called out, "Go 'head on!" The organist pounded out the chords to what could have been the theme song of a TV game show.

She looked to see what Sister Drusella's and Sister Maxwell's unsaved guests were doing. Drusella's unsaved guest was her son, which made him easy to bring into the fold: he was living in her shed and had no car. He was busy turning over one of the cardboard fans donated by Hamblin and Sons Funeral Parlor, reading the words intently, then flipping it over again to stare at the picture of a gleaming casket and grieving family. Sister Donna Maxwell's guest was an ex-con she'd written to and tried to save while he was in prison. The ex-con seemed to watch the scene with approval, though one could never really know what was going on in the criminal mind. For all Sister Clareese knew, he could be counting all the pockets he planned to pick.

And they called themselves missionaries. Family members and ex-cons were easy to convince of God's will. As soon as Drusella's son took note of the pretty young Sisters his age, he'd be back. And everyone knew you could convert an ex-con with a few well-timed pecan pies.

Wednesday was her only day off besides Sunday, and though a phone call or two was her policy on days off, she very seldom visited the hospital. And yet, last Wednesday, she'd had to. The more she'd considered Cleophus's situation—his loss of limb, his devil's music, his unsettling laughter—the more she grew convinced that he was her Missionary Challenge. That he was especially in need of Saving.

Minutes after she'd talked with him on the phone, she took the number 42 bus and transferred to the crosstown H, then walked the rest of the way to the hospital.

Edwina had taken over for Patty as nurses' station attendant, and she'd said, "We have an ETOH in—where's your uniform?"

"It's not my shift," she called behind her as she rushed past Edwina and into Room 204.

She opened the door to find Cleophus sitting on the bed, still plucking chords on his unplugged electric guitar that she'd heard him playing over the phone half an hour earlier. Mr. Toomey's bed was empty; one of the nurses must have already taken him to O.R., so Cleophus had the room to himself. The right leg of Cleophus's hospital pants hung down limp and empty, and it was the first time she'd seen his guitar, curvy and shiny as a sportscar. He did not acknowledge her when she entered. He was still picking away at his guitar, singing a song about a man whose woman had left him so high and dry, she'd taken the car, the dog, the furniture. Even the wallpaper. Only when he'd strummed the final chords did Cleophus look up, as if noticing her for the first time.

"Sister *Clare-reeeese!*" He said it as if he were introducing a showgirl.

"It's your soul," Clareese said. "God wants me to help save your soul." The urgency of God's message struck her so hard, she felt the wind knocked out of her. She sat on the bed next to him.

"Really?" he said, cocking his head a little.

"Really and truly," Clareese said. "I know I said I liked your music, but I said it because God gave you that gift for you to use. For Him."

"Uhnn-huh," Cleophus said. "How about this, little lady. How about if God lets me keep this knee, I'll come to church with you. We can go out and get some dinner afterwards. Like a proper couple."

She tried not to be flattered. "The Lord does *not make* deals, Mr. Sanders. But I'm sure the Lord would love to see you in church regardless of what happens to your knee."

"Well, since you seem to be His receptionist, how about you ask the Lord if he can give you the day off. I can take you out on the town. See, if I go to church, I *know* the Lord won't show. But I'm positive you will."

"Believe you me, Mr. Sanders, the Lord is at every service. *Where two or three are gathered together in my name, there am I in the midst of them.*" She sighed, trying to remember what she came to say. *"He is the Way, the Truth and the Life. No man—"*

"...cometh to the father," Cleophus said, *"but by me."*

She looked at him. "You know your Bible."

"Naw. You were speaking and I just heard it." He absently strummed his guitar. "You were talking, saying that verse, and the rest of it came to me. Not even a voice," he said, "more like ... kind of like music."

She stared. Her hands clapped his, preventing him from playing further. For a moment, she was breathless. He looked at her, suddenly seeming to comprehend what he'd just said, that the Lord had actually spoken to him. For a minute, they sat there, both overjoyed at what the Lord had done, but then he had to go ruin it. He burst out laughing his biggest, most sinful laugh yet.

"Awww!" he cried, doubled over, and then flopped backward onto his hospital bed. Then he closed his eyes, laughing without sound.

She stood up, chest heaving, wondering why she even bothered with him.

"Clareese," he said, trying to clear his voice of any leftover laughter, "don't go." He looked at her with pleading eyes, then patted the space beside him on the bed.

She looked around the room for some cue. Whenever she needed an answer, she relied on some sign from the Lord; a fresh beam of sunlight through the window, the hands of a clock folded in prayer, or the flush of a commode. These were signs that whatever she was thinking of doing was right. If there was a storm cloud, or something in her path, then that was a bad sign. But nothing in the room gave her any indication whether she should stay and witness to Mr. Sanders, or go.

"What, Mr. Sanders, do you want from me? It's my day off. I decided to come by and offer you an invitation to my church because God has given you a gift. A musical gift." She dug into her purse, then pulled out a pocket-sized Bible. "But I'll leave you with this. If you need to find us—our church—the name and number is printed inside."

He took the Bible with a little smile, turning it over, then flipping through it, as if some money might be tucked away inside. "Seriously, though," he'd said, "let me ask you a question that's gonna seem dumb. Childish. Now, I want you to think long and hard about it. Why the hell's there so much suffering in the world if God's doing his job? I mean, look at me. Take old Toomey, too. We done anything *that* bad to deserve all this put on us?"

She sighed. "Because of people, that's why. Not God. It's *people* who allow suffering, people who create it. Perpetrate it."

"Maybe that explains Hitler and all them others, but I'm talking about—" He gestured at the room, the hospital in general.

Clareese tried to see what he saw when he looked at the room. At one time, the white and pale green walls of the hospital rooms had given her solace; the way everything was clean, clean, clean; the many patients that had been in each room, some nice, some dying, some willing to accept the Lord. But most, like Mr. Toomey, cast the Lord aside like wilted lettuce, and now the clean hospital room was just a reminder of the emptiness, the barrenness, of her patients' souls. Cleophus Sanders was just another patient who disrespected the Lord.

"Why does He allow natural disasters to kill people?" Clareese said, knowing that her voice was raised louder than what she meant it to be. "Why are little children born to get some rare blood disease and die? Why," she yelled, waving her arms, "does a crane fall on your leg and smash it? I don't know, Mr. Sanders. And I don't like it. But I'll say this! No one has a *right* to live! The only right we have is to die. That's it! If you get plucked out of the universe and given a chance to become a life, that's more than not having become anything at all, and for that, Mr. Sanders, you should be grateful!"

She had not known where this last bit had come from, and, she could tell, neither had he, but she could hear the other nurses coming down the hall to see who was yelling, and though Cleophus Sanders looked to have more pity on his face than true belief, he had come after her when she turned to leave. She'd heard the clatter of him gathering his crutches, and even when she heard the meaty weight of him slam onto the floor, she did not turn back.

THEN there it was. Pastor Everett's silly motion of cupping his hand to his ear, like he was eavesdropping on the choir, his signal that he was waiting for Sister Clareese to sing her solo, waiting to hear the voice that would send the congregation shouting, "Thank you, Jesus, Blessed Savior!"

How could she do it? She thought of Cleophus on the floor and felt ashamed. She hadn't seen him since; her yelling had been brought to the attention of the administrators, and although the hospital was understaffed, the administration had suggested that she not return until next week. They handed her the card of the staff psychiatrist. She had not told anyone at church what had happened. Not even her aunt Alma.

She didn't want to sing. Didn't feel like it, but, she thought, *I will freely sacrifice myself unto Thee: I will praise Thy name, O Lord, for it is good.* Usually thinking of a scripture would give her strength, but this time it just made her realize how much strength she was always needing.

She didn't want to, but she'd do it. She'd sing a stupid solo part— the Waterfall, they called it—not even something she'd *invented* or *planned* to do who knows how many years ago when she'd had to sneeze her brains out, but oh no, she'd tried holding it in, and when she had to sing her solo, those years ago, her near-sneeze had made the words come out tumbling in a series of staccato notes that were almost fluid, and ever since then, she'd had to sing *all* solos that way, it was expected of her, everyone loved it, it was her trademark. She sang: "All-hall other-her her grooouund—is sink-king sand!"

The congregation applauded.

"S A I N T S ," the Pastor said, winding down, "you know this world will soon be *over*! Jesus will come back to this tired, sorry Earth in *a moment and a twinkling of an eye*! So you can't use call-waiting on the Lord! *Jeeee-zus,* my friends, does not accept conference calls! You are Children of God! You need to PRAY! Put down your phone! Say goodbye to AT&T! You cannot go in God's *direction,* without a little—*genuflection!*"

The congregation went wild, clapping and banging tambourines, whirling in the aisles. But the choir remained standing in case Pastor Everett wanted another song. For the first time, Clareese found that her monthly troubles had settled down. And now that she had the wherewithal to concentrate, she couldn't. Her cross-eyes wouldn't keep steady, they roamed like the wheels of a defective shopping cart, and from one roving eye she saw her aunt Alma, waving her arms as though listening to leftover strains of Clareese's solo.

What would she do? She didn't know if she'd still have her job when she went back on Monday, didn't know what the staff psychiatrist would try to pry out of her. More important, she didn't know what her aunt Alma would do without the special medical referrals Clareese could get her. What was a Sister to do?

Clareese's gaze must have found him just a moment after everyone else's had. A stranger at the far end of the aisle, standing directly opposite Pastor Everett as though about to engage him in a duel. There was Cleophus Sanders with his crutches, the right leg of his pinstriped pants hollow, wagging after him. Over his shoulder was a strap, attached to which was his guitar. Even Deacon Mc-Creedy was looking.

What in heaven's name was Cleophus doing here? To bring his soul to salvation? To ridicule her? For another argument? Perhaps the doctors had told him he did not need the operation after all, and Cleophus was keeping his end of the deal with God. But he didn't seem like the type to keep promises. She saw his eyes search the congregation, and when he saw her, they locked eyes as if he had come to claim her. He did not come to get Saved, didn't care about his soul in that way, all he cared about was—

Now she knew why he'd come. He'd come for her. He'd come

despite what she'd told him, despite his disbelief. Anyhow, she disapproved. It was God he needed, not her. Nevertheless, she remained standing for a few moments, even after the rest of the choir had already seated themselves, waving their cardboard fans to cool their sweaty faces.

Our Lady of Peace

❧

THE CHROME-TOPPED vending machine in the Baltimore Travel Plaza flashed *Chips! Chips! Chips!* but no one
could have known it was broken unless they'd been there for a long
time, like Lynnea, having just escaped lackluster Kentucky, waiting for a taxi, watching a pale, chain-smoking white girl whose life
seemed to be brought to a grinding halt by an inability to obtain
Fritos.

The white girl kicked the vending machine, then cracked her
knuckles. After a few spells of kicking and pouting, she found her
way to the row of seats where Lynnea was sitting, then plunked
down next to her.

"I'm going to kill myself," the white girl said.

Lynnea turned in the girl's direction, which was invitation

enough for the girl to begin rattling off the story of her life: running away, razor blades, ibuprofen; living day to day on cigarettes and Ritz crackers.

Outside the Travel Plaza, Baltimore stretched black and row-house brown. Traffic signals changed, dusk arrived in inky blue smudges, and slow-moving junkies stuttered their way across the sidewalk as though rethinking decisions they'd already made. This, she thought lamely, had been what was waiting for her in Baltimore.

But any place was better than Odair County, Kentucky. She'd hated how everyone there oozed out their words, and how humble everyone pretended to be, and how all anyone ever cared about was watching basketball and waiting for the next Kentucky Derby. Her grandparents had been born in Odair and so had their parents. Her family was one of four black families in the county, and if another white person ever told her how "interesting" her hair was, or how good it was that she didn't have to worry about getting a tan— ha ha—or asked her opinion anytime Jesse Jackson farted, she'd strangle them.

Nevertheless, she'd gone back to Odair County after college and started working at the Quickie Mart. One night—while in the middle of reminding herself that the job was beneath her, and that once she'd saved up enough, she'd move to a big city—four high school boys wearing masks held up the place with plastic guns, taking all the Miller Light they could fit in their Radio Flyer wagons. She hadn't been scared, and the manager had said she'd done the right thing. Still, she smoked her first cigarette that night, and spread a map of the country over her mother's kitchen table.

When she'd ruled out the first tier of cities—New York (too expensive), L.A. (she had no car), Chicago (she couldn't think of any reason why not Chicago, but it just seemed wrong)—Lynnea had settled on Baltimore. She took an apartment sight-unseen, her last few hundred dollars devoured by a cashier's check for a security deposit, signed to a landlady named Venus.

Now that she had arrived in Baltimore, she'd begun to have doubts. There was no taxi in sight, and the white girl next to her droned on, describing preferable methods of suicide.

"Tibetan monks light themselves on fire," the girl said.

Lynnea held her head in her hands and tried to ignore the girl. She stared at the floor, its checkered tiles marbleized by filth; she looked outside to see if any taxis had arrived. She even cast her eyes about the bus station crowd, but the white girl *still* would not shut up.

"Eskimos kill themselves by floating away on icebergs," the white girl said.

"If you can find an iceberg anywhere near Baltimore," Lynnea finally said, "I'd be glad to strap you to it."

H ER L A N D L A D Y , Venus, was a tiny sixtyish woman who walked in quiet, jerky steps. Her complexion was the solemn brown of leatherbound books—nearly the same shade as Lynnea's—but atop her head, where presumably black hair should have been, Venus wore a triumphant blond wig. Lynnea had been living in a damp efficiency below Venus for nearly three months when she spotted the woman taking out the garbage, readjusting her wig as though Lynnea were an unexpected guest.

"Oh my. Shocked me near to death. How's the moving going?"

"I moved in three months ago," Lynnea said. "I'm pretty much finished moving in."

"I thought you were moving out."

"No. Not that I know of."

Lynnea always paid her rent late and hadn't paid last month's at all. She slurped black bean soup straight from the can, used newsprint for toilet paper, had tried foreign coins and wooden nickels in the quarters-only laundromat. By the end of three months she'd decided freelancing at the weekly paper was not enough; she would need a job that paid for dentist visits, health insurance, toilet paper.

Then she read about a teaching program that promised to cut the certification time from two years to a single summer. This, she knew, was for her. Inner-city Baltimore students would be nothing like the whiny white girl from the bus station. Lynnea would become an employee of the city, and have—at long last—benefits.

"We're going to do a few exercises," the director said on the first day of the certification program. "What you're trying to do," she said widening her eyes, "is disappear."

Lynnea waited for her to explain what she meant by "disappear" but the director just smiled as though disappearing were easy and fun. Lynnea looked around the classroom to see if others were as lost as she. A man who had previously introduced himself to Lynnea simply as Robert the Cop stared at Evelyn, then winced as though he'd been asked for a urine sample.

"Miss Evelyn," Robert the Cop said, his hands holding a box of imaginary no-nonsense. "I'm a cop. I'm new at this teaching business. You gotta break it down for me. What do you mean by 'disappear'?"

"Disappear. You know. To go away, to vanish."

Lynnea sighed and looked down, watching a roach scramble across the floor. Then Jake Bonza, the man second-in-charge, a teacher for twenty years, took over. "What Ms. Evelyn Hardy means is this: one a y'all is going to pretend to be the teacher. The rest of y'all are going to abandon your adult selves and act like students. Not the goody-two-shoe students, but the kinda fucked-up students you know y'all were or wanted to be." He paused, looking at them as if to sear his words into their heads before he continued, "This'll prepare you for the freaks of nature who'll throw spit wads at you while you try to take attendance."

Bonza browsed the room, flashing an ornery grin. "Yeah." He nodded. "We'll see which one a y'alls cracks and bleeds. Which one a y'alls bends over and takes it from behind."

DURING THE training sessions, adults playing students took their roles as miscreants to heart: they got out of their seats, wanting to pee and eat and smoke: Robert the Cop stood and lit a Marlboro while some pink farm girl from Vermont went through her lesson on subtraction in tears, her shaky hand gripping the chalk so hard it broke. They'd ask questions like how much wood could a wood-chuck chuck; one teacher felt liberated enough to discharge a sulfurous fart. Lynnea sat with her chin resting on her desk, eyes trained on the chalkboard, refusing to believe her students would act this way, refusing to participate in team-spirit badness.

But after eight weeks of role-play, Lynnea was in front of a real classroom. Freshman English. After she'd written her name on the chalkboard, a tall boy, the color of a paper bag, hitched up his droopy jeans and exclaimed, "Two G's, yo!" splaying two fingers like a sign of victory, the other hand in an arthritic semblance of a "G." The replies were immediate and high-pitched. "Yeaah boyeee!"

"What up, yo!" Then a trio found each other from the maze of Lynnea's carefully organized seats and high-fived elaborately before leisurely sitting back down, happily grabbing their crotches.

Throughout the first day, she kept hearing this phrase; students in the hallway yelling, "2 G's! 2 G's!" She finally pulled two girls aside and asked what it meant. The girls looked at each other, tottering coltishly in their clunky Day-Glo shoes, all enlarged eyes and grins, muffling giggles on each other's shoulders. Finally one girl composed herself enough to explain, "It mean two grand. Two thousand dollars. Like the Class of 2000. Get it?"

Lynnea nodded her head quickly, feigning remembrance of something she'd momentarily forgotten. She had wondered what the Class of 2000 would call themselves when she and people she called friends gathered in the Taco Bell parking lot to celebrate their own graduation. "What're they gonna call themselves? The class of Double Nothing?"

A T T H E end of the first week of teaching, Lynnea found herself having to raise her voice to get their attention—something she wasn't used to doing. They didn't quite yell and scream, but their collective whimsical talk was the unsettling buzz of a far-off carnival. When she sent them to the principal's office, they snickered and bugged out cartoon eyes, heading toward the office for a few paces, then bolting in the opposite direction. She found herself sharking the room, telling duos here and trios there that they should not be talking about their neon fingernail polish or the Mos Def lyrics in front of them, but the novel at hand, *Their Eyes Were Watching God*. They were quiet for a moment, controlling their grins as if they were hiding something live and wriggling between the covers of their notebooks.

One day into her second week of school, students had begun slipping to the edges of their seats during the lesson, stunt-falling to the floor whenever an anonymous ringleader gave the signal.

"STOP IT," Lynnea said, teeth clenched. As soon as she spoke, a wave of students dropped to the floor, stricken by an invisible three-second plague. She gritted her teeth and tugged at her hair. The students hushed and slid back into their chairs, then sat straight again as if watching to see what gesture of pain she'd make next. She tried counting to ten, but only got to five when she caught the unmistakable scent of marijuana.

"All right. Who's been smoking?"

"Smoking's bad for you," someone said.

First came guarded giggles, then a blossoming of laughter.

E v e r y F r i d a y after school all the teachers in the program met at a bar called The Rendezvous Lounge, ostensibly to swap teaching stories and commiserate before they got drunk. The first time she'd gone to The Rendezvous, she and Robert the Cop had smoked together, making fun of Bonza.

"Forget that crack-and-bleed song and dance," Robert the Cop said. "All I want is for the students to do what I tell them. All I want is for my fucking health care to kick in so I can get rid of this rotten molar."

Just a week ago, Lynnea would have agreed, but now, at the end of her second week of teaching, she just wanted to be able to teach without having to shout above the students. One of the teachers at her school had said that whenever the students got loud, he whispered, forcing the students to shut up in order to make out what he said. But this little trick didn't work for Lynnea. Her whispers went as unheeded as her yells.

She ordered a DeGroen's and scanned the crowd of teachers, the barroom air smelling of beer and smoke. Then, to Lynnea's surprised joy, Jake Bonza strode through The Rendezvous in a pantomime of majesty, glancing right and left; surveying the crowd before picking the person he believed would soonest buckle under the pressure of his loud piss stream of talk.

"How's it hanging, Davis?" Bonza called out to Lynnea. Bonza took out a cigarette and lit it, blowing smoke from his nostrils like a hero in an old western before aiming the cigarette Lynnea's way. "You think you gone pull through this, hon?"

"Of course I'll pull through," Lynnea said. "Why shouldn't I?"

She hadn't told him anything about the past two weeks, and now felt insulted that he'd assumed—correctly—that something was wrong. Lynnea searched Bonza for an elaboration, but Bonza just winked at Evelyn, then downed half of his beer.

"I've been through some tough times," Lynnea said, thinking back to her days of working at the Odair Quickie Mart. She would have to pull through: she wouldn't get paid until the end of the month. And she was running out of toilet paper.

A few days later, Lynnea caught two girls nonchalantly plunking packages of fake hair onto their desks. The packages were labeled by color: Burnished Rum, Foxy Black, Champagne Kiss.

"What do you think you're going to do with those?" she asked mid-lesson, her shaky finger still pointing to a vocabulary word on the chalkboard: *expiate.*

One of the girls, Ebony, looked her up and down, then rested her eyes at a point beyond Lynnea's glare. "Whatever the hell I want to." Ebony took out a strip of hair from the long plastic bag, doubled it, and hooked it around a spongy black clump of Kyra's hair, then proceeded to braid. The room was quiet.

"Out!" Lynnea said.

"No," Ebony said, then sucked her teeth as though annoyed she'd been forced to answer. Ebony kept braiding at a steady pace, as if determined to show the rest of the class she wasn't paying attention to Lynnea. It was this calm, this nonchalance, that infuriated Lynnea most of all, and she gripped Ebony's bony shoulder, leaned until her mouth was flush against Ebony's ear, and blared, "OUT!"

Ebony whipped up from her seat and backhanded her, strands of Foxy Black slapping across Lynnea's face. Chairs clattered to floor, students stood, screaming like cheerleaders. "*Shit!* Did you see that! Ms. Davis got *banked!*"

Lynnea felt her face. No blood. Barely a sting. The girl was gone. Lynnea blinked slowly, then walked out of the classroom. Behind her the class had become a noisy party, and ahead of her, a few yards down the hallway, she saw Ebony make the corner—a flash of short skirt, yellow plastic go-go boots, a trail of fake hair. She heard the squeak of sneakers and knew half her class was on its way down two flights of stairs and out the massive doors.

LYNNEA WROTE out a suspension sheet for Ebony, though no one in the school could track the girl down to give it to her. When the final bell rang, Mr. Morocco, the principal, sat down with Lynnea in her empty classroom. In low, clear tones, he spoke about the need for "greater classroom management." Then he left, closing the door the way a parent might after grounding a child.

Alone in her classroom, Lynnea thought of Charlesetta Flew, the history teacher down the hall who carried a dish towel to wipe sweat from her face. She was a stocky, penny-colored woman, her looks reminding Lynnea of her quiet aunt Selma, but when a student so much as whispered in Ms. Flew's class, Charlesetta Flew threatened to sit on them. They believed her and sat at their desks with the solemnity of pieces on a chessboard.

Mrs. Flew would laugh at Lynnea, how Lynnea approached the chalkboard crabwise, afraid that if she turned her back to write anything on it, the students would rearrange their desks. Or a student might just up and leave, or curse her out. Or hit her.

Without quite knowing what led her, Lynnea made her way past a sprinkling of after-school students in the lime green halls, nearly slipping on confetti left over from a pep rally before finally reaching the main office. She plunked her quarter in the normally broken pay phone and called Bonza, who promised to meet her as soon as he could.

She waited outside for Bonza in the gray weather. The front of the school was deserted and the four skimpy trees that dotted the dirt-packed school lawn evaded any pretense of bright New Englandesque fall colors, heading straight to dried-out beige. She could just make out the thunk and dribble of a basketball game getting started on the far eastern side of the school. The boys preferred to primp on the basketball courts where teachers would be less likely to catch them smoking blunts packed with weed. Lynnea had seen—and smelled—them once, watching the boys swirl and fake each other out. Most of the audience comprised girls she'd seen leisurely walking the halls. They wore their makeup like stains, propped themselves against the school walls, yelling names and dares and sexy invitations. But no one loitered where she waited on the school's front steps, the wind making her eyes water.

Bonza drove up in a Pinto that looked like it had been dipped in acid. He rolled—then pushed—down his broken car window.

"Having problems?" Bonza drawled. He lit a cigarette and slammed the car door. His head bobbed up and down, as if in agreement with himself. "Thought you said you'd seen some tough times." He began to walk the perimeter of the school and she followed.

"They mill around whenever they want, they won't shut up, they—they couldn't care less about—I mean, when you're teaching, don't you ever see a—light in their eyes?"

The Baltimore Public School System ran a series of Vaseline-smeared camera shots of students eagerly raising their hands to answer questions, students traipsing through fields to release butterflies into the wild, smiling students clad in black graduation robes, a teary-eyed teacher, beaming from the front row. In each of these shots, the camera zooms in on one student, until their eyes are the size of fists on the television screen, with a twinkling star of light flashing through each retina.

"A light?" Bonza covered his mouth with his hand, then doubled over in an exaggerated bow, and when he finally came up, his hair flew back like that of a Labrador flicking off the waters of a mountain stream.

"Ohhh boy." Bonza shook his head.

Lynnea felt her eyes narrow on him. "What's so funny?"

He regarded the burning ash, turning serious. "Maybe," he said, "you became a teacher for all the wrong reasons, hon. Maybe you just don't care enough about them."

"Listen," Lynnea said. "I care. It's the students who don't care."

"All right. So they don't care. Whaddya do?"

She knew this was one of his little tests. She stuttered, but didn't answer. He snapped his fingers to signal she was out of time and smiled his disapproval. She'd expected him to come up with one of his handy one-liners about teaching—*teachers don't teach, they coach; dilemmas aren't solved, they're managed*—but all he said was:

"Robert the Cop quit teaching."

Lynnea looked at him. "Doesn't surprise me," she said.

"Yeah. He's a cop down in his blood." Bonza seemed to lament this, and she could see why: during Robert the Cop's role-play as teacher that summer, all the adults pretending to be students in his class pulled the same antics they'd pulled in other role-plays. But Robert the Cop never lost his composure. He gave them all detention, goose-stepping to each pretend student, pounding his fist on their desks for quiet. He ended by telling them they were all sorry motherfuckers, said they'd all amount to nothing, zero, zilch, nada, if they didn't respect authority.

Before he began teaching school, Robert took night shifts so he could attend his classes during the day. After his turn at role-play teaching, he drove to a black part of town called Hollander Ridge and parked his unmarked Mazda at an intersection where the traffic lights never worked.

"Yep. I nabbed 'em," he admitted the day after he'd given the tickets. "I needed to get my quota." He'd handed out eleven speeding tickets and three vagrancy charges. Fourteen in all. "Payback."

Lynnea knew it was revenge on the fourteen pretend students

who'd given him hell in role-play, and she somehow felt complicit, as though she'd had the power to stop him but didn't.

"It's better that he quit." Bonza leaned toward her, his black hair battered by the wind. "Robert didn't have the heart for it. Not like you, hon."

The wind jerked the four trees of the schoolyard until it gathered a shower of dead leaves to carry away; it swung open the flaps of Lynnea's cheap green jacket so hard the lapels hit her face. She could see Bonza's eyes scanning the school steps: no students. He threw his cigarette to the concrete, snuffed it out with his shoe, then grabbed her, kissing her with full, sloppy thrusts of tongue, his mustache scrubbing her face with its bristles. Lynnea pushed him away and gasped for air, trying to wipe away the saliva ringing her mouth, only to find both hands locked solidly in Bonza's.

"C'mon. Let's blow this joint."

"*Joint?* I'm sure you have to get back home to your wife." She used the steady bad-ass eyes she'd practiced in the mirror for her class. Bonza chucked his head to the side as though his wife were some sort of poem he'd read, hadn't understood, and had dismissed.

Lynnea tried to pull away, but couldn't. "No," she said. "And I mean it."

Bonza let go and looked at her as though he was tired and she was keeping him from getting his sleep. "Listen. Do you wanna learn all the right tricks or what?"

Two weeks after the Bonza incident, Lynnea got a new student. The guidance counselor, Mr. Knight, handed her a thick, bulging folder.

"Sheba Simmons. Those are all her records, transfers."

As Lynnea glanced down at the heavy folder, the guidance counselor whispered into her ear, "She knifed a teacher at her old school."

"Yippee," Lynnea said.

A girl walked into the office. She was over six feet tall and the legs under her miniskirt looked like those of a bodybuilder.

"Are you my new student?" Lynnea asked.

"Question is, You my new teacher?"

Mr. Knight pulled Lynnea outside the office and gave her the rundown on Sheba: Sheba did not live with a family but in a home for girls. Every afternoon a bus with iron grillework on the windows was going to pick her up, take her to Hollander Ridge. According to Mr. Knight, the place was a large formstone building with OUR LADY OF PEACE in bas-relief above the entrance.

Before Sheba entered the classroom, Lynnea told everyone that they would have a new student, and as soon as she said the name "Sheba," Terra Undertaker howled, "Sheba. That a *dog's* name!" The class began to bark wildly in various pitches, ranging from Chihuahua to Doberman.

When Sheba stepped into the room, the barking trailed off to nothing. Sheba sat in the chair closest to Lynnea's desk, took out her notebook and pen, eyed the board, and began copying the day's notes. No one moved, Lynnea included. Sheba, sensing that it was a bit too quiet, turned her head around to the class.

"Why y'all all back there?"

Lynnea didn't know what she was talking about until she noticed that the desks and seats had traveled to the back half of the room, leaving her and Sheba in the front.

"Everyone," Lynnea began, using her orchestra-conducting voice, "move your desks forward."

A few pushed their desks, but that was it. Five students had come forward. Sheba stood and scanned the classroom.

"Y'all hear the woman! The woman say *move!*"

Desks clattered, seats edged across the tiled floor with persistent fart noises, girls dragged large fake designer handbags behind them like migrant workers told to flee the land. Sheba flitted her eyes as though all of this wasn't quick enough for her, but would suffice. The students sat straight in their desks, not daring to speak. Sheba sat back down slowly, primly smoothing down her short skirt against her thighs before edging into her seat. Lynnea stood. The silence lasted almost a full minute. Finally, Sheba looked at Lynnea and said, "Is you gone teach us or what?"

VENUS WAS raking the same patch of leaves over and over. The leaves leapt from the broken prongs of the rake and settled back to where they'd originally lain. "Hello," Lynnea said. "Venus. Venus? Hello?"

"Oh." Venus turned, still raking. "How you doing?"

"Fine. Teaching. You know how that goes."

"Ohhhh do I. They all crack babies. None a them's got a bit a sense to them. Ought a skip schooling and send them all to the military."

Without looking up from the leaves she said, "So. When you say you was moving out?"

IN THE following weeks, they finished reading *Their Eyes Were Watching God* and moved on to *The Great Gatsby*. The class was quiet with Sheba in it. If a student began to talk, Sheba would stand and say, "Y'all need to shut up and learn something." Everyone would remain seated.

One day after school, Lynnea lifted her head from its defeated position on her desk and found a pair of eyes staring at her, as though she were a problem Sheba was trying to solve.

"Miz Davis, I got to talk to you."

"Yes," Lynnea said, glancing at the clock.

"We can't go on like this. I mean, nobody want to learn about no metaphors and symbolisms and—I don't know what all."

"Well, that's what we have to learn for exams."

"*You* don't have to learn nothing. We the ones—"

"Anything," Lynnea corrected.

"What?"

"Go on." Lynnea sneaked another glance at the clock.

"Maybe we can learn it, but not by you just yapping at us. Nobody wanna hear nobody else talk for no hour. It just get boring. Maybe we could act out some of the book, like a soap opera or something. Or when people wanna say their opinions, like a talk show."

So they tried the soap operas and talk shows in class.

"I still think Myrtle is a ho and Daisy—" Jerron searched the ceiling for words. "If she tried that shit—I mean stuff—where I live, some guy woulda clocked her long ago."

"But you gotta understand," Ramona said, "them was white folks, back in the twenties, when they just had invented cars. Daisy didn't even know she'd run Myrtle over. They just did stupid shit like that."

"All right," Lynnea said. "Could you quit it with the cursing? We're not on the streets."

"I don't live on no street!" an anonymous voice piped up.

In return, Sheba glared at the class and said, "If you don't *live* in no street, then don't *act like* you live in *no street*!"

The class was absolutely silent. Lynnea felt awkward and feeble breaking the silence. "Thank you, Sheba. Very well put."

The rest of the class they discussed *The Great Gatsby* with the quiet reserve of golf commentators describing a stroke. When the bell rang, they shambled out of the room quietly, but Sheba stayed.

Though class had ended well, it had still been a long day. Lynnea slumped over her desk, forehead resting on a pile of ungraded homework.

"Well," Sheba finally said, "they read the book. They understand. That's what you gotta keep in mind."

Lynnea raised her head and slowly nodded in reply, though Sheba was gone.

For a few weeks things went well. She was finally finishing her copying and lesson planning early enough to leave when the other teachers left; she was finally able to pack up her lessons and leave the building before the janitors kicked her out. Before Sheba, she used to spend at least an hour at her desk, paralyzed, recovering from her day. Now when she passed the school basketball court, she smiled and waved.

T H E N S H E B A stopped coming to class regularly. When she did come, she would smack her lips, occasionally casting a feeble glance Lynnea's way. One day when Lynnea was trying to explain etymologies to the class, the class grew noisier and noisier, books scattered on the students' desks, wads of papers strewn about the floor. Lynnea couldn't even hear herself speaking; the room sounded like a football arena, everyone talking—all save Sheba, who'd come to class after three weeks of spotty attendance. Sheba sat in her chair, the cuffs of her too-small rabbit fur jacket starting way past her wrists. In the midst of the noise and confusion, Sheba surveyed the scene, arms folded like a cigar-store Indian.

Lynnea heard a girl yell, "He pushed his thang up against my jeans and *whooo*!"

"All right, April," Lynnea said. "Out! Now!"

April stood, and for a moment looked as if she was going to say something, but shook her head, furiously, as though what she would have said would have been too foulmouthed even for her.

"Hurry up, April," Lynnea said. "We don't have all day."

Sheba stood up from her chair so suddenly the chair nearly toppled backward. She glared at Lynnea. "Now, everybody else *in here* talking. Why you gone call on April? If you had your *act* together you'da stopped the yakking before it got to this!"

The class applauded.

"Sit down, Sheba."

"Make me," Sheba said.

Lynnea considered this. Why couldn't she make Sheba sit down? Wasn't that one of the basic things a teacher should be able to do? "Well, Sheba. You can leave with April. Out."

"I'll get out. I don't care no more. Sick a this class."

Lynnea sighed. "Well, get out." She'd felt that up until now, up until Sheba's absences, she and Sheba had been a team: a crazy, lopsided one, but a team nonetheless. For a moment, she dared to meet Sheba's gaze head-on, and in that moment thought they'd reached some sort of détente of stares. It was then that Lynnea knew she would have gladly endured Sheba telling her off, cursing her out, stomping her foot, as long as Sheba stayed. *Stay,* she wanted to plead, but Sheba was the one to twist her eyes away first, and Lynnea heard herself say, "GET OUT!"

And so Sheba made a production of leaving: stashing papers into her notebook with grand, though haphazard, flourishes, slamming each book onto her desk before stuffing it into her bag. April's eyes followed Sheba slamming books and she began packing her supplies as well. Just as the girls got to the door, the guidance counselor arrived.

"Ms. Davis. I'm here for Sheba."

"That was fast. I was just sending her out. April needs to go, too."

The guidance counselor turned to April and narrowed his eyes with mock seriousness, "April, what you doing getting in trouble? I thought we put a end to that." He winked at April as though to remind her of a secret deal.

April tottered her head and flashed a set of lipstick-stained horse-teeth for him.

"Oh Mistah Knight!"

Mr. Knight straightened to all his six-five bulk and resumed his guidance-counselor voice for Lynnea. "I wasn't coming here to take Sheba to the principal's office. She's got a doctor's appointment, but I'll take both these young ladies downstairs." They left chattering on either side of him.

As soon as they had gone, Ebony, the girl who'd hit Lynnea, cheerily called out, "Miz Day-vis!"

"Yes, Ebony. What do you want?"

"You don't know Sheba got a baby in the oven?"

Lynnea tried not to let her surprise show. "That's not a matter for classroom discussion."

The students thought it was a perfect matter for discussion.

"Uhh uhhn!" one girl squealed. "Sheba pregnant! No she *didn't* go and get knocked up!"

"And she a big girl, too," one boy said. "I'd be afraid to steer that wheel."

~o

A F E W days before the winter break, while she was sitting in her car thinking, she spotted Sheba through the frost of her windshield. Sheba was watching the boys' basketball game, her hands clutching the chain-link that fenced in the basketball court. Though Sheba was no less than a few feet away from a crowd of people, she looked utterly alone. Winter was beginning to chill the air but Sheba still wore miniskirts, fishnet stockings, high heels.

Lynnea tried to see what it was that Sheba saw, but when she looked at the basketball court all she saw was gray concrete, the long-faded free-throw line, the school mascot painted in the center so weathered and chipped that the whole thing looked like an ancient mosaic. The boys who smoked weed all through the fall had vanished, leaving behind two short, skinny boys playing a hard, fast game. Perhaps Sheba only cared about the boys. More likely than not, she cared about how hard they were playing, that they could want to win so badly that neither dared back down.

Lynnea got out of her car and walked over to Sheba. A few students she recognized looked at her, but she pretended not to see them. "C'mon," Lynnea said, "I'll give you a ride home."

Sheba looked at Lynnea with annoyance, then resignation, as though she'd weighed her options and had decided she might as well get a free ride. Sheba walked with Lynnea to the parking lot, and got in the car without speaking.

"Where do you live?" Lynnea asked.

"You know where I live."

"Our Lady of Peace. I know *that*," Lynnea said, "but where is it?"

"Hollander Ridge."

"Where in Hollander Ridge?"

Sheba's eyes bugged out. "C'mon, Miz Davis. You really don't know?"

"No, I don't." They stared at each other. Sheba sighed. A cloud of her breath hung in the cold car interior.

Lynnea pulled off and headed down Thirty-third Street in the general direction of Hollander Ridge.

Sheba gave her a jumble of directions: Erdman, Moravia, Bel Air Road, and Frankford Avenue. Then the streets got small and narrow, with turns where Lynnea hadn't expected streets to be at all.

"Scared yet?"

Lynnea didn't answer. Sheba called out turns; otherwise the rest of the ride was silent.

Our Lady of Peace was its own planet: singular, immense, imposing. The statue of the Virgin Mary was larger than Lynnea thought statues of Virgins should be, and was covered with pigeon droppings. A sign with a picture of a lightning bolt on it was attached to the high electric fence that ran around the building. A whitewash of floodlights illuminated the sign. Next to it, another sign, wooden and hand-painted, read: TRY TO GET IN OR OUT WITHOUT PERMISSION AND DIE.

"Well. Here you are," Lynnea said. She thought for a moment, then said, "If you need something, or want me to visit you, give me a call."

"I don't think I'll be needing your help. But thanks for the ride." Sheba slammed the car door and clomped up the sidewalk.

Lynnea stretched her head over to the passenger window and clumsily rolled it down. "Be good. Take care of that baby."

Sheba stood, eyes still and unblinking.

O F C O U R S E she had said the wrong thing: Sheba obviously hadn't wanted the baby, but what was said was said, Lynnea thought. On the way back, Lynnea sailed through the red lights hoping to get home as quickly as possible. There she could think. Cry. Maybe fry herself an egg. She went the wrong way down one-way roads. Streetlamps buzzed here and there, but most were broken and did not flicker at all.

She came to an intersection where the traffic lights were out, looked both ways, and zoomed through. The single *Whuurp!* of a police siren stunned her for a moment, but she kept driving, only slower now. She thought of herself as an ant, foolish enough to believe that if she kept ambling along, the giant foot above wouldn't come smashing down. The police car trailed her. A voice barked through megaphone static, "Pull over."

The policeman got out and his door made its official-sounding slam. He walked over to her car, hitching up his pants as if preparing to recite a blasé Miranda. She rolled down the window. The policeman bent his head down to greet her. It was Robert the Cop.

"Hey, man. How's it going?" She smiled up at him.

Robert the Cop whipped out his ticket pad. "You were speeding."

Lynnea kept the smile pasted on her face. Robert the Cop wrote something on his pad. When he flipped the page and kept writing, her smile deserted her. "I just dropped off a student, O.K.?"

He walked to the back of her car to take down her license plate number. She thought about running him over. No one in Hollander Ridge would care. One less cop.

He came back around driver side and stuck his head in again.

"It's Lynnea. Lynnea Davis. Remember me? Teacher training? Bonza? Role-play?"

"Yep. I remember. Did you know you were speeding? Through red lights?"

Lynnea tried counting to ten to calm herself, but only got to three. "Do you know what it feels like to want to go home?" she asked. "To have worked one long motherfucking day with a bunch of kids who want to strangle your ass and you want to strangle theirs and you think about that sentimental shit—that 'if I can only reach one' shit—and you don't reach anyone?"

He nodded once. "Yep," he said. He tore the ticket from the pad.

SHE SPED out of the maze of streets. There was a green light and she whooshed through it faster than the reds. She could see the outlines of two boys walking across the street the way Baltimore kids walk, sauntering and primping and strolling all at once. They were the sort of kids who thought they had all the time in the world; time to play around, time to disobey, time to do whatever they wanted. They were the types of kids who seemed to love watching faces curse noiselessly on the other side of the windshield, their vengeance against the world. Lynnea knew they weren't going to make it across at the speed she was driving. She would have to slow down. She pressed on the horn so hard it braced her in the seat. The horn bleated.

"It's a green light! Get out of the way!" She knew the kids could only see her yelling, that they heard none of the words. One short outline flashed her the finger like a hearty salute. The taller one saw that she was going too fast and tried to limp a bit quicker, but the finger-flasher held on to him, as though to say, *They gone stop. Make 'em wait and get mad and shit.*

She had a chance to slow down, and she didn't want to. She'd scare them, for once. *Make* them run. Her foot slammed the accelerator for what seemed like no time at all, but when she changed her mind, trying to brake, she knew it was too late, she couldn't stop in time.

Somehow she heard the strange hissing before she heard the brakes screech. She'd never associated hissing with car wrecks, at least not the ones she'd seen in movies, where metal crunched, tires squealed. On television, cars spun like compasses gone haywire, only to regain their sense of direction, speeding off to create other wrecks. She no longer saw the boys—the limper, the finger-flasher.

She promised herself that if these boys lived, if they turned out all right, she'd visit Sheba at Our Lady of Peace; she wouldn't just pretend to care but would actually do something about it.

Just as she made this promise to herself, she heard the boys cursing and wailing somewhere near the front of the car's grille. One boy howled, struggling to one foot, holding his knee, hopping around as though he were searching for someone in a crowd. The other one banged the passenger window with heavy thumps and curses. They were alive.

Lynnea closed her eyes. Of course she knew leaving the accident scene would be the wrong thing to do, just as she knew she'd never see Sheba again, knew that her teaching days were over.

She could still hear the boys, even as she reversed, even as she took off. Even as she imagined how ridiculous it would be to visit Sheba, to watch as the girl hitched up her scary fishnet stockings, her eyes narrowed and unforgiving, speaking up for every pissed-off kid in the world, "C'mon. *Make me.*"

The Ant of the Self

❧

O PPORTUNITIES," my father says after I bail him out of
jail. He's banging words into the dash as if trying to get them
through my thick skull, "You've got to invest your money if you
want opportunities." It's October of '95, and we're driving around
Louisville, Kentucky, in my mother's car. Who knows why he came
down here, forty miles south of where he lives, but I don't ask questions that are sure to have too many answers. I just try to get my father, Ray Bivens Jr., back across the river to his place in Indiana.
Once we're on the Watterson Expressway, it seems as if we're about to
crash into the horizon. The sunset has ignited the bellies of clouds; the
mirrored windows of downtown buildings distort the flame-colored
city into a funhouse. I can already see that it'll be one of those days
when the sunset is extra-brilliant, though without staying power.

My father just got a DUI—again—though that didn't stop him from asking for the keys. When I didn't give them up, he sighed and shook his head as though I withheld keys from him daily. "C'mon, Spurge," he'd said. "The pigs aren't even looking."

He's the only person I know who still calls cops "pigs," a holdover from what he refers to as his Black Panther days, when "the brothers" raked their globes of hair with black-fisted Afro picks, then left them stuck there like javelins. When, as he tells it, he and Huey P. Newton would meet in basements and wear leather jackets and stick it to whitey. Having given me investment advice, he now watches the world outside the Honda a little too jubilantly. I take the curve around the city, past the backsides of chain restaurants and malls, office parks and the shitty Louisville zoo.

"That's your future," he says winding down from his rant. "Sound investments."

"Maybe you should ask the pigs for your bail money back," I say. "We could invest that."

He doesn't respond; by now he's too busy checking out my mom's new car. Ray Bivens Jr. doesn't own a car. The one he just got his DUI in was borrowed, he'd told me, from a friend.

Now he takes out the Honda's cigarette lighter from its round home, looking into the unlit burner as though staring into the future. He puts the lighter back as if he'd thought about pocketing it but has decided against it. He drums a little syncopation on the dash, then, bored, starts adjusting his seat as though he's on the Concorde. He wants to say something about the car, wants to ask how much it costs and how the hell Mama could afford it, but he doesn't. Instead, out of the blue, voice almost pure, he says, "Is that my old dress jacket? I loved that thing."

"It's not yours. Mama bought it. I needed a blazer for debate."

The words come out chilly, but I don't say anything else to warm them up. And I feel a twinge of childishness mentioning my mother, like she's beside me, worrying the jacket hem, smoothing down the sleeves. I make myself feel better by recalling that when I went to post bail, the woman behind the bulletproof glass asked if I was a reporter.

"You keep getting money from debate, we could invest."

When most people talk about investing, they mean stocks or bonds or mutual funds. What my father means is his friend Splo's cockfighting arena, or some dude who goes door to door selling exercise equipment that does all the exercise for you. He'd invested in a woman who tried selling African cichlids to pet shops, but all she'd done was dye ordinary goldfish so that they looked tropical. "Didn't you just win some cash?" he asks. "From debate?"

"Bail," I say. "I used it to pay your bail."

He's quiet for a while. I wait for him to stumble out a thanks. I wait for him to promise to pay me back with money he knows he'll never have. Finally he sighs and says, "Most investors buy low and sell high. Know why they do that?" With my father there are not only trick questions, but trick answers. Before I can respond, I hear his voice, loud and naked. "I *axed* you, 'Do you know why they do that?'" He's shaking my arm as if trying to wake me. "You *answer me* when I ask you something."

I twist my arm from his grasp to show I'm not afraid. We swerve out of our lane. Cars behind us swerve as well, then zoom around us and pull ahead as if we are a rock in a stream.

"Do you know who this *is*?" he says. "Do you know who you're *talking to*?"

I haven't been talking to anyone, but I keep this to myself.

"I'll tell you who you're talking to—Ray Bivens Junior!"

He used to be this way with Mama. Never hitting, but always grabbing, groping, his halitosis forever in her face. After the divorce he insisted on partial custody. At first all I had to do was take the bus across town. Then, when he couldn't afford an apartment in the city, I had to take the Greyhound into backwoods Indiana. I'd spend Saturday and Sunday so bored I'd work ahead in textbooks, assign myself homework, whatever there was to do while waiting for Ray Bivens Jr. to fart himself awake and take me back to the bus station.

That was how debate started. Every year there was a different topic, and when they made the announcement last year, it was like an Army recruitment campaign, warning students that they'd be expected to dedicate even their weekends to the cause. I rejoiced, thinking that I would never have to visit Ray Bivens Jr. again. And I was good at debate. My brain naturally frowned at illogic. But I don't think for a minute that my teachers liked me because of my logical mind; they liked me because I was quiet and small, and not rowdy like they expected black guys to be. Sometimes, though, the teachers slipped. Once, my history teacher, Mrs. Ampersand, said, "You stay away from those drugs, Spurgeon, and you'll go far." That was the kind of thing that could stick in my stomach for days, weeks. I could always think of things to say about a debate topic like U.S.–China diplomatic relations, or deliver a damning rebuttal on prison overcrowding, but it was different with someone like Mrs. Ampersand— all debate logic fell away, and in my head I'd call her a bitch, tell her that the strongest stuff in my mother's house was a bottle of Nyquil.

WE'VE CROSSED the bridge into Indiana but my father is still going. "THAT'S RIGHT! YOU'RE TALKING TO RAY BIVENS *JUNIOR!* AND DON'T YOU FORGET IT!"

Outside, autumn is over, and yet it's not quite winter. Indiana farmlands speed past in black and white. Beautiful. Until you remember that the world is supposed to be in color.

L A T E R , calm again, he says, "Imagine a stock. Let's say the stock is the one I was telling you about, Scudder MidCap. The stock is at fifty bucks. If it's a winner, it doesn't stay at fifty bucks for long. It goes to a hundred let's say, or two hundred. But first it's gotta get to fifty-one, fifty-two, and so on. So a stock *increasing* in price is a good sign. That's when you buy."

I make sure to tell him thanks for telling me this.

"Doesn't matter what you invest in, either," Ray Bivens Jr. says. "That's the beauty. Don't gotta even think about it. That's something you won't hear from an accountant."

"You mean stockbroker. A stockbroker advises about stocks. Not an accountant."

His face turns bitter, as though he's about to slap me, but then he thinks the better of it and says, "So you know who to go to when you get some extra cash."

"Look. I just told you I don't have any money." I try to concentrate on looking for gas station signs in the dark.

"You will, Spurgeon," he says. He puts an arm around me like a prom date, and I can smell his odor from the jail. I don't have to see his face to know exactly how it looks right now. Urgently earnest, a little too sincere. Like a man explaining to his wife why he's late coming home. "I'll pay back every penny. I mean that."

"I believe you," I say, prying his arm from where it rests on my neck.

"You believe me," he says, "but do you believe *in* me?" He puts his arm back where it was, like he's some suburban dad, a Little League coach congratulating his charge.

"I believe in you."

His arm falls away of its own accord as he settles deeper into his car seat with this knowledge, the leather sighing and complaining under him. I take the exit that promises a Citgo, park at a gas pump. You don't usually see insects in this weather, but the garbage can between the diesel and unleaded swarms with flies. The fluorescent lights stutter off and on as I begin pumping gas. I can hear what my mother would say, that my father is a cross I have to bear, that the Good Book says, "A child shall lead them," and all that crap, which basically boils down to "He's *your* father. Your blood, not mine." Ray Bivens Jr. leans against the car and stretches. Then he cleans the windshield with a squeegee. After that he sniffs and looks around as though he's checking out the scenery. When I'm finished filling the tank he says, "Hey, Spurgeon. How about breaking off a few bills? You know they frisked me clean in lockdown."

I give him a twenty and wait in the car. He's in the Citgo for what seems like half an hour. He's in there so long I get out and wipe off the squeegee streaks he left on the windshield. Finally, he comes back with a six-pack of Schlitz and a family-sized bag of Funyuns. "Listen," he says, handing me a beer, "we have to make a quick stop to Jasper."

Jasper, Indiana, is where his ex-girlfriend Lupita lives.

"I knew it," I say, and hand back the unopened beer before starting the car. "You're in trouble."

He opens the can, looking as though both the Schlitz and I have disappointed him. One of the fluorescent lights overhead blinks out. "What the hell are you talking about?"

"Why do we have to go to Jasper all of a sudden?"

"If you *shut your mouth* and go to Jasper you'll find out."

"This is mama's car," I remind him. "She wants it back."

"Why you gotta act like everything I ask you to do is gonna kill you? You my *son*. I tell you to do something, you obey."

I *do* obey, and hate myself for it, turning the car out to the service road. I try to imagine the worst that can await him in Seymour, figure out what he's running from: men who'll tie him up at gunpoint and demand the twenty dollars that he owes them, policemen waiting at his door, but those thoughts give way to the only thing we'll find in Jasper: Lupita, watching TV, painting her toenails. I've been to Lupita's place twice, but that's more than enough. It's full of birds. Huge blue-and-gold macaws. Yellow-naped Amazons. Rainbow lorikeets who squirt their putrid frugiverous shit on you. Tons of birds, and not in cages either. I don't think my father liked them perching on his shoulders any more than I did, but the birds could land anywhere on Lupita and she'd wear them like jewelry.

Then it occurs to me that this is the only reason he cleaned the windshield. "You're going to make me drive you and Lupita around so the two of you can get drunk. I knew it."

"If you don't shut up—"

I don't speak to him, he doesn't speak to me. We pass a billboard that reads, WHEN LIFE GIVES YOU LEMONS, MAKE LEMONADE. I try to think of what my mother will say. She knows I had to get him out of jail, that's why she let me borrow the car. But she wasn't about to pay bail, and she definitely won't want me coming home at midnight, her car smelling of cigarettes and Mad Dog.

My father sees me fuming and says, "I told you I was going to get your money back, right? Well, there's going to be a march, tomorrow. A million people in Washington, D.C. One. Million. People."

"No," I say. "Dear God, no."

"Exactly," he says.

Even though the windows are closed, I feel a breeze pass through me. At one point, I wanted to go to the March; I imagined it would be as historic as King's march on Washington, as historic as the dismantling of the Wall. The men's choir of my mother's church was going, but I didn't want to be trapped on a bus with a bunch of men singing hymns, feeling sorry for me being born with Ray Bivens Jr. for a father. And what's more, I have a debate tournament. I imagine Sarah Vogedes, my debate partner, prepping for our debate on U.S. foreign policy toward China, checking her watch. She'd have to use our second stringers, or perhaps even Derron Ellersby, a basketball player so certain he'd make the NBA that he'd joined the speech and debate team "to sound smooth for all those postgame interviews." This was the same Derron Ellersby who ended his rebuttals by pointing at me, saying, "Little Man over here's going to break it down for ya," or who'd single me out in the cafeteria, telling his friends, "Little Man's got skills, yo! Break off some a your skills!" as if expecting me to carry on a debate with my tuna casserole.

I'd never missed a day of school in my life, and my mother had the framed perfect-attendance certificates to prove it, but the thought of Sarah Vogedes's composed face growing rumpled as Derron agreed with our opponent makes me feel something like bliss; I imagine Derron, index cards scattered in front of him, looking as confused as if he'd been faked out before a lay-up, saying, "Yo! Sarah V! Where's Little Man? Where he at!"

For once I'm glad Ray Bivens Jr. is scheming so hard he doesn't see me smiling. If he could—if he sensed in *any* way that I might be willing—he'd find a way to call the whole thing off.

"That's in Washington, D.C.," I remind him, "nearly seven hundred miles away."

"I know. But first we're going to Jasper," he says. "To get the birds."

TECHNICALLY, the birds are my father's, not Lupita's. He bought them when he was convinced that the animals were an Investment. He tried selling them door to door. When that didn't work and he couldn't afford to keep them, Lupita volunteered to take care of them. Lupita knew about birds, she'd said, because she'd once owned a rooster when she was five back in Guatemala.

It is completely dark and the road is revealing its secrets one at a time. I ask, once more, what he plans on doing with these birds.

He tells me he plans on selling them.

"But you couldn't sell them the first time."

"I didn't have a million potential buyers the first time."

For a brief moment I'd wanted to go to the March, perhaps even see if Ray Bivens Jr. got something out of it, but no longer. I tell him that I can take him to Jasper, Indiana. I can take him home, even, which was what I was supposed to do in the first place, but that I absolutely cannot, under any circumstances, cut school and miss my debate tournament to drive him to D.C.

"Don't you want your money back?" he says. "One macaw alone will pay back that bail money three times over."

"What are a million black men going to do with a bunch of birds? Even if you could sell them, how're you going to get them there?"

"Would you just drive?" he says, then sucks his teeth, making a noise that might as well be a curse. He stretches out in his seat, then starts up, explaining things to me as if I'd had a particularly stupefy-

ing bout of amnesia: "You're gonna have Afrocentric folks there. Afrocentrics and Africans, *tons* of Africans. And what do Africans miss most? That's right. The Motherland. And what does the Mother Africa have tons of? Monkeys, lions, and guess what else? *Birds.* Not no street pigeons, but real birds, like the kind I'm selling. Macaws and African grays. Lorikeets and yellow napes and shit." He might as well have added, *Take that.*

He's so stupid, he's brilliant; so outside of the realm of any rationality that reason stammers and stutters when facing him. I say nothing, nothing at all, just continue on, thinking quickly, but driving slowly. He hits the dash like he's knocking on a door to make me speed up.

Off the interstate, the road turns so narrow and insignificant it could peter out into someone's driveway. The occasional crop of stores along the roadside look closed. We pass through Paoli Peaks and Hoosier National Forest before finally arriving in Jasper.

We pull into Lupita's driveway. In the dark, her lawn ornaments resemble gravestones. Motion-detector floodlights buzz on as my father walks up to the house. Lupita stands on her porch, wielding a shotgun. She's wearing satiny pajamas that show her nipples. Pink curlers droop from her hair like blossoms.

"What do *joo* want?" Her eyes narrow in on him. She slits her eyes even more to see who's in the car with him, straightening herself up a little bit, but when she sees that it's just me, just nerdy ol' Spurgeon, she drops all signs of primping.

I stay in the car. She and my father disappear into the house while I watch the pinwheel lawn daisies spin in the dark. The yelling from inside the house is mostly Lupita: "I am tired of your blag ass! Enough eez enough!" Then it stops. They've argued their way to the bedroom, where the door slams shut and all is quiet.

But the calm doesn't hold. Lupita breaks out with some beautiful, deadly Spanish threats, and the screen door bangs open. My father comes out clutching cages, each crammed two apiece with birds. I can hear birdseed and little gravelly rocks from the cages spill all over the car interior when he puts them on the backseat. The whole time he doesn't say a word. Looks straight ahead.

He makes another trip into the house, but Lupita doesn't go in with him. He comes back with another cageful of birds.

Lupita follows him for a bit, but she stops halfway from the car. She stands there in her ensemble of sexy pajamas and pink sponge curlers and shotgun.

"Don't get out," Ray Bivens Jr. says to me. "We're going to drive off. Slowly."

I do as my father says and back out of the driveway.

Lupita yells after us, "Joo are never thinking about maybe what Lupita feels!" For a moment I think she's going to come after us, but all she does is plop down on her porch step, holding her head in her hands.

O N C E   T H E Y get used to the rhythm of the road, the birds swap crude, disjointed conversations with one another. The blue-and-gold macaw sings "Love Me Do," but recent immigrant that it is, it gets the inflections all wrong. The lorikeet says, repeatedly, "Where the dickens is my pocket watch?" then does what passes for a man's lewd laugh. If there's a lull, one will say, *"Arriba, 'riba, 'riba!"* and get them all going again.

"Bird crap doesn't have an odor," my father says. "That's the paradox of birds."

"She loved those birds," I say. "And you just took them away."

"They learn best when stressed out," he says. "Why do you think they say '*Arriba!*' all the time? They get it from the Mexicans who're all in a rush to get them exported."

He almost knocks me off kilter with that one, but I stick to the point. "Don't try to make excuses. You hurt her. And what about the birds? You didn't think to get food, did you?"

"You are a complete pussy, you know that?"

He'd only used that word once before, when I was twelve and refused to fight another boy, and said if I didn't whup that boy the next day that he'd whup me.

"You *need* to go to this March. When you go, check in at the pussy booth and tell 'em you want to exchange yours for a johnson."

I check the rearview mirror, then cross all lanes of I-65 North until I'm on the shoulder. It's the kind of boldness he'd always wanted me to show to everyone else but him.

"You better have a good reason for stopping," he says.

"Get out," I say, as soon as I stop the car. The birds also stop their chatter, and when I turn around they're looking from me to him as though they've placed bets on who will go down in flames.

Ray Bivens Jr. clamps his hand to his forehead in mock dumbfoundedness. "You ain't heard that before? Don't *tell me* nobody never called you no pussy?"

"Get out, *sir,*" I say.

"Yeah. I'll *get out* all right." He opens the passenger-side door just as a semi whooshes by, and even I can feel it. He slams the door and traps the cold air with me.

IT'S LATE: past midnight. I stop at the next exit to call my mother. She says if I don't get my tail back in her house tonight, she'll skin me alive. I tell her I love her too. She likes to pretend that I'm the man of the house, and says as much when she asks me if I've locked all the doors at night, or tells me to drive her to church so she can show off what a good son she has. But it's times like this when it's clear that the only man of the house is Jesus.

I buy a Ho Ho at the gas station and as I separate the cake part from the creamy insides with my teeth, I think about how Derron would have shrugged Ray Bivens Jr.'s schemes away with a good-hearted hunch of the shoulders. "Pops is crazy," he'd say to the mike in an NBA postgame interview, then put his gently clenched fist over his heart like someone accepting an award, "but I love the guy."

I get back in the car and the birds squawk and complain at having been left alone. I return to the last exit before heading north again, going slow in the right-hand lane. When I see my father, I pull off to the shoulder, pop open the electronic locks. He acts as though he knew I would come back for him all along. We don't talk for nearly an hour, but everything is completely clear: if I am not a pussy, I will cut school, forget about debate, and go to D.C.

JUST OUTSIDE Clarksburg, West Virginia, I pull over. I can't make it to the exit. Twice I almost nodded off. When I slump onto the steering wheel my father gets out and rouses me enough for us to exchange places, even though he's not supposed to be driving.

I don't know how long I've been asleep, but I wake to the umbrella cockatoo chanting, "Sexy, sexy!" My eyes adjust to the dim light, first making out the electric glow of the dash panels, and then the scenery beyond the cool of the windows. We are on a small hilly road. It is so dark and so full of conifers I feel like we're traveling through velvet.

Ray Bivens Jr., I can tell, has been waiting for me to wake. At first I think he wants me to take over the wheel, but then I realize he wants company. He raps on the car window and says, "In ancient Mesopotamia it was hot. There was no glass. What they did have was the wheel—"

The yellow-naped Amazon breaks into the Oscar Mayer wiener jingle before I can ask my father what the hell he's talking about.

"Shut up!" he yells, and at first I sit up, startled, thinking that he's yelling at me. The bird says "Rawrk!" and starts the jingle over, from the beginning.

He sits through the jingle, and as a reward, there is a peculiar silence that comes after someone speaks. For once in his life, he has had to use patience. "Here's why windows are called windows," he says with strained calmness, but the lorikeet interrupts: "Advil works," the bird says, "better than Tylenol."

My father blindly gropes the backseat for a cage, seizes one, and slams it against another cage. All the birds revolt, screeching and shuffling feathers, sounding like bricks hitting a chain-link fence. One of them says, almost angrily, "And here's to *you*, Mrs. Robinson!"

But Ray Bivens Jr. raises his voice over the din. "The Mesopotamians cut out circles, or O's, in their homes to mimic the shape of the wheel, but also to let in the wind," he yells. "And there you have it. Your modern day window. Get it? Wind-o."

I look to see if he is taking himself seriously. He used to say shit like this when I was little. I could never tell whether he was kidding me or himself. "You're trying to tell me that the Mesopotamians spoke English? And that they created little O's in their homes to let in the wind?"

"All right. Don't believe me, then."

◦◦

WE MAKE it into Arlington at seven in the morning, park the car at a garage, and take the Metro into D.C. with the morning commuters. White men with their briefcases and mushroom-colored trenchcoats. White women with fleet haircuts, their chic lipstick darker than blood. The occasional Asian, Hispanic—wearing the same costume but somehow looking nervous about it. More than anything though, we see black men—everywhere—groups of black men wearing identical T-shirts with the names of churches and youth groups emblazoned on them. Men in big, loose kente-cloth robes; men in full-on suits with the traditional Nation of Islam bow tie.

My father hands me two cages. He hefts two. While the morning commuters eye us, he breaks down the bird prices loudly, as though we're the only people in the world.

When we get to the Mall, all you can hear from where we stand are African drums, gospel music blaring from the loudspeakers, and someone playing rap with bass so heavy it hurts your heart. Everything has an early-morning smell to it, cold and wet with dew, but already thousands have marked their territory with portable chairs and signs. Voter registration booths are everywhere; vendors balance basketfuls of T-shirts on their heads; D.C. kids nudge us, trying to sell us water for a dollar a cup. The Washington Monument stands in front of us like a big granite pencil, miles away, it seems, and everywhere, everywhere, men shake hands, laugh like they haven't seen one another in years. They make pitches, exchange business cards, and congratulate one another for just getting here. But most of all they speak in passwords: *Keep Strong, Stay Black, Love Your Black Nation.*

The birds are so unnaturally quiet I can't tell if they don't mind being jostled about amid the legs of a million strangers or if they're dying. As we work our way through the masses, Ray Bivens Jr. keeps looking off into the distance in perpetual search for the perfect customer. I try to follow my father, but it's hard to plow through the crowd holding the cages.

"Brother," one man says, shaking his head at me, "I don't know if them birds males or not, but they *sho ain't* black!"

I nod in my father's direction and say, "Looks like you've got a customer."

He shoots me an annoyed look. "Let's split up," he says. "We'll cover more area if we're spread out."

"O.K., chief," I say. But I pretty much stay where I've been.

AFTER A few speeches from Christian ministers, a stiff-looking bow-tied man gives an introduction for Farrakhan and the Nation of Islam. I'm so far back that I have to look at the large-screen TVs, but as Farrakhan takes to the stage, the Fruit of Islam phalanx behind him applauds so violently that their clapping resembles some sort of martial art.

I make my way toward the edge of the crowd to get some air. Though I'm already as far from the main stage as one can be, it still takes me a good half hour to push through the crowd of men, most of them patting me on the back like uncles at a family reunion. Although I've seen a sprinkling of women at the march, some black women cheer as they stand on the other side of Independence Avenue, but others wave placards reading "Let Us In!" or "Remember Those You Left Home." Quite a few whites also stop to look as if to see what this thing is all about, and their hard, nervous hard smiles fit into two categories: the "Don't mug me!" smile, or the "Gee, aren't black folks something!" smile. It occurs to me that I can stay here on the sidelines for the entire march. A hush falls over the crowd, then they erupt into whistles and cheering and catcalls, and though I can barely see the large convention screen anymore, people begin chanting, "Jesse! Jesse!"

I look at the screen and see him clasping hands with Farrakhan, but he doesn't do much more than that. If anything, I'd like the chance to hear him speak in person, purely for speech and debate purposes, but it seems as though the day will be a long one, with major speakers bookended by lesser-known ones.

Now a preacher from a small town takes to the platform. "Brothers, we have to work it out with each other! How are we going to go back to our wives, our babies' mothers, and tell them that we love *them* if we can't tell our own brothers that we love them?"

At first it sounds like what everyone else has been saying, breaking a cardinal rule of public speaking: One should reiterate, not regurgitate. He reads from a letter written in 1712 by William Lynch, a white slave owner from Virginia. It occurs to me that Farrakhan read from this same letter, the content of which got lost in his nearly three-hour speech. The letter explains how to control slaves by pitting dark ones against light ones, big plantation slaves against small plantation slaves, female slaves against male ones. The preacher ends by telling everyone that freedom is attained only when the ant of the self—that small, blind, crumb-seeking part of ourselves—casts off slavery and its legacy, becoming a huge brave ox.

"Well, well, well!" An elbow nudges me. "Wasn't that powerful, brother?" A man wearing a fez extends his hand for me to shake.

I shake his hand, but he doesn't let go, as if he's waiting for me to agree with him.

"Powerful!" the fezzed man shouts above the applause.

"Yes," I say, and turn away from him.

But I can feel him looking at me, staring through me so hard that I'm forced to turn toward him again. "Powerful," I say. "Indeed."

I must not be convincing enough because the guy looks at me pleadingly and says, "*Feel* this! The *power* here! This is *powerful!*"

I look around for someone to save me from this man, but everyone is cheering and clapping for the next speaker. I decide that my only recourse is to shut the man up with the truth. Maybe then he'll leave me alone. "Don't get me wrong. I love my Black Nation," I say, adding the mandatory chest thump, "but I'm just here because my father made me come."

The fezzed man screws up his face in the sunlight, features bunched in confusion. He puts his hand to his ear like he's hard of hearing.

"My father!" I yell. "My father made me come!"

People twenty deep turn around to shoot me annoyed looks. One man looks like he wants to beat the crap out me, but then looks apologetic. I in turn duck my head in apology and murmur, "Sorry."

"*Made* you come? *Made you?* This, my brother," he nearly yells, "is a day of atonement! You got to cut your father a little slack for caring for your sorry self!"

Everyone's eyes are on me again, but I'll be damned if this man who doesn't even *know me* sides with Ray Bivens Jr. "I thought the whole point of all this was to take responsibility. Put an end to asking for slack. If you knew my father you'd know that his whole damn life is as slack as a pantsuit from JCPenney!"

"Hold up, hold up, hold up," a voice says. The voice comes from a man with a bullet-smooth head, the man who earlier looked as if he wanted to stomp my face into the ground. Now that he's turned toward me, the pistils and stamens of his monstrous Hawaiian flower-print shirt seem to stare at me, and suddenly his face is so close I can smell the mint of his breath.

"You need to learn that responsi*bility* is a two-way street!" The Hawaiian-shirt guy points to my chest. "*You* have to take responsibility and reach out to *him*."

Now many, many people have turned to look at us, and though I try not to look guilty, people know the Hawaiian-shirted guy is talking to *somebody,* somebody who caused a disturbance. The Phalanx of Islam is on its way, moving in the form of crisp, gray-suited men wearing stern looks and prison muscles. The Hawaiian-shirted guy sees them and waves me away with his hand as though I'm not worth his time. Then, suddenly—despite the Fruit of Islam weaving through the crowd toward us—he decides to have another go at it. "Let me ask you a question, my brother. Why are you here? You don't seem to *want* to atone—not with your pops, not with anybody."

Those around me have formed a sideshow of which I seem to be the villain, and they look at me expectantly. The Hawaiian-shirted man folds his arms across his chest and jerks his chin up, daring me to answer him.

"Atoning for one's wrongs is different from apologizing," I begin. "One involves words, the other, actions." I don't want to dignify all this attention with a further response; don't want the four men who are now brisk-walking straight toward me to hurt me; don't want to say anything now that the air around me is silent, listening, now that the sun in my eyes is so hot I feel like crying. I continue, delivering a hurried, jibbering philippic on the nuances between atonement and apology, repentance and remorse. What I'm saying is right and true. Good and important. But I can feel myself getting flustered, can feel the debate judge mouthing *Time's up,* see the disbelief and disappointment in the men's faces, nearly twenty in all, and more turn around to see what the disturbance is about. An Oxford-shirted security guard grabs me by the arm.

"What," he says, "seems to be the problem, son?"

"Look," I say finally to him and anyone else who'll listen, "I'm not here to atone. I'm here to sell birds."

I finally spot my father, the cages balanced on his shoulders, when the marchless march is pretty much finished. The sky is moving toward dusk, and though there are still speakers on the podium, you'd stick around to listen only if they were your relatives or something. My father and I get pushed along with other people trying to leave.

I don't bother telling him how security clamped me on the shoulder and sat me down on the curb like a five-year-old and gave me a talking-to, reminding me of the point of the March. I don't tell him how they fed me warm flatbread and hard honey in a hot plastic tent that served as some sort of headquarters, or how they gave me three bean pies, some pamphlets, and a Koran. I know he can tell how pissed off I am. Anyone can.

And he can see I haven't sold any birds, and I see he hasn't either. I wonder if word got around to his section about how security took me out of the crowd for "safety purposes," but apparently he doesn't give a shit. Ray Bivens Jr. grabs a passing man by the arm. The man's T-shirt reads: "Volunteer—Washington D.C."

"Where's a good bar?" my father asks. "That's cheap?"

The man raises his eyebrows and says, "Brotherman, we're trying to keep away from all that poison. At least for one day." His voice is smooth and kind, that of a guy from the streets who became a counselor, determined to give back to the community. He smiles. "You think you can make it for one day without the sauce, my brother?"

᎒

THE BAR we end up in is called The Haven, and it's nowhere near where we left the car. Before we left the March, I asked Ray Bivens Jr. how he felt knowing that he'd come nearly seven hundred miles and hadn't sold a single bird. He didn't speak to me on the Metro ride to the bar, not even when the birds started embarrassing us on the subway.

The bartender looks at the birds and shakes his head as if his patrons never cease to amuse him.

Even though he's sitting in the place he loves most, Ray Bivens Jr. still seems mad at me. So do the birds. None of them are speaking, just making noises in their throats as though they're plotting something. I ask the bartender if the birds are safe outside; if someone will steal them.

"Not if it's something that needs feeding," the bartender says.

"Speaking of feeding," my father says, "I'm going to get some Funyuns. Want any?" He says this more to the bartender than to me, but I shake my head though all I've eaten are the bean pies and honey. The bartender spray-guns a 7 Up in a glass for me without my even asking, then resumes conversation with the trio of men at the end of the counter. One man has a goiter. One has processed waves that look like cake frosting. While those two seem to be smiling and arguing at the same time, the third man says nothing, smoking his cigarette as though it's part of his search for enlightenment.

The smoker ashes his cigarette with a pert tap. "You been at the March, youngblood?"

"Yeah. How'd you know?"

They all laugh, but no one tells me why.

The bartender towels down some beer glasses. "Anybody here

go?" When nobody says anything, he says to me, with a knowing wink, "These some *shift*less niggers up in here!"

There's general grumbling, and to make them feel less bad about missing the March I say, "I didn't get all pumped up by the speeches, but in a way I was glad I was there. I think I felt more relieved than anything else."

"Relieved? What about?" the smoker asks, his voice wise and deep, even though he's just asking a question.

I try to think. "I don't know. I'm the only black kid in my class. Like a fucking mascot or something," I say, surprised that I said the f-word out loud, but shaking my head as though I said words like that every day. "I just get tired of it. You skip it for a day and it feels like a vacation. That's why I was glad."

There's a round of nodding. Not sympathy, just acknowledgment.

"Man," the guy with the goiter says, "I'm happy to hear that. You got the *luxury* of feeling tired. Back in the day, before you were born, couldn't that type of shit *happen*."

He seems to be saying less than he means, and looks at me, his eyes piercing, his goiter looking like he's swallowed a lightbulb. "We the ones *fought* for you to be in school with the white folks." He looks behind him, as if checking if any white people are around, though that's about as likely as Ray Bivens Jr. going sober for good. He lowers his voice so that he almost sounds kind. "We sent you to go spy on them. See how the hell those white folks make all that money! Now you talking 'bout a *va*cation!"

They all laugh like it's some sort of secret code that got broken.

"You'll be all right, youngblood," says the smoker. "You'll be all right."

Just as I begin to realize that they're humoring me, Ray Bivens Jr.

comes blustering in through the door like he lives there. He flashes a wad of money. "Luck," he says smiling, "is sometimes lucky."

The trio at the bar high-five one another and laugh in anticipation of free drinks.

"Who," I say, "did you take that from?"

"Take?" He chucks his thumb toward me as if to say, *Get a load of this guy.* He counts out the bills so fast that he can't actually be counting them. "Sold a bird. Rich white dude. Convenient store. I said, 'I got birds.' He said, 'I got money.' Six hundred bones."

I'm upset, though I don't know why. Six hundred bucks. Who in this neighborhood even *has* six hundred bucks? I lean toward him and whisper, "I bailed you out of jail, remember."

"Don't worry," he says, "I'll buy you a drink."

THREE HOURS pass, and my father has beaten all the regulars trying to win money from him at pinochle when a woman appears out of nowhere. Her skin is the color of good scotch. She sits between me and my father, twirls around on her barstool once, and points a red-enameled finger toward the goiter man changing songs on the jukebox. "Play 'Love the One You're With.' Isley Brothers."

"I was going to," says the Goiter, "just for you."

She spins around on the barstool again so that she's facing the bottles lined up on display. "Farrah," she says and extends a tiny limp hand in my direction. "Farrah Falana."

"That's not," I say, "your real name."

"Yes it is," she says dreamily. "Farrah Falana. I was named after that show."

Now I see that she's going on fifty. She smiles at me with her mouth closed, and for a moment she looks like a beautiful frog.

My father takes a long, admiring look at her seated behind. "Farrah and Ray," my father says. "I like how that sounds." For a moment, he looks like Billy Dee Williams. The smile is the same, that same slick look.

"I like how it sounds, too," Farrah says. She actually slides on her barstool and leans toward him, leans so close it looks as if she might kiss him.

"Farrah and Ray," I say. "That sounds like a Vegas act."

"It *does!*" she squeals.

M Y F A T H E R and Farrah get drunk while I play an electronic trivia game with the Goiter. He knows more than I gave him credit for, but he's losing to me because he bets all his bonus points whenever he gets a chance. The Goiter and I are on our tenth game when Ray Bivens Jr. taps me on the shoulder. I look over to see him standing very straight and tall, trying not to look drunk.

"You don't love me," he says sloppily. "You don't under*stand* me."

"*You* don't understand you," I say.

Farrah is still at the bar, and though she's not saying anything, her face goes through a series of exaggerated expressions as if it were she responding to someone's questions. I plunk three quarters in the game machine. "Your go," I say to the Goiter.

"Does anybody understand themselves?" he says to me softly, and for a second he looks perfectly lucid. Then he says it louder, for the benefit of the whole bar, with a gravity only the drunk can muster. "Does *anybody,* I say, under*stand* themselves?"

The men at the bar look at him and decide it's one of their many jokes, and laugh, though my father is staring straight at me, straight through me as though I were nothing but a clear glass of whiskey into which he could see the past and future.

I grip my father's elbow and try to speak with him one on one. "I'm sorry about what I said at the March."

"No you ain't."

"Yes," I say, "I am. But you've got to tell me how to understand you." I feel silly saying it, but he's drunk, and so is everybody else but me.

He lurches back then leans in forward again. "Tell you? I can't *tell* you." He drums each word out on the counter, "That's. Not. What. It's. A-bout. I can *tell* you about Paris, but you won't know 'less you been there. You simply under-*stand*. Or you don't." He raises an eyebrow in clairvoyant drunkenness before continuing. "You either take me, or you *don't*." He throws his hands up, smiling as though he's finally solved some grand equation in a few simple steps.

"Please," I say, giving up on him. I beckon the Goiter for another game of electronic trivia, but he shakes his head and smiles solemnly, a smile that says he's more weary for me than for himself.

"Let me tell you something," Ray Bivens Jr. says, practically spitting in my face, "Lupita *understands* me. That woman," he says, suddenly sounding drunk again, "*understands*. She's It."

Farrah, suddenly sober, smacks him on the shoulder and says, "What about me? What the fuck about me?"

ANOTHER HOUR later he says, all cool, "Gimme the keys. Farrah and I are going for a ride."

I've had many 7 Ups and I've twice asked my father if we could go, told him that we either had to find a motel outside the city or plan on driving back soon. But now he's asking for the keys at nearly three a.m., the car all the way over in Arlington, and even the Metro has stopped running.

"Sir," I say. "We need to drive back."

"I said, Spurgeon, dear son, that Farrah and I are going for a ride. Now give me the keys, dear son."

A ride means they're going to her place, wherever that is. Him going to her place means I have to find my own place to stay. Giving him the keys not only means he'll be driving illegally, which I no longer care about, but that the car will end up on the other side of the country, stripped for parts.

"No," I say. "It's Mama's car."

"Mama's car," he mimics.

"Sir."

"Maaaamaaa's caaaaar!"

I leave the bar. I'm walking for a good minute before I hear him coming after me. I speed up but don't run. I don't even know how I'm going to get back to the car, but I pick a direction and walk purposefully. I hear the *click click click* of what are surely Farrah's heels, hear her voice screaming something that doesn't make sense, hear his footfalls close in on me, but all I see are the streetlights glowing amber, and the puffs of smoke my breath makes in the October air. All I feel is that someone has spun me around as if for inspection, and that's when I see his face—handsome, hard-edged, not the least bit sloppy from liquor.

Sure. He's hit me before, but this is hard. Not the back of the hand, not with a belt, but punching. A punch meant for my face, but lands on my shoulder, like he's congratulating me, then another hit, this one all knuckles, and my jaw pops open, automatically, like the trunk of a car. I try to close my mouth, try to call time out, but he's ramming into me, not with his fists, but with his head. I try to pry him from where his head butts, inside my stomach, right under my windpipe, but he stays that way, leaning into me, tucked as if fighting against a strong wind, both of us wobbling together like lovers. Finally, I push him away, and wipe what feels like yogurt running from my nose into the raw cut of my lip. I start to lick my lips, thinking that it's all over, when he rushes straight at me and rams me into something that topples over with a toyish metal clank. Sheaves of weekly newspapers fan the ground like spilled cards from a deck. I kick him anywhere my foot will land, shouting at him, so strangely mad that I'm happy, until I finally kick at air, hard, and trip myself. I don't know how long I'm down, how long my eyes are closed, but he's now holding me like a rag doll. "What the hell are you talking about?" he says as if to shake the answer out of me. "What the *hell* are you talking about?"

I only now realize what I've been screaming the whole time. "Wind-o!" I yell at him. "You and your goddamn 'wind-o'! There was never any 'wind-o'! And you don't know *shit* about birds! *Arriba! Arriba!*" I say mockingly.

When he grabs my collar, almost lifting me from the ground, I feel as though I'm floating upward, then I feel some part of me drowning. I remember something, something I know will kill my father. My father dodged the draft. They weren't going to get this nigger, was his view of Vietnam. It was the one thing I'd respected him for, and yet somehow I said it, "You didn't know fucking Huey P. Newton. You never even *went* to Vietnam!"

That does it. I had turned into something ugly, and of all the millions of words I've ever spoken to him in all my life, this is the one that blows him to pieces.

"Vietnam?" he says, once, as if making sure I'd said the word.

I'm quiet. He says the word again, "Vietnam," and his eyes somehow look sightless.

I try to pull him back, begging in the only way you can beg without words. I go to put my hand on his shoulder, but a torrent of people, fresh from the March, it seems, has been loosed from a nearby restaurant. They slap one another's backs, smelling of Brut and Old Spice, musk-scented African oils and sweat. I go to put my hand on his shoulder, but already my father has gone.

R a y B i v e n s J r . left with the car and Farrah left with someone else. The birds are gone. My blazer is gone. After I have a scotch, the bartender says, "Look. I can float you the drinks, but who's going to pay for that, youngblood?" He points to one of the bar's smashed windowpanes.

After I pay him, I have no money left for a cab or a bus. The bridge over the Potomac isn't meant for pedestrians, and it takes me half an hour to walk across it. For a long time I'm on New Hampshire Avenue, then for a long time I'm on Georgia. I ask for directions to the train station and someone finally gives them to me.

I wonder if he's right about Lupita. When she sat on the porch and held her head, it seemed she felt more sorry for him than she did for herself; not pity, but sympathy.

I pass by an old-fashioned movie theater whose marquee looks like one giant erection lit in parti-colored lights. People pass by, wondering how to go about mugging me. A well-dressed man asks if I'm a pitcher or a catcher, and I have no idea what he means. I tell myself that it's good that Ray Bivens Jr. and I fought. Most people think that you find something that matters, something that's worth fighting for, and if necessary, you fight. But it must be the fighting, I tell myself, that decides what matters, even if you're left on the sidewalk to discover that what you thought mattered means nothing after all.

"WHERE DO you want to go?" the Amtrak ticket officer asks.

"East," I say. "Any train that goes east this time of night."

"You're in D.C., sir. Any further east and you'll be in the Atlantic."

Of course I'm not going east anymore. I'd been going east the last day and a half, and it's just now hitting me that I can finally go west. Go home.

After the events of the day, I'm not surprised that I get the snottiest ticket officer of the whole damn railway system. I look into the his gray eyes. "West, motherfucker."

The ticket officer stares at me and I stare right back.

The ticket officer sighs. He looks down at his computer, and then at me again. "Where, pray tell, do you want to go? West, I'm afraid, is a direction, not a destination."

"Louisville, Kentucky," I finally say. "Home."

He enters something into his computer. Tilts his head. He smiles when he tells me there is no train that goes to Louisville. The closest one is Cincinnati.

I walk away from the counter and sit down, trying to think of how I'm going to pay to get to Cincinnati, then from Cincinnati to Louisville. The only other white person in the station besides the ticket officer is an old woman in a rainbow knit cap. She's having quite an intelligent conversation with herself.

I'll have to call home, ask my mother to give her credit card number to this prick. I start to try to find a phone when a man approaches the ticket counter, his half-asleep son riding on his back. He probably just came from the March. Probably listened to all the poems and speeches about ants and oxen and African drumming, but still had this kid out in the hot sun for hours, then in the cold night for longer. It's almost five o'clock in the morning, and all this little boy wants, I can tell, is some goddamned sleep.

"Hey," I say to the man. When he doesn't respond, I tap him on the non-kid shoulder. "It's pretty late to have a kid out. Don't you think?"

He puts his hand up like a traffic cop, but apparently decides I'm harmless and says to me, "Son. I want you to promise me you'll go clean yourself up. Get something to eat." He produces a wallet from his back pocket. He hands me a twenty. "Now, don't go spending it on nothing that'll make you *worse*. Promise me."

It's not enough to get me where I'm going, but it's just what I need. I sit down on a wooden bench. The old white woman next to me carefully pours imaginary liquid into an imaginary cup. The man with the kid goes up to the ticket officer, who stops staring into space long enough to say, "May I help *you*, sir?"

"Do y'all still say 'All aboard'?"

"Excuse me?" the ticket officer says.

"My son wants to know if y'all say 'All aboard.' Like in the movies."

"Yes," the ticket officer says wearily. "We *do* say 'All aboard.' How else would people know to board the train?"

Now the boy jiggles up and down on his father's back, suddenly animated, as if he's riding a pony. The ticket officer sighs, hands grazing the sides of his face as though checking for stubble. Finally he throws his arms up in a "Sure, what the hell" kind of way, and disappears into the Amtrak offices for what seems like an hour. The father sets the boy down, feet first, onto the ground. An intercom crackles and a voice says:

"All aboard!"

The voice is hearty and successful. The boy jumps up and down with delight. He is the happiest I've seen anyone, ever. And though the urge to weep comes over me, I wait—holding my head in my hands—and it passes.

Drinking Coffee
Elsewhere

≈

ORIENTATION GAMES BEGAN the day I arrived at Yale from Baltimore. In my group we played heady, frustrating games for smart people. One game appeared to be charades reinterpreted by existentialists; another involved listening to rocks. Then a freshman counselor made everyone play Trust. The idea was that if you had the faith to fall backward and wait for four scrawny former high school geniuses to catch you, just before your head cracked on the slate sidewalk, then you might learn to trust your fellow students. Russian roulette sounded like a better way to go.

"No way," I said. The white boys were waiting for me to fall, holding their arms out for me, sincerely, gallantly. "No fucking way."

"It's all cool, it's all cool," the counselor said. Her hair was a shade of blond I'd seen only on *Playboy* covers, and she raised her hands as though backing away from a growling dog. "Sister," she said, in an I'm-down-with-the-struggle voice, "you don't have to play this game. As a person of color, you shouldn't have to fit into any white, patriarchal system."

I said, "It's a bit too late for that."

In the next game, all I had to do was wait in a circle until it was my turn to say what inanimate object I wanted to be. One guy said he'd like to be a gadfly, like Socrates. "Stop me if I wax Platonic," he said. I didn't bother mentioning that gadflies weren't inanimate—it didn't seem to make a difference. The girl next to him was eating a rice cake. She wanted to be the Earth, she said. Earth with a capital E.

There was one other black person in the circle. He wore an Exeter T-shirt and his overly elastic expressions resembled a series of facial exercises. At the end of each person's turn, he smiled and bobbed his head with unfettered enthusiasm. "Oh, that was good," he said, as if the game were an experiment he'd set up and the results were turning out better than he'd expected. "Good, good, good!"

When it was my turn I said, "My name is Dina, and if I had to be any object, I guess I'd be a revolver." The sunlight dulled as if on cue. Clouds passed rapidly overhead, presaging rain. I don't know why I said it. Until that moment I'd been good in all the ways that were meant to matter. I was an honor roll student—though I'd learned long ago not to mention it in the part of Baltimore where I lived. Suddenly I was hard-bitten and recalcitrant, the kind of kid who took pleasure in sticking pins into cats; the kind who chased down smart kids to spray them with Mace.

"A revolver," a counselor said, stroking his chin, as if it had grown a rabbinical beard. "Could you please elaborate?"

The black guy cocked his head and frowned, as if the beakers and Erlenmeyer flasks of his experiment had grown legs and scurried off.

"Y o u w e r e just kidding," the dean said, "about wiping out all of mankind. That, I suppose, was a joke." She squinted at me. One of her hands curved atop the other to form a pink, freckled molehill on her desk.

"Well," I said, "maybe I meant it at the time." I quickly saw that this was not the answer she wanted. "I don't know. I think it's the architecture."

Through the dimming light of the dean's office window, I could see the fortress of the old campus. On my ride from the bus station to the campus, I'd barely glimpsed New Haven—a flash of crumpled building here, a trio of straggly kids there. A lot like Baltimore. But everything had changed when we reached those streets hooded by gothic buildings. I imagined how the college must have looked when it was founded, when most of the students owned slaves. I pictured men wearing tights and knickers, smoking pipes.

"The architecture," the dean repeated. She bit her lip and seemed to be making a calculation of some sort. I noticed that she blinked less often than most people. I sat there, intrigued, waiting to see how long it would be before she blinked again.

M y r e v o l v e r comment won me a year's worth of psychiatric counseling, weekly meetings with Dean Guest, and—since the parents of the roommate I'd never met weren't too hip on the idea of

their Amy sharing a bunk bed with a budding homicidal loony—
my very own room.

Shortly after getting my first C ever, I also received the first knock
on my door. The female counselors never knocked. The dean had
spoken to them; I was a priority. Every other day, right before din-
nertime, they'd look in on me, unannounced. "Just checking up," a
counselor would say. It was the voice of a suburban mother in training. By the second week, I had made a point of sitting in a chair in
front of the door, just when I expected a counselor to pop her head
around. This was intended to startle them. I also made a point of being naked. The unannounced visits ended.

The knocking persisted. Through the peephole I saw a white
face, distorted and balloonish.

"Let me in." The person looked like a boy but it sounded like a
girl. "Let me in," the voice repeated.

"Not a chance," I said. I had a suicide single, and I wanted to keep
it that way. No roommates, no visitors.

Then the person began to sob, and I heard a back slump against
the door. If I hadn't known the person was white from the peephole,
I'd have known it from a display like this. Black people didn't knock
on strangers' doors, crying. Not that I understood the black people
at Yale. Most of them were from New York and tried hard to pretend
that they hadn't gone to prep schools. And there was something piti-
ful in how cool they were. Occasionally one would reach out to me
with missionary zeal, but I'd rebuff the person with haughty silence.

"I don't have anyone to talk to!" the person on the other side of
the door cried.

"That is correct."

"When I was a child," the person said, "I played by myself in a
corner of the schoolyard all alone. I hated dolls and I hated games,

animals were not friendly and birds flew away. If anyone was looking for me I hid behind a tree and cried out 'I am an orphan—'"

I opened the door. It was a she.

"Plagiarist!" I yelled. She had just recited a Frank O'Hara poem
as though she'd thought it up herself. I knew the poem because it
was one of the few things I'd been forced to read that I wished I'd
written myself.

The girl turned to face me, smiling weakly, as though her triumph was not in getting me to open the door but in the fact that she
was able to smile at all when she was so accustomed to crying. She
was large but not obese, and crying had turned her face the color of
raw chicken. She blew her nose into the waist end of her T-shirt, revealing a pale belly.

"How do you know that poem?"

She sniffed. "I'm in your Contemporary Poetry class."

She said she was Canadian and her name was Heidi, although she
said she wanted people to call her Henrik. "That's a guy's name," I
said. "What do you want? A sex change?"

She looked at me with so little surprise that I suspected she hadn't
discounted this as an option. Then her story came out in teary,
hiccup-like bursts. She had sucked some "cute guy's dick" and he'd
told everybody and now people thought she was "a slut."

"Why'd you suck his dick? Aren't you a lesbian?"

She fit the bill. Short hair, hard, roach-stomping shoes. Dressed
like an aspiring plumber. And then there was the name Henrik.
The lesbians I'd seen on TV were wiry, thin strips of muscle, but
Heidi was round and soft and had a moonlike face. Drab henna-
colored hair. And lesbians had cats. "Do you have a cat?" I asked.

Her eyes turned glossy with new tears. "No," she said, her voice
quavering, "and I'm not a lesbian. Are you?"

"Do I look like one?" I said.

She didn't answer.

"O.K.," I said. "I could suck a guy's dick, too, if I wanted. But I don't. The human penis is one of the most germ-ridden objects there is." Heidi looked at me, unconvinced. "What I meant to say," I began again, "is that I don't like anybody. Period. Guys or girls. I'm a misanthrope."

"I am, too."

"No," I said, guiding her back through my door and out into the hallway. "You're not."

"Have you had dinner?" she asked. "Let's go to Commons."

I pointed to a pyramid of ramen noodle packages on my windowsill. "See that? That means I never have to go to Commons. Aside from class, I have contact with no one."

"I hate it here, too," she said. "I should have gone to McGill, eh."

"The way to feel better," I said, "is to get some ramen and lock yourself in your room. Everyone will forget about you and that guy's dick and you won't have to see anyone ever again. If anyone looks for you—"

"I'll hide behind a tree."

"A REVOLVER?" Dr. Raeburn said, flipping through a manila folder. He looked up at me as if to ask another question, but he didn't.

Dr. Raeburn was the psychiatrist. He had the gray hair and whiskers of a Civil War general. He was also a chain smoker with beige teeth and a navy wool jacket smeared with ash. He asked about the revolver at the beginning of my first visit. When I was unable to explain myself, he smiled, as if this were perfectly reasonable.

"Tell me about your parents."

I wondered what he already had on file. The folder was thick, though I hadn't said a thing of significance since Day One.

"My father was a dick and my mother seemed to like him."

He patted his pockets for his cigarettes. "That's some heavy stuff," he said. "How do you feel about Dad?" The man couldn't say the word "father." "Is Dad someone you see often?"

"I hate my father almost as much as I hate the word 'Dad.'"

He started tapping his cigarette.

"You can't smoke in here."

"That's right," he said, and slipped the cigarette back into the packet. He smiled, widening his eyes brightly. "Don't ever start."

I THOUGHT that that first encounter would be the last of Heidi or Henrik, or whatever, but then her head appeared in a window of Linsly-Chit during my Chaucer class. A few days later, she swooped down a flight of stairs in Harkness, following me. She hailed me from across Elm Street and found me in the Sterling Library stacks. After one of my meetings with Dr. Raeburn, she was waiting for me outside Health Services, legs crossed, cleaning her fingernails.

"You know," she said, as we walked through Old Campus, "you've got to stop eating ramen. Not only does it lack a single nutrient but it's full of MSG."

I wondered why she even bothered, and was vaguely flattered she cared, but I said, "I like eating chemicals. It keeps the skin radiant."

"There's also hepatitis." She knew how to get my attention— mention a disease.

"You get hepatitis from unwashed lettuce," I said. "If there's anything safe from the perils of the food chain, it's ramen."

"But do you refrigerate what you don't eat? Each time you reheat it, you're killing good bacteria, which then can't keep the bad bacteria in check. A guy got sick from reheating Chinese noodles, and his son died from it. I read it in the *Times*." With this, she put a jovial arm around my neck. I continued walking, a little stunned. Then, just as quickly, she dropped her arm and stopped walking. I stopped, too.

"Did you notice that I put my arm around you?"

"Yes," I said. "Next time, I'll have to chop it off."

"I don't want you to get sick," she said. "Let's eat at Commons."

In the cold air, her arm had felt good.

THE PROBLEM with Commons was that it was too big; its ceiling was as high as a cathedral's, but below it there were no awestruck worshippers, only eighteen-year-olds at heavy wooden tables, chatting over veal patties and Jell-O.

We got our food, tacos stuffed with meat substitute, and made our way through the maze of tables. The Koreans had a table. Each singing group had a table. The crew team sat at a long table of its own. We passed the black table. Heidi was so plump and moonfaced that the sheer quantity of her flesh accentuated just how white she was. The black students gave me a long, hard stare.

"How you doing, sista?" a guy asked, his voice full of accusation, eyeballing me as though I were clad in a Klansman's sheet and hood. "I guess we won't see you till graduation."

"If," I said, "you graduate."

The remark was not well received. As I walked past, I heard

protests, angry and loud as if they'd discovered a cheat at their poker game. Heidi and I found an unoccupied table along the periphery, which was isolated and dark. We sat down. Heidi prayed over her tacos.

"I thought you didn't believe in God," I said.

"Not in the God depicted in the Judeo-Christian Bible, but I do believe that nature's essence is a spirit that—"

"All right," I said. I had begun to eat, and cubes of diced tomato fell from my mouth when I spoke. "Stop right there. Tacos and spirits don't mix."

"You've always got to be so flip," she said. "I'm going to apply for another friend."

"There's always Mr. Dick," I said. "Slurp, slurp."

"You are so lame. So unbelievably lame. I'm going out with Mr. Dick. Thursday night at Atticus. His name is Keith."

Heidi hadn't mentioned Mr. Dick since the day I'd met her. That was more than a month ago and we'd spent a lot of that time together. I checked for signs that she was lying; her habit of smiling too much, her eyes bright and cheeks full so that she looked like a chipmunk. But she looked normal. Pleased, even, to see me so flustered.

"You're insane! What are you going to do this time?" I asked. "Sleep with him? Then when he makes fun of you, what? Come pound your head on my door reciting the collected poems of Sylvia Plath?"

"He's going to apologize for before. And don't call me insane. You're the one going to the psychiatrist."

"Well, I'm not going to suck his dick, that's for sure."

She put her arm around me in mock comfort, but I pushed it off, and ignored her. She touched my shoulder again, and I turned, annoyed, but it wasn't Heidi after all; a sepia-toned boy dressed in khakis and a crisp plaid shirt was standing behind me. He thrust a hot-pink square of paper toward me without a word, then briskly made his way toward the other end of Commons, where the crowds blossomed. Heidi leaned over and read it: "Wear Black Leather—the Less, the Better."

"It's a gay party," I said, crumpling the card. "He thinks we're fucking gay."

HEIDI AND I signed on to work at the Saybrook dining hall as dishwashers. The job consisted of dumping food from plates and trays into a vat of rushing water. It seemed straightforward, but then I learned better. You wouldn't believe what people could do with food until you worked in a dish room. Lettuce and crackers and soup would be bullied into a pulp in the bowl of some bored anorexic; ziti would be mixed with honey and granola; trays would appear heaped with mashed potato snow women with melted chocolate ice cream for hair. Frat boys arrived at the dish-room window, en masse. They liked to fill glasses with food, then seal them, air-tight, onto their trays. If you tried to prize them off, milk, Worcestershire sauce, peas, chunks of bread vomited onto your dish-room uniform.

When this happened one day in the middle of the lunch rush, for what seemed like the hundredth time, I tipped the tray toward one of the frat boys as he turned to walk away, popping the glasses off so that the mess spurted onto his Shetland sweater.

He looked down at his sweater. "Lesbo bitch!"

"No," I said, "that would be your mother."

Heidi, next to me, clenched my arm in support, but I remained motionless, waiting to see what the frat boy would do. He glared at me for a minute, then walked away.

"Let's take a smoke break," Heidi said.

I didn't smoke, but Heidi had begun to, because she thought it would help her lose weight. As I hefted a stack of glasses through the steamer, she lit up.

"Soft packs remind me of you," she said. "Just when you've smoked them all and you think there's none left, there's always one more, hiding in that little crushed corner." Before I could respond she said, "Oh, God. Not another mouse. You know whose job that is."

By the end of the rush, the floor mats got full and slippery with food. This was when mice tended to appear, scurrying over our shoes; more often than not, a mouse got caught in the grating that covered the drains in the floor. Sometimes the mouse was already dead by the time we noticed it. This one was alive.

"No way," I said. "This time you're going to help. Get some gloves and a trash bag."

"That's all I'm getting. I'm not getting that mouse out of there."

"Put on the gloves," I ordered. She winced, but put them on. "Reach down," I said. "At an angle, so you get at its middle. Otherwise, if you try to get it by its tail, the tail will break off."

"This is filthy, eh."

"That's why we're here," I said. "To clean up filth. Eh."

She reached down, but would not touch the mouse. I put my hand around her arm and pushed it till her hand made contact. The cries from the mouse were soft, songlike. "Oh, my God," she said. "Oh, my God, ohmigod." She wrestled it out of the grating and turned her head away.

"Don't you let it go," I said.

"Where's the food bag? It'll smother itself if I drop it in the food bag. Quick," she said, her head still turned away, her eyes closed. "Lead me to it."

"No. We are not going to smother this mouse. We've got to break its neck."

"You're one heartless bitch."

I wondered how to explain that if death is unavoidable it should be quick and painless. My mother had died slowly. At the hospital, they'd said it was kidney failure, but I knew, in the end, it was my father. He made her so scared to live in her own home that she was finally driven away from it in an ambulance.

"Breaking its neck will save it the pain of smothering," I said. "Breaking its neck is more humane. Take the trash bag and cover it so you won't get any blood on you, then crush."

The loud jets of the steamer had shut off automatically and the dish room grew quiet. Heidi breathed in deeply, then crushed the mouse. She shuddered, disgusted. "Now what?"

"What do you mean, 'now what?' Throw the little bastard in the trash."

A T o u r third session, I told Dr. Raeburn I didn't mind if he smoked. He sat on the sill of his open window, smoking behind a jungle screen of office plants.

We spent the first ten minutes discussing the Iliad, and whether or not the text actually states that Achilles had been dipped in the River Styx. He said it did, and I said it didn't. After we'd finished with the Iliad, and with my new job in what he called "the scullery," he asked questions about my parents. I told him nothing. It was none of his business. Instead, I talked about Heidi. I told him about that day in Commons, Heidi's plan to go on a date with Mr. Dick, and the invitation we'd been given to the gay party.

"You seem preoccupied by this soirée." He arched his eyebrows at the word "soirée."

"Wouldn't you be?"

"Dina," he said slowly, in a way that made my name seem like a song title, "have you ever had a romantic interest?"

"You want to know if I've ever had a boyfriend?" I said. "Just go ahead and ask if I've ever fucked anybody."

This appeared to surprise him. "I think that you are having a crisis of identity," he said.

"Oh, is that what this is?"

His profession had taught him not to roll his eyes. Instead, his exasperation revealed itself in a tiny pursing of his lips, as though he'd just tasted something awful and was trying very hard not to offend the cook.

"It doesn't have to be, as you say, someone you've fucked, it doesn't have to be a boyfriend," he said.

"Well, what are you trying to say? If it's not a boy, then you're saying it's a girl—"

"Calm down. It could be a crush, Dina." He lit one cigarette off another. "A crush on a male teacher, a crush on a dog, for heaven's sake. An interest. Not necessarily a relationship."

It was sacrifice time. If I could spend the next half hour talking about some boy, then I'd have given him what he wanted.

So I told him about the boy with the nice shoes.

I was sixteen and had spent the last few coins in my pocket on bus fare to buy groceries. I didn't like going to the Super Fresh two blocks away from my house, plunking government food stamps into the hands of the cashiers.

"There she go reading," one of them once said, even though I was only carrying a book. "Don't your eyes get tired?"

On Greenmount Avenue you could read schoolbooks—that was understandable. The government and your teachers forced you to read them. But anything else was antisocial. It meant you'd rather submit to the words of some white dude than shoot the breeze with your neighbors.

I hated those cashiers, and I hated them seeing me with food stamps, so I took the bus and shopped elsewhere. That day, I got off the bus at Govans, and though the neighborhood was black like my own—hair salon after hair salon of airbrushed signs promising arabesque hair styles and inch-long fingernails—the houses were neat and orderly, nothing at all like Greenmount, where every other house had at least one shattered window. The store was well swept, and people quietly checked long grocery lists—no screaming kids, no loud cashier-customer altercations. I got the groceries and left the store.

I decided to walk back. It was a fall day, and I walked for blocks. Then I sensed someone following me. I walked more quickly, my arms around the sack, the leafy lettuce tickling my nose. I didn't want to hold the sack so close that it would break the eggs or squash the hamburger buns, but it was slipping, and as I looked behind me a boy my age, maybe older, rushed toward me.

"Let me help you," he said.

"That's all right." I set the bag on the sidewalk. Maybe I saw his face, maybe it was handsome enough, but what I noticed first, splayed on either side of the bag, were his shoes. They were nice shoes, real leather, a stitched design like a widow's peak on each one, or like birds' wings, and for the first time in my life I understood what people meant when they said "wing-tip shoes."

"I watched you carry them groceries out that store, then you look around, like you're lost, but like you liked being lost, then you walk down the sidewalk for blocks and blocks. Rearranging that bag, it almost gone to slip, then hefting it back up again."

"Uh-huh," I said.

"And then I passed my own house and was still following you. And then your bag really look like it was gone crash and everything. So I just thought I'd help." He sucked in his bottom lip, as if to keep it from making a smile. "What's your name?" When I told him, he said, "Dina, my name is Cecil." Then he said, "D comes right after C."

"Yes," I said, "it does, doesn't it."

Then, half question, half statement, he said, "I could carry your groceries for you? And walk you home?"

I stopped the story there. Dr. Raeburn kept looking at me. "Then what happened?"

I couldn't tell him the rest: that I had not wanted the boy to walk me home, that I didn't want someone with such nice shoes to see where I lived.

Dr. Raeburn would only have pitied me if I'd told him that I ran down the sidewalk after I told the boy no, that I fell, the bag slipped, and the eggs cracked, their yolks running all over the lettuce. Clear amniotic fluid coated the can of cinnamon rolls. I left the bag there on the sidewalk, the groceries spilled out randomly like cards loosed from a deck. When I returned home, I told my mother that I'd lost the food stamps.

"Lost?" she said. I'd expected her to get angry, I'd wanted her to get angry, but she hadn't. "Lost?" she repeated. Why had I been so clumsy and nervous around a harmless boy? I could have brought the groceries home and washed off the egg yolk, but instead I'd just left them there. "Come on," Mama said, snuffing her tears, pulling my arm, trying to get me to join her and start yanking cushions off the couch. "We'll find enough change here. We got to get something for dinner before your father gets back."

We'd already searched the couch for money the previous week, and I knew there'd be nothing now, but I began to push my fingers into the couch's boniest corners, pretending that it was only a matter of time before I'd find some change or a lost watch or an earring. Something pawnable, perhaps.

"What happened next?" Dr. Raeburn asked again. "Did you let the boy walk you home?"

"My house was far, so we went to his house instead." Though I was sure Dr. Raeburn knew that I was making this part up, I continued. "We made out on his sofa. He kissed me."

Dr. Raeburn lit his next cigarette like a detective. Cool, suspicious. "How did it feel?"

"You know," I said. "Like a kiss feels. It felt nice. The kiss felt very, very nice."

Raeburn smiled gently, though he seemed unconvinced. When he called time on our session, his cigarette had become one long pole of ash. I left his office, walking quickly down the corridor, afraid to look back. It would be like him to trot after me, his navy blazer flapping, just to get the truth out of me. *You never kissed anyone.* The words slid from my brain, and knotted in my stomach.

When I reached my dorm, I found an old record player blocking my door and a Charles Mingus LP propped beside it. I carried them inside and then, lying on the floor, I played the Mingus over and over again until I fell asleep. I slept feeling as though Dr. Raeburn had attached electrodes to my head, willing into my mind a dream about my mother. I saw the lemon meringue of her skin, the long bone of her arm as she reached down to clip her toenails. I'd come home from a school trip to an aquarium, and I was explaining the differences between baleen and sperm whales according to the size of their heads, the range of their habitats, their feeding patterns.

I awoke remembering the expression on her face after I'd finished my dizzying whale lecture. She looked like a tourist who'd asked for directions to a place she thought was simple enough to get to only to hear a series of hypothetical turns, alleys, one-way streets. Her response was to nod politely at the perilous elaborateness of it all; to nod and save herself from the knowledge that she would never be able to get where she wanted to go.

THE DISHWASHERS always closed down the dining hall. One night, after everyone else had punched out, Heidi and I took a break, and though I wasn't a smoker, we set two milk crates upside down on the floor and smoked cigarettes.

The dishwashing machines were off, but steam still rose from them like a jungle mist. Outside in the winter air, students were singing carols in their groomed and tailored singing-group voices. The Whiffenpoofs were back in New Haven after a tour around the world, and I guess their return was a huge deal. Heidi and I craned our necks to watch the year's first snow through an open window.

"What are you going to do when you're finished?" Heidi asked. Sexy question marks of smoke drifted up to the windows before vanishing.

"Take a bath."

She swatted me with her free hand. "No, silly. Three years from now. When you leave Yale."

"I don't know. Open up a library. Somewhere where no one comes in for books. A library in a desert."

She looked at me as though she'd expected this sort of answer and didn't know why she'd asked in the first place.

"What are you going to do?" I asked her.

"Open up a psych clinic. In a desert. And my only patient will be some wacko who runs a library."

"Ha," I said. "Whatever you do, don't work in a dish room ever again. You're no good." I got up from the crate. "C'mon. Let's hose the place down."

We put out our cigarettes on the floor, since it was our job to clean it anyway. We held squirt guns in one hand and used the other to douse the floors with the standard-issue, eye-burning cleaning solution. We hosed the dish room, the kitchen, the serving line, sending the water and crud and suds into the drains. Then we hosed them again so the solution wouldn't eat holes in our shoes as we left. Then I had an idea. I unbuckled my belt.

"What the hell are you doing?" Heidi said.

"Listen, it's too cold to go outside with our uniforms all wet. We could just take a shower right here. There's nobody but us."

"What the fuck, eh?"

I let my pants drop, then took off my shirt and panties. I didn't wear a bra, since I didn't have much to fill one. I took off my shoes and hung my clothes on the stepladder.

"You've flipped," Heidi said. "I mean, really, psych-ward flipped."

I soaped up with the liquid hand soap until I felt as glazed as a ham. "Stand back and spray me."

"Oh, my God," she said. I didn't know whether she was confused or delighted, but she picked up the squirt gun and sprayed me. She was laughing. Then she got too close and the water started to sting.

"God damn it!" I said. "That hurt!"

"I was wondering what it would take to make you say that."

When all the soap had been rinsed off, I put on my regular clothes and said, "O.K. You're up next."

"No way," she said.

"Yes way."

She started to take off her uniform shirt, then stopped.

"What?"

"I'm too fat."

"You goddam right." She always said she was fat. One time I'd told her that she should shut up about it, that large black women wore their fat like mink coats. "You're big as a house," I said now. "Frozen yogurt may be low in calories, but not if you eat five tubs of it. Take your clothes off. I want to get out of here."

She began taking off her uniform, then stood there, hands cupped over her breasts, crouching at the pubic bone.

"Open up," I said, "or we'll never get done."

Her hands remained where they were. I threw the bottle of liquid soap at her, and she had to catch it, revealing herself as she did.

I turned on the squirt gun, and she stood there, stiff, arms at her side, eyes closed, as though awaiting mummification. I began with the water on low, and she turned around in a full circle, hesitantly, letting the droplets from the spray fall on her as if she were submitting to a death by stoning.

When I increased the water pressure, she slipped and fell on the sudsy floor. She stood up and then slipped again. This time she laughed and remained on the floor, rolling around on it as I sprayed.

I think I began to love Heidi that night in the dish room, but who is to say that I hadn't begun to love her the first time I met her? I sprayed her and sprayed her, and she turned over and over like a large beautiful dolphin, lolling about in the sun.

HEIDI STARTED sleeping at my place. Sometimes she slept on the floor; sometimes we slept sardinelike, my feet at her head, until she complained that my feet were "taunting" her. When we finally slept head to head, she said, "Much better." She was so close I could smell her toothpaste. "I like your hair," she told me, touching it through the darkness. "You should wear it out more often."

"White people always say that about black people's hair. The worse it looks, the more they say they like it."

I'd expected her to disagree, but she kept touching my hair, her hands passing through it till my scalp tingled. When she began to touch the hair around the edge of my face, I felt myself quake. Her fingertips stopped for a moment, as if checking my pulse, then resumed.

"I like how it feels right here. See, mine just starts with the same old texture as the rest of my hair." She found my hand under the blanket and brought it to her hairline. "See," she said.

It was dark. As I touched her hair, it seemed as though I could smell it, too. Not a shampoo smell. Something richer, murkier. A bit dead, but sweet, like the decaying wood of a ship. She guided my hand.

"I see," I said. The record she'd given me was playing in my mind, and I kept trying to shut it off. I could also hear my mother saying that this is what happens when you've been around white people: things get weird. So weird I could hear the stylus etching its way into the flat vinyl of the record. "Listen," I said finally, when the bass and saxes started up. I heard Heidi breathe deeply, but she said nothing.

WE SPENT the winter and some of the spring in my room— never hers—missing tests, listening to music, looking out my window to comment on people who wouldn't have given us a second thought. We read books related to none of our classes. I got riled up by *The Autobiography of Malcolm X* and *The Chomsky Reader*; Heidi read aloud passages from *The Anxiety of Influence*. We guiltily read mysteries and *Clan of the Cave Bear,* then immediately threw them away. Once we looked up from our books at exactly the same moment, as though trapped at a dinner table with nothing to say. A pleasant trap of silence.

THEN ONE weekend I went back to Baltimore and stayed with my father. He asked me how school was going, but besides that, we didn't talk much. He knew what I thought of him. I stopped by the Enoch Pratt Library, where my favorite librarian, Mrs. Ardelia, cornered me into giving a little talk to the after-school kids, telling them to stay in school. They just looked at me like I was crazy; they were only nine or ten, and it hadn't even occurred to them to bail.

When I returned to Yale—to a sleepy, tree-scented spring—a group of students were holding what was called "Coming Out Day." I watched it from my room.

The emcee was the sepia boy who'd given us the invitation months back. His speech was strident but still smooth and peppered with jokes. There was a speech about AIDS, with lots of statistics: nothing that seemed to make "coming out" worth it. Then the women spoke. One girl pronounced herself "out" as casually as if she'd announced the time. Another said nothing at all: she came to the microphone with a woman who began cutting off her waist-length, bleached-blond hair. The woman doing the cutting tossed the shorn hair in every direction as she cut. People were clapping and cheering and catching the locks of hair.

And then there was Heidi. She was proud that she liked girls, she said when she reached the microphone. She loved them, wanted to sleep with them. She was a dyke, she said repeatedly, stabbing her finger to her chest in case anyone was unsure to whom she was referring. She could not have seen me. I was across the street, three stories up. And yet, when everyone clapped for her, she seemed to be looking straight at me.

HEIDI KNOCKED. "Let me in."

It was like the first time I met her. The tears, the raw pink of her face.

We hadn't spoken in weeks. Outside, pink-and-white blossoms hung from the Old Campus trees. Students played Hacky Sack in T-shirts and shorts. Though I was the one who'd broken away after she went up to that podium, I still half expected her to poke her head out a window in Linsly-Chit, or tap on my back in Harkness, or even join me in the Commons dining hall, where I'd asked for my dish-room shift to be transferred. She did none of these.

"Well," I said, "what is it?"

She looked at me. "My mother," she said.

She continued to cry, but seemed to have grown so silent in my room I wondered if I could hear the numbers change on my digital clock.

"When my parents were getting divorced," she said, "my mother bought a car. A used one. An El Dorado. It was filthy. It looked like a huge crushed can coming up the street. She kept trying to clean it out. I mean—"

I nodded and tried to think what to say in the pause she left behind. Finally I said, "We had one of those," though I was sure ours was an Impala.

She looked at me, eyes steely from trying not to cry. "Anyway, she'd drive me around in it and although she didn't like me to eat in it, I always did. One day I was eating cantaloupe slices, spitting the seeds on the floor. Maybe a month later, I saw this little sprout, growing right up from the car floor. I just started laughing and she kept saying what, what? I was laughing and then I saw she was so—"

She didn't finish. So what? So sad? So awful? Heidi looked at me with what seemed to be a renewed vigor. "We could have gotten a better car, eh?"

"It's all right. It's not a big deal," I said.

Of course, that was the wrong thing to say. And I really didn't mean it to sound the way it had come out.

I TOLD Dr. Raeburn about Heidi's mother having cancer and how I'd said it wasn't a big deal, though I'd wanted to say the opposite. I told Dr. Raeburn how I meant to tell Heidi that my mother had died, that I knew how one eventually accustoms oneself to the physical world's lack of sympathy: the buses that are still running late, the kids who still play in the street, the clocks that won't stop ticking for the person who's gone.

"You're pretending," Dr. Raeburn said, not sage or professional, but a little shocked by the discovery, as if I'd been trying to hide a pack of his cigarettes behind my back.

"I'm pretending?" I shook my head. "All those years of psych grad," I said. "And to tell me *that*?"

"What I mean is that you construct stories about yourself and dish them out—one for you, one for you—" Here he reenacted this process, showing me handing out lies as if they were apples.

"Pretending. I believe the professional name for it might be denial," I said. "Are you calling me gay?"

He pursed his lips noncommittally, then finally said, "No, Dina. I don't think you're gay."

I checked his eyes. I couldn't read them.

"No. Not at all," he said, sounding as if he were telling a subtle joke. "But maybe you'll finally understand."

"Understand what?"

"Oh, just that constantly saying what one doesn't mean accustoms the mouth to meaningless phrases." His eyes narrowed. "Maybe you'll understand that when you finally need to express something truly significant your mouth will revert to the insignificant nonsense it knows so well." He looked at me, his hands sputtering in the air in a gesture of defeat. "Who knows?" he asked with a glib, psychiatric smile I'd never seen before. "Maybe it's your survival mechanism. Black living in a white world."

I heard him, but only vaguely. I'd hooked on to that one word, pretending. Dr. Raeburn would never realize that "pretending" was what had got me this far. I remembered the morning of my mother's funeral. I'd been given milk to settle my stomach; I'd pretended it was coffee. I imagined I was drinking coffee elsewhere. Some Arabic-speaking country where the thick coffee served in little cups was so strong it could keep you awake for days.

❧

HEIDI WANTED me to go with her to the funeral. She'd sent this message through the dean. "We'll pay for your ticket to Vancouver," the dean said.

These people wanted you to owe them for everything. "What about my return ticket?" I asked the dean. "Maybe the shrink will chip in for that."

The dean looked at me as though I were an insect she'd like to squash. "We'll pay for the whole thing. We might even pay for some lessons in manners."

So I packed my suitcase and walked from my suicide single dorm to Heidi's room. A thin wispy girl in ragged cutoffs and a shirt that read "LSBN!" answered the door. A group of short-haired girls in thick black leather jackets, bundled up despite the summer heat, encircled Heidi in a protective fairy ring. They looked at me critically, clearly wondering if Heidi was too fragile for my company.

"You've got our numbers," one said, holding on to Heidi's shoulder. "And Vancouver's got a great gay community."

"Oh, God," I said. "She's going to a funeral, not a Save the Dykes rally."

One of the girls stepped in front of me.

"It's O.K., Cynthia," Heidi said. Then she ushered me into her bedroom and closed the door. A suitcase was on her bed, half packed.

"I could just uninvite you," Heidi said. "How about that? You want that?" She folded a polka-dotted T-shirt that was wrong for any occasion and put it in her suitcase. "Why haven't you talked to me?" she said, looking at the shirt instead of me. "Why haven't you talked to me in two months?"

"I don't know," I said.

"You don't know," she said, each syllable steeped in sarcasm. "You don't know. Well, *I* know. You thought I was going to try to sleep with you."

"Try to? We slept together all winter!"

"If you call smelling your feet sleeping together, you've got a lot to learn." She seemed thinner and meaner; every line of her body held me at bay.

"So tell me," I said. "What can you show me that I need to learn?" But as soon as I said it I somehow knew she still hadn't slept with anyone. "Am I supposed to come over there and sweep your enraged self into my arms?" I said. "Like in the movies? Is this the part where we're both so mad we kiss each other?"

She shook her head and smiled weakly. "You don't get it," she said. "My mother is dead." She closed her suitcase, clicking shut the old-fashioned locks. "My mother is dead," she said again, this time reminding herself. She set her suitcase upright on the floor and sat on it. She looked like someone waiting for a train.

"Fine," I said. "And she's going to be dead for a long time." Though it sounded stupid, I felt good saying it. As though I had my own locks to click shut.

HEIDI WENT to Vancouver for her mother's funeral. I didn't go with her. Instead, I went back to Baltimore and moved in with an aunt I barely knew. Every day was the same: I read and smoked outside my aunt's apartment, studying the row of hair salons across the street, where girls in denim cutoffs and tank tops would troop in and come out hours later, a flash of neon nails, coifs the color and sheen of patent leather. And every day I imagined Heidi's house in

Vancouver. Her place would not be large, but it would be clean. Flowery shrubs would line the walks. The Canadian wind would whip us about like pennants. I'd be visiting her in some vague time in the future, deliberately vague, for people like me, who realign past events to suit themselves. In that future time, you always have a chance to catch the groceries before they fall; your words can always be rewound and erased, rewritten and revised.

Then I'd imagine Heidi visiting me. There are no psychiatrists or deans, no boys with nice shoes or flip cashiers. Just me in my single room. She knocks on the door and says, "Open up."

Speaking in Tongues

❧

AFTER SUNDAY SCHOOL, Tia usually went outside, where she'd talk with her best friend Marcelle. They would lean against the white brick of the church, silently hoping that Morning Service would never begin. Tia had only known Marcelle since the summer, when the two had met in band camp, Tia playing the clarinet, Marcelle the trumpet. They were also the only saved students in Rutherford B. Hayes High, roaming the halls together in their ankle-length skirts, their long-sleeved ruffled blouses, while the others watched them: the other black girls who leaned sexily against lockers as though auditioning for parts in a play, the white girls who traded pocket mirrors, lipsticking themselves like four-year-olds determined to crayon one spot to a waxy patch. These were the people Tia and Marcelle gossiped about after Sunday school, but that Sunday Tia knew she was in trouble. Instead of heading outside, she searched the sanctuary, trying to get to her great-aunt Roberta before Sister Gwendolyn did.

The trouble had started in Sunday school. Tia was sitting next to Marcelle, who was reading aloud from the lesson: "God's Special Message for Teens."

The other girls in Sunday school had read their passages, but Tia had been gazing at the stained-glass Paul: behind his frozen image of sudden blindness and supplication, shadows passed, turning the picture of Paul dark and opaque. Marcelle had kicked Tia's shin.

"'God's Special Message for Teens,'" Tia began.

"I already read that," Marcelle whispered, tapping her pencil to a passage ten paragraphs down the page. Next to the passage was a picture of a young Jesus sitting on a grassy hill with a dreamy Nazarene look in his eyes. Marcelle leaned over Tia as if the words in Tia's book were different and more engrossing than her own. Marcelle began to draw a cartoon bubble above Jesus' head. Tia read the passage:

"As a teen, you may believe that no one understands your problems. You may say to yourself, 'I'm all alone.' But this is NOT TRUE! God understands your problems. Remember, Jesus was a teen, just like you! Modern teens face many challenges, but just think: when Jesus was a teen, he already knew he would have to save the world from SIN. And as though that weren't enough, the elder rabbis gave him homework, too— just like you!"

All the Sunday school books Tia had read were written this way, but this was the first time they seemed so ridiculous to her. Perhaps, as her aunt Roberta never ceased to remind her, this was Marcelle's bad influence. Perhaps, as she'd learned in her high school biology class, all bodies' cells regenerate, and within seven years' time, all cells have died and been reborn, and you are truly a new person. Tia stopped reading and looked up from the page, glancing at Sister Gwendolyn, who held her book in front of her as if she were about to begin singing carols from it. "Continue," she said.

Marcelle now had the book in her lap and Tia had to lean over to see the words. Marcelle made an arrow from the word "homework" to the cartoon bubble she'd drawn. In the bubble next to Jesus' head she'd written out a quadratic equation.

"Tia, Marcelle is busy taking notes and you can't even concentrate on a simple passage. *Read.* Please."

Tia continued, trying to read with a revitalized sense of duty:

"You, being a teenager, may be asked to drink alcohol, smoke drugs and other things, or 'have a little fun.' DON'T DO IT! Doing these things may seem 'far out' and 'groovy,' but they are not only dangerous to your health, they are also dangerous to your life as a Christian. When someone asks you to go to a party, you should ask yourself, 'Would Jesus go to this party?' If he wouldn't, then that's God's way of telling you that the party is not for you."

When Tia finished, Marcelle was putting the final touches on a crude drawing of three guys in bandannas asking the sketch of Jesus to attend their party.

Though Tia did not laugh very loud, or for a long time, the other girls, including Marcelle, looked at her, their eyes blinking the slow and steady concerned flashes of car hazard lights. All these other girls in her Sunday school had begun speaking in tongues, but Tia could not. You couldn't fake it, though she had tried to at home. The fake tongues sounded like something between Pig Latin and a record played in reverse.

You could only truly speak in tongues when all worldly matters were emptied from your mind, or else there was no room for God. To do that, you had to be thinking about him, praising him, or singing to him. She had tried at church and she had tried at home, but nothing worked. In her room, she would genuflect, pushing her head against her bed ruffle, reciting scriptures, praying, singing, concluding it all with a deep, waiting silence. But nothing would come out. Her only solace was that Marcelle was three years older and hadn't spoken in tongues either.

Tia could not afford to laugh, and yet she had done it.

"Sister Tia Townsend. May I remind you that the fool hath said in his heart, *there is no God.*"

By the time Tia wove through the clusters of church members, Sister Gwendolyn and Tia's aunt Roberta were already talking about her. Sister Gwendolyn wore a hat that looked like a strawberry birthday cake. Roberta's hat was dove-gray, sleek as an airplane. At each angry quake of Sister Gwendolyn's curls, Tia's aunt Roberta furrowed her brow deeply, shook her head heartily, held her Bible so tight against her chest one might think it could ward off a heart attack.

Tia watched their hats drift away from each other. She knew what they were thinking: Tia did not Believe, thus Tia Laughed in her Heart, thus Tia was not able to Speak in Tongues. Their thoughts headed toward the same conclusion as tiny ants march toward the same mammoth crumb of bread.

◦〜◦

TIA FOLLOWED Sister Gwendolyn past the sanctuary, past the pastor's office. When they reached the hymnbook closet, Sister Gwendolyn took out a ring of keys and unlocked the door. "In here," she said with a smile that never reached her eyes. She turned on the light, gesturing to the only chair in the closet, one used as a step stool for reaching the top shelves.

Sister Gwendolyn wedged herself in between Tia and the shelf of hymnbooks, wheezing the way big people do in small places. All the smells of the closet were buoyed by its heat: the hymnbooks, musty with years of sweaty palms, the bottles of anointing oil that had seeped through their boxes, marking the cardboard with round, greasy stains. And then there was Sister Gwendolyn's signature odor: fig-smelling perfume, armpit sweat, cough drops.

By now the congregation would be filing into the sanctuary for Morning Service. Soon someone would begin jangling a tambourine and the choir would sing. Robin-breasted women would swell their bosoms, inhaling God.

"Sister Townsend," Sister Gwendolyn said, "do you believe that you will ever receive the Holy Ghost?"

She knew the answer to that one. "Yes, ma'am," she said.

Sister Gwendolyn held her hands behind her back, sharking around Tia as best she could without her haunches threatening to unpry books from the shelves. Sister Gwendolyn raised her palms to either side of Tia's head, as though Tia's skull were a fly she was determined to trap with her bare hands. Tia had seen this done before, a more aggressive sort of laying-on-of-hands, usually performed on new members. Or the sick-hearted older ones, Brothers who refused to stay with wives, Sisters who refused to obey their husbands. Sister Gwendolyn began: *This child oh Lord is not following in your path oh Lord show her the way oh Lord you died on the Cross at Calvary oh Lord and you came resurrected oh Lord but this child laughs at you oh Lord, spare her oh—*

"I wasn't laughing *at* Him," Tia said.

Sister Gwendolyn started once more, clamping the heels of her hands onto Tia's temples, harder now: *Oh Lord she has laughed oh Lord at your loving kindness oh Lord . . .*

"I WASN'T LAUGHING *AT* HIM."

Sister Gwendolyn stopped. Tia shook off Sister Gwendolyn's hands. Sister Gwendolyn relaxed. "No?" Sister Gwendolyn said, her wreath of beauty-parlor curls quivering. She reached for a hymnbook and opened it to a random page as if to suggest that, with reading material, she could wait forever. "I suppose you're going to tell me you weren't laughing *at* him, you were laughing *with* Him."

"Something like that," Tia said.

Sister Gwendolyn threw the hymnbook on the floor, where it slapped the concrete. Once it was thrown, she refused to look at it. "I want you to say the Lord's Prayer for me, Tia Townsend." She said it with a quiet steadiness that did not dam the anger behind it. "I want you to say the Lord's Prayer. I want you to cry tears for Jesus."

Tia said the Lord's Prayer. Then the scripture about God giving his only begotten Son. Then the one from Revelation that foretold of rivers flowing blood and seven angels opening seven seals that would end the world.

After a time, no tears in sight, she was allowed to leave.

❧

TIA AND her aunt Roberta walked home from church on the old rural road. Oaks spread their huge, trophy-shaped crowns, branches of bayberry looking like fans. Beyond this was bottlebrush weed, and beyond the weed, the endless green nap of the cemetery. It was a beautiful day outside; the sky was a color Marcelle called Aqua Velva blue. It seemed a colossal injustice that her internal weather never matched the one outside.

As they walked, Tia briskly and impatiently ahead, her great-aunt unhurried and elephantine behind, Roberta hummed an old tune, a spiritual so mournful people sang it only at wakes, and the only word Tia could make out was "Nebuchadnezzar." Roberta did not mention her conversation with Sister Gwendolyn; Tia did not mention the closet.

"I want," Tia said, "to live with my mother."

She had been working up to these words for a long time. Her mother, as far as she knew, lived in Atlanta, but Tia had only seen her once since Roberta had become her legal guardian. Tia had been seven then, though she hadn't remembered that last visit as well as she would have liked; she had expected that more visits would follow. But she remembered her mother in a hazy soft-focus way. How her mother would absently stroke her hair, wherever she happened to be, like a starlet. How she would hold Tia's face with both hands, as if it were a big blossom. Once, Tia recalled to Roberta her mother's game of making Tia recite the days of the week and months of the year at random. Roberta snapped, "She was trying to make sure you weren't high on her stuff. She kept it laying around so much it's a wonder you didn't get high from the dust bunnies."

After that, Tia kept her questions about her mother to the essential few, and after a while, living with Roberta seemed less like an arrangement and more like the way things simply had to be.

Tia felt emboldened from her time in the closet with Sister Gwendolyn, and repeated, slowly, forcefully, as if accommodating a lip reader. "I want. To live. With my mother."

The insolence of her tone was enough to merit a single sharp slap on the face, though Roberta had hit her only twice before. But Roberta did not stop humming, nor did she signal in any way that she'd heard Tia, and when they'd reached home, Roberta took the thawed-out chicken from the Frigidaire and served it baked with green beans as planned.

The next day, Tia walked to the Montgomery Greyhound bus station instead of catching the school bus. She had stuffed all that would fit into her backpack without looking suspicious: five skirts, five blouses, and stockings. Deodorant, a toothbrush, a washcloth, soap, and all the underwear she owned. She opened her clarinet case and laid her sheet music atop the clarinet pieces. She stashed her books under her bed and thought about how it might be her last time smelling the lemony Murphy oil soap that rose from the cool hardwood floor. She had thirty-four dollars. A bus ticket to Atlanta cost thirty-two.

She'd been in the station before, but never as a passenger, always with Roberta to drop off or pick up church members who didn't want to pay the five-dollar cab fare. Now that she had two hours of waiting ahead of her, she had time to notice how outdated it seemed, the bus arrival and departure tables on the same corrugated plastic as corner-store menu boards; the seat in which she sat—huge and spoon-shaped, rendered in taffy-orange plasticine—must have once seemed like the height of space-age decor. Perhaps this was exactly how it looked when King lived here, and she tried to imagine where the "Colored" and "Whites Only" signs would have hung, then realized she didn't have to. All five blacks waited in one area, all three whites in another.

She decided to call Marcelle, who lived so close to school that she'd still be home.

"Mrs. Barnes, is Marcelle there? It's Tia."

"Who?"

Mrs. Barnes, Marcelle's mother, was what people at church called "sick and shut in." She had some ailment that wasn't serious enough for hospitalization, but was serious enough that she stayed in bed all day. Marcelle said it was depression, and that nobody in her family wanted to admit it. Finally, Mrs. Barnes put Marcelle on the phone. Tia told Marcelle she was leaving.

"What are you going to tell them when they ask about me?" Tia said.

"Which time? When you don't come home or when your face is on a milk carton?"

"Look, they didn't lock you in a closet, so I don't even want to hear it." She'd expected Marcelle to be happy for her; it was exactly the kind of thing she thought Marcelle would have done.

"I'll be down there in twenty minutes." Marcelle said.

It took Marcelle nearly an hour. When Tia suggested they get some orange juice in the bus station diner, Marcelle refused. "Hell, naw! The longer you stay in the station, the more likely they are to remember your face."

So they walked the periphery of the station grounds, Marcelle asking questions Tia should have known the answers to.

"You don't know where your mother lives?"

"I told you, she lives in Atlanta."

"Her and twenty billion other people."

But Marcelle didn't try to talk her out of it, and for that, Tia was grateful. When it was time to board the bus, Marcelle gave her forty-two dollars, all one-dollar bills.

"You were saving this for your prom dress."

Though church members weren't allowed to dance, and though Marcelle wouldn't be a senior for two years, she was working on a way of going to the prom, stealing a dollar here and there from her zonked-out mother's purse.

"What was I supposed to do? You only got like two dollars." Marcelle tried not to show disappointment at giving up the money, but Tia could see it, and felt powerless, since she knew she was not about to refuse the money. "I got two more years to save," Marcelle said, and with a wicked grin added, "Long as those SDI checks keep coming in!"

"Don't talk about your mother that way."

"She's *my* mama!" Marcelle grinned as broadly as ever, then moved to hug her, but Tia pulled back.

"Like you said, they'll remember us."

Marcelle glanced at the white bus driver, talking about transmissions with a black lady midget. "He won't notice," Marcelle said, hugging her. "We all look the same to them anyway."

WHEN THEY reached Columbus, Georgia, the bus driver took an exit and switched to low gear. The machinery of the bus fought against moving so slowly, moaning until it came to a complete stop in a Burger King parking lot.

"Fifteen minutes, folks," the driver said. Before he could even open the door, people pushed impatiently down the aisle.

The driver stepped outside and lit a cigarette while passengers hustled into the Burger King. Tia did not want to spend her money quickly, so she stayed in her seat and watched the driver. He walked to the edge of the parking lot where weeds rose up in a growth of densely packed stalks. It seemed as though he were sizing up the weeds to see if the brush would make a path for him. Tia could see only the back of his head, but he seemed to be thinking, *I will leave you all behind, and then where will you be? I will enter this here growth of weed and disappear forever.*

"Go," Tia whispered, looking out the window. "Go." She was rooting for him, knowing she would be the only person who understood what he was doing and why, until she saw him unzip his pants and loose his urine in a series of arcs so elaborate he seemed to be spelling out his name.

Everyone returned with Whoppers and Cokes. The driver yawned, making motions for dawdlers to hurry onto the bus. He sat in his seat, looked at his watch, then closed the door. He had already swung the bus into a slow reverse when someone in back told him that one man was inside the Burger King, still waiting for his food.

"Fifteen minutes," said the bus driver. "I'm no joke, folks. I say fifteen minutes, that means fifteen minutes." He turned out of the parking lot.

"Lordy, lordy. Buses sure have changed," said the white woman across the aisle from Tia. "*No* kind of manners." Tia was about to agree until she realized that the white woman was talking to herself.

The bus had just made the turn out onto the service road when the abandoned passenger came flying out of the Burger King with his bag of food.

"He's just back there, Chuckie. *Wait* for him!"

The bus driver continued at a slow crawl toward the interstate sign. The abandoned man crossed the road, and a car he'd dodged honked madly. Once he'd gotten on the right side of the road, he caught up to the bus just a few yards from the door. The driver braked and the bus halted with a hydraulic sigh.

The man, exhausted, stopped running and lowered his head to catch his breath. Just as he'd made it inches from the door, the driver kicked into drive again.

"No he *didn't*!" one woman squealed.

"Girrrrrl. We should report this one! Report his ass to the Greyhound people!"

The abandoned man began running once more, and the whole busload of passengers were either pressed against the windows or standing in the aisle. "Run! Run! Run!" they chanted to the man who was already running. The bus driver stopped for the man once more—another tease—and drove off again. This time the passengers began yelling at the bus driver, cursing him while he checked his rearview mirror as if to make sure they didn't hit him. "All I can say," hollered one woman, "is that you is wrong, Mr. Bus Driver. I don't know who you or Mr. Greyhound is, but you is both *wrong*!"

Tia could feel herself smiling from the excitement of it all. It was different from church, where everyone felt something she wished she could feel but didn't. She thought she felt God the most when she was quiet, or when she wondered whether there was a God at all. But here on the bus, everyone was rooting for a man whom none of them knew, but there he was, real and running. When everyone began banging the windows as if to break them, she banged on them too, yelling, "Run! Run! Run!"

The third time the driver stopped, he opened the door and the man boarded the bus to wild cheering. Whatever food he'd bought had fallen out the bottom of the bag. He heaved, trying to stare at the driver murderously, but tears streamed down his face. As he made his way down the aisle, people applauded; men clamped him on the shoulder as if to affirm his manhood.

In his delirium, perhaps, the man passed his original seat, and when he'd gotten to Tia's row, he sniffed up his tears and sat next to her. Another shock of excitement hit her, as if she were sitting next to a celebrity. But he soon feel asleep, his head nodding off on her shoulder, and when a rivulet of drool, thin as spider silk, trickled onto her collar, she hadn't the heart to nudge him awake.

THEY APPROACHED Atlanta; her insides jumped when she saw the skyline. She tried to figure out why it hit her so hard. They were just buildings. But in each one, someone worked, someone sang, someone complained; someone shuttled away the trash, the storehouse of banalities, secrets, and cravings. When the lights were out, she thought, surely some couple would creep up or down a stairwell, stopping on a landing to embrace. The buildings breathed and exhaled possibilities; that was why a skyline like this one could stop your heart. As the bus entered the city's center, threading its way in, the skyline seemed to whisper, *You too are possible.*

The nearly abandoned man's celebrity had faded by the time people stumbled out of the bus and into hot, gleaming Atlanta. Tia stood in the Atlanta bus station as streams of people with destinations whizzed past her, bumped into her, crowded around her. She found a carousel of phones and shrugged off her backpack, set down her clarinet case. Atlanta had two separate phone books, A through M and N through Z, each over a thousand pages. When she found the right phone book she counted twenty-two Dunloveys, no Rosalyns, but four R's.

The first R. Dunlovey's phone was busy; the second, she found out from the answering machine, belonged to a gaggle of college students. On her third call, a black man answered the phone.

"Yeah," the voice said. "Who is it?"

"I'm looking for Rosalyn Dunlovey."

"I'm asking *who you is,* not who you *want.*" In the background she heard children. Something smashed, and the phone on the other end tumbled and fell.

When things settled down she said, "This is Tia."

"Well, Tia, there's a Rosa here, but no Rosalyn. How you know Rosa?"

Tia had never heard her aunt Roberta call her mother Rosa. Her mother would have been Roz, not Rosa. And kids. What if her mother had other children, and hadn't bothered to visit Tia now that she had younger children? Tia didn't want to think about it. She preferred the image of her mother on an anonymous street corner, doing—she didn't know what her mother would be doing—to that of her mother living a real life without her. Then, for the first time, it occurred to her that her mother might be dead.

"I'm sorry. I have the wrong number."

"Wait a minute," the man said, suddenly buttering his words, "you sound good. Rosa ain't gone be off work till ten. Why don't you come—"

Tia hung up. She closed her eyes. She did not know why she'd expected there to be fewer people, less noise, less ugliness when she opened them again, but she had.

SHE DECIDED that she'd leave the bus station and call hotels from pay phones elsewhere.

"What's your price range?" one hotel desk clerk asked.

She told him.

"Ten dollars?" He whistled, high and arch. He'd been the only one to stay on the phone after she'd announced how much money she had. "What you're looking for is a *motel*. You're looking for, like, a roach motel." The clerk laughed, and when Tia did not, he said, "I was just kidding."

Tia pictured her aunt Roberta in the kitchen, singing along with the gospel station on the radio. About now, she would notice that Tia was late coming home from school.

"O.K.," the man sighed, gathering patience. "Are you trying to find a job here or something?"

Yes. That was it. She was looking for a job. She obviously would have to start looking for a job. "Yes, I am. Do you have one?"

"Doll, I got two jobs, but they're mine. How old are you?"

Tia told him she was fourteen.

"You like a runaway or something?"

"More like a run-a-to," she said, proud of her wit, but the hotel clerk didn't even break a laugh. She called the places he told her to call: the YMCA said they didn't have rooms, just a swimming pool; the shelter told her to come on down, but she thought anyone so willing to take her would be more than willing to ship her away. Finally, she'd booked a room with the Atlanta Dream Youth Hostel for fifteen dollars until their desk clerk told her to bring two forms of ID.

"I don't have an ID."

"Well, we can't give you a room. You need two forms of identification." Tia wanted to know why, and the clerk told her, "To prove that you are who you say you are."

"But I told you. I'm Tia Townsend."

"But we need pictures. Like a driver's license. Or a passport. We need picture identification."

"Why do you need a picture?" Tia asked. "You'll see me when I get there."

B e s i d e s , the youth hostel was in Decatur, too far away to conduct a search for her mother. By nightfall, she had walked around most of downtown Atlanta and ridden five MARTA buses. She plopped down in a hard McDonald's chair to rest before ordering food. It had rained during the day, and though she'd folded newspapers into a tent over her head, she was soaked. She'd slipped in mud taking the shortcut over the small hill on her way into the McDonald's, and she was too tired to go to the restroom to change. She knew her hair was a mess, and when she reached for her comb, remembered that she'd given it away to a homeless man. "But I'm homeless, too," she'd protested. The man argued that he was *professionally* homeless.

Only the day before, her aunt Roberta forced her to pray for two hours straight after they'd come home from church, and most of her half hour of silent prayer included thinking of a way to get to Atlanta. Now that she was in Atlanta, she prayed, her head bowed over the table's yellow Formica.

Then she felt someone staring at her. When she lifted her head, she saw that the man doing the staring wore one of those nylon running suits that swished with every movement. She tried to stare back, hoping he'd realize his rudeness, but his gaze was unflagging. He gurgled up the last bit of drink with his straw, then grinned as though he were proud of this accomplishment, and she should be too.

"Rough day?"

Tia nodded.

"Well, keep your pretty self smiling." He got up and tossed his cup in the trash. He spoke a few words to the bored cashier, then swished out the door.

When Tia finally summoned the energy to order and pay for her food, the cashier waved her hand.

"It's free," the cashier said.

"Thank you," Tia said. "Thank you so much."

"I ain't do nothing. He paid for it." The cashier girl pushed the tray of food toward Tia as though the meal had offended her in some way.

At first Tia thought "He" meant God. For people at church, "He" always meant God. *He touched me, He spoke to me, He healed me.* But people in the World, Tia knew, never used "He" to refer to God.

"'He' who?"

The girl waved a lazy hand toward the door. "Him who just left. Dezi. It's on him."

The man who'd spoken to her, who'd said she was pretty. The last time anyone had called her pretty was when she was five years old. Her mother lay next to her on a stained, sheetless mattress and said, "You so pretty." Her eyes were glazed, their whites not white at all but the color of old piano keys. "You so pretty," she'd said, patting Tia's face harder than she must have intended.

TAVERNS AND bars lined Virginia Avenue, their interiors leaking a dim tungsten glow. Tia passed restaurants where waiters and waitresses zipped around the linened tables like dragonflies through a maze of lily pads. An Oriental grocery advertised itself in both

149

English and Chinese, and Tia stood transfixed at the complex darning of saber-shaped strokes. The large window displayed an oversized bird of some sort, hanging by its feet, its corpse glossed molasses-black down to its headless neck. Tia walked down the sidewalk, against the northward flow of pedestrian traffic. She found a pay phone and dialed the R. Dunlovey that had previously been busy. A young boy answered the phone.

"Hello!" the voice shouted, loud and confident, as if this were one of the few words he knew.

"Hello," Tia said. "May I speak to your mother?"

After almost a full minute, she heard a sibling argument over a Popsicle ensue in the distance, and just as she was about to hang up, a woman's amber-toned voice answered. Tia recognized it, but tried to control herself.

"Ma'am. Do you know a Tia Townsend?"

The woman was silent, and as the silence grew Tia envisioned their reunion, hugs, smiles, shopping sprees so that Tia could get normal clothes, a little adorable brother whom Tia would teach to play the clarinet.

"Atiya, Atiya . . ." the woman said, "I don't think so."

Tia turned onto another street, then another, and another, but she did not cry, not even when she saw a squirrel on the sidewalk, dead, clutching the branch that had failed it. She kept walking until she entered a residential section where it looked like bills were paid on time. Then she saw the quiet streets as Marcelle would have, and suddenly she knew what to do. She checked to see which cars were locked. After the first car alarm, she panicked, her clarinet case banging against her side for the four whole blocks she ran.

She began to look for cars with clubs on their steering wheels.

These, she figured, would not be locked as often as the ones without, and when she brushed past them, no alarms sounded. The one she opened had plush-looking seats, but it turned out the seats did not matter. If she didn't want anyone noticing her, she'd have to lie on the floor and cover herself. The floor was matted with what seemed like a week's worth of old newspapers, and she arranged these over herself in a thin tissuey blanket.

It was Monday, so Tia's aunt Roberta would be home from church and would have made pork chops. When they asked about her, Marcelle would have played it cool, *She talked about going to Atlanta but I never thought she'd do it.* At church, Aunt Roberta would have prayed with the Saints for Tia to come home, for Tia to be safe, for God to guide her. They loved her and she loved them, but it was a smothering sort of love: love because you had to, never getting the chance to find out whether you wanted to or not.

Through a rip in the newspaper, she could see out the window. The sky remained a muddy, light-polluted purple-brown, refusing to turn black and starry the way it did in Alabama. The lights from downtown winked at her, the crescent moon like a castaway cuticle, discarded by God.

TIA WAS certain the morning sun would wake her before the owner got into the car to go to work. Instead, the car door slammed, the engine turned over, and the sun streamed through the newsprint as it would stained glass.

The car began moving. Tia wished whoever was driving would hum or turn on the radio so she could stretch without the paper making noise. She felt paralyzed, a vague tingle in her leg. If she could not get her circulation going soon, she feared it would stay limp and immobile forever. Then the person—a white woman—began singing to herself.

Is this love, is this love, is this love,
Is this love that I'm feeling . . .

Tia recognized it as part of a song the Rasta-hatted boys sang. She stretched and scratched. She could hear the newspaper crinkle and tear, but she didn't think the woman would be able to hear it over her singing. Tia stopped scratching, a moment after the woman stopped singing. The silence in the car seemed to double. The car swerved and came to a halt.

The front door opened but did not slam shut. The back door opened, and Tia could feel a draft of air rush up her skirt. She sat up. The woman screamed and ran down the sidewalk. She wanted to tell the woman that she was Tia, that she wasn't going to steal or molest the woman, but all this was not possible. At some point, Tia got out of the car and began running in the opposite direction, tugging her backpack behind her like a child who couldn't keep up. The woman had fallen onto the concrete, and amid her screams, Tia realized she'd left her clarinet in the car. By the time she recovered it, the woman's hyperventilating and repeated pointing had sent two men running after her.

She ran, her skirt chopping off her natural stride. Then she hiked it up, nearly dropping everything in the process. Suddenly she re-membered what Marcelle had said at the bus station, *We all look the same to them anyway.* She had an idea. She stopped running, and the white men, perplexed, stopped shy of her.

"Why's she screaming at *me?*"

"You were trying to steal her car."

She was out of breath but did her best to look aghast, wronged, mortified. "You must think we *all* look alike!"

Then it was their turn to look aghast, wronged, mortified. Then one snapped out of it and started the chase anew.

She had not realized she could run so fast in her skirt once it was hiked past her thighs, and cursed herself for all the times in gym when she'd fallen, unable to wear shorts like everyone else. She ran and she beat them. Ha! she wanted to say to the two men who couldn't keep up. When she felt a safe distance away, she slumped next to a dumpster, sitting amid pizza crusts, half-eaten sausages, and scampering cockroaches.

She took stock of herself; her sleeve was dotted with blood the whole length of her forearm. She cleaned up in a park restroom, raking her hair as well as she could with her fingers. In the park, she stopped to listen to a man playing a saxophone. His case was open, and as people passed by, they dropped money inside. Tia headed toward an unshaded spot in a park where the sky was the color of a suburban swimming pool. Tia opened her clarinet case and began to play. For the first hour, no one put money in her case, so instead of trying to play through the whole *Marriage of Figaro*—most of which consisted of uneventful passages for clarinets—she waited until she saw people approaching before she began to play, concentrating on the dramatic swells and crests. Occasionally, someone would drop a quarter, but more often than not, they dropped wholly unhelpful items, as though her case were an opportunity for them to clean their pockets: a stick of chewing gum from an elderly man, the business card of a personal-injuries lawyer, a single earring with the glued-in rhinestone missing, and several times, lint. But a few times someone dropped—she was overjoyed—a dollar.

❧

SHE'D MADE over ten dollars, and to celebrate, she wanted to buy something. Certain she could make another ten before nightfall, she considered buying a pair of jeans she'd seen in a store called Herbie's. Unlike the other thrift shops on Virginia Avenue, Herbie's was inexpensive. She still hadn't found a very cheap store like a Kmart, and figured she'd have to go to the outer reaches of the city, and that she could not do.

Reason took hold of her, and the power of food was more immediate than the intense desire for her first pair of jeans. She walked back to the same McDonald's at which she'd eaten the day before, the streets now feeling homey and welcoming. She was on her second Big Mac—relishing how two mass-produced patties could bring such joy—when the man from yesterday tapped on the window, mouthing overzealous surprise. He—Dezi—looked younger than she'd remembered. His head, shaved to a bullet-like smoothness, gave his skull the raw beauty of a lynx or a panther. Before, she had put him at thirty; today she thought mid-twenties. He came inside and sat across from her, then boomed his order in the general direction of the cashier. One of the managers brought it over in seconds. She wanted to ask what made him so special, but he spoke first.

"Looking more upbeat, girlfriend."

"Yeah," she said, surprised and a little worried that he was being so familiar with her, but she felt obligated to return the casual tone, "Thanks, man, for yesterday."

While she silently mocked herself—she'd never called anyone "man"—Dezi looked as though he was trying to remember what he'd done that was so remarkable. "Oh. *That*. Sweetheart. Don't even sweat it. I take care of people I like." Dezi sucked on his Coke, but he looked at Tia as though making sure she wouldn't suddenly leave.

It was strange to have a man across from her. But then again, there was something in the way Dezi sucked his Coke—head bent, yet his eyes on her—that reminded her of Richie Cunningham sitting with his dates on *Happy Days*. This wasn't a date, but it felt like how she thought one would feel. She grew flushed, suddenly feeling cumbersome in her long, ankle-grazing skirt, her ruffled blouse. She cursed herself for not stopping in that store to buy jeans instead of food.

"Well. I'm thanking you anyway," she said. "You didn't have to pay for my food. I have my own money."

"I know you do, girl. You a modern woman. Inde*pen*dent."

"True," she said.

"An independent woman," he said. "But a church girl, too." He nodded knowingly, and his lips slowly parted to reveal beautiful white teeth, one capped with gold.

"No. I'm not," she said, lying before she'd even realized it. It was the first lie she'd ever told, and it slipped from her mouth easily, as though it had been waiting to get out all along.

He affected a British gentleman's disbelief, a single dainty hand on his neck as if tugging an ascot.

"No," she said, more forcefully. Not exactly a second lie, she thought, more like one and a half. She'd heard that adding something true to a lie would make it more believable, so she said, "Actually, when the cashier yesterday said, 'He paid for it,' 'he' meaning you, I thought she meant—" Tia pointed to the ceiling and rolled her eyes, mocking her stupidity.

"God?"

"Dumb. I know."

"Well, you know what Brother Farrakhan say: the black man *is* God." Before she could ask whether he was Muslim or not, Dezi fingered his thin gold chain, plucking the cross attached to it from under his shirt. "See. I'm real tight with God, *you know?*" He held up two joined fingers to signify their close relationship.

He talked a little like Marcelle, one idea after another, like facts in an almanac. She was wondering whether she should call Marcelle when he interrupted her thoughts.

"Why'd I say that?" He smiled. "I shouldn't have even mentioned church. You just look—I don't know. Special. You look real special."

"Special *retarded* special?"

He laughed. "Special *pretty* special," he said, "pretty special, in an *especially* pretty way."

He liked her.

And she liked the way he talked to her, easy and slow, like how she'd seen guys talking to girls at their lockers. The thought of this made her feel muggy: the clothes themselves weren't making her hot, but the thought of them was. She broke off his intense love-stare and looked out the window, hoping his eyes would follow suit and that any attention to her clothes would be, for the moment, deflected. When the window trick didn't work, she picked up her burger with an expression of renewed interest, but he kept staring, and the more he stared at her, the more troubled his face became.

"Your arm," he said. "What happened?" His voice had suddenly gone gruff, as if he were prepared to pummel the sidewalk that had done this to her.

In the park, she'd rolled her blouse sleeves to her elbows to air the wide scrape on her arm, and now she saw that it looked worse than the last time she'd checked it. Her brown skin had been stripped away to reveal the raw pink underneath. "I don't know," she said, trying to sound casual about it. She didn't want to go into the details of the day: the screaming woman, the men chasing her. "I don't even remember."

She could tell Dezi didn't buy it, but he let it go. "That could get infected. You got to get that cleaned up. Where you live? I'll take you home."

She ate the rest of her burger. "That's all right. I live a long ways away."

Dezi wiggled his pinky finger in his ear. "What's your name?"

She hesitated, stunned that she hadn't told him earlier, then realized that she somehow expected him to just *know* it, the way he seemed to know everything. "Tia," she said. "It means 'aunt' in Spanish."

"All right, Tia. Let me put it this way. I know you don't have a place to stay." He looked at her significantly, giving her time to protest if she felt like it. "I'll make sure that it gets disinfected. But if you want to sleep on the street—fine." Dezi held his hands up like a man getting frisked. "You can sleep on the street, but I'd rather you didn't. I try to watch over people." He studied her face as if making sure she was following him.

"No offense," she said, "but I don't know you." The words surprised her, her tone was strong. She tried to make her face match it.

Dezi looked as though he was hurt by this, but determined not to show it. "My bad, my bad. I just felt a connection."

She felt suddenly wise, even grateful, that this was happening to her, that one day she'd be able to rasp hoarsely at some young girl, telling her all the things she'd learned on the streets, the hard way. She was not going to be lured by some man who felt "a connection."

"A connection?" she said, emboldened. "How can you just *feel* a connection? A connection doesn't just *exist* in the air, in outer space, by *itself*." She waved her arms wildly.

Dezi raised his eyebrows, smiled painfully. "Girlfriend, you think I'm *into* you. *Nuh-uh*. I just—" His voice quavered, as though he was on the verge of tears. "I just . . . it's just that you're so *young*. I tell you what—I don't have no babies running around by three different mamas like some a these hand-to-dick men out here. Not Dezi. What I *do* got is a niece. Younger than you. But guess what? You remind me of her. Big pretty eyes, hair in a ponytail. I see you here with your Happy Meal and that scrape on your arm and I want to do something for you. Like I'd do for my niece."

He read her face and held up a single hand to put a stop to any apologies she might make. "As I aforementioned, I don't want you out on no street, no place to lay your head, trying to scrape up enough money for the next hamburger." He felt the pocket of his synthetic jumpsuit, pulled out a wad thicker than any billfold she'd seen, and peeled off a fifty. "Take it, honey. You don't have to talk to me ever again. If I see you here, I'll pretend I don't know you. But I want you to take this so *I* can sleep easy tonight."

She was dumbstruck.

He insisted. "Take it for my sake. So I won't have to *imagine* my niece out in the cold."

Besides the fact that it wasn't cold out at all, she couldn't believe how wrong she'd been about Dezi. She was no better than her aunt Roberta, who railed against all men who weren't church members, calling them low-life no-good, no-account fathers. A surge of affection rose in her for Dezi, for his protectiveness, for the pain in his eyes. This man had paid for her food out of anonymous generosity, and though she badly needed the fifty dollars, she forced herself to say, "I can't take your money."

Dezi put the bill back in his pocket. "Then, at the very least," he said, "allow me to clean your wound."

DEZI DROVE her to his apartment on Northside Drive. He drove a tan Celica, and the whole ride he talked on a cellular phone in the deep voice of a midnight deejay. He mostly talked about some ball game, but sometimes he would just say, "Yeah," in a way that seemed shorthand for things he didn't want her to hear.

The staid stores of Virginia Avenue gave way to grillework-caged liquor stores with names like Max's and The Place, and more to the point, Liquor Here. Some businesses gave no indication as to what they might be selling, their signposts were signless, their neon neonless.

The only spots of color were the billboards and the prostitutes. The billboards all advertised Kools or Newports, and against the green backdrops, beautiful black people wore toy-colored clothes. They were shown sledding, or skiing, or some other activity involving snow, all of them somehow managing to hold on to their cigarettes.

It was a hot autumn, and the girls wore outfits that would have made Aunt Roberta shut her eyes and shake her head. Denim sets with short fringed skirts and shirts with sleeveless, plunging necklines. Bandeaus and skintight pants that outlined their pubic bones like an X ray. The guys wore the same style of swishy synthetic jumpsuit that Dezi wore, or else low-riding jeans with big boxy designer T-shirts.

The prostitutes—Tia assumed they were prostitutes—wiped sweat from their faces, slinking around in abbreviated versions of evening wear. It shocked her that not all the prostitutes were women in the strictest sense: men—transvestites, she imagined—looked like catwalk versions of the real women: their legs longer, their skirts shorter, their faces more carefully drawn on. When men cruised up to the curbs, they were so nonchalant about their business it seemed as if they were merely giving directions to a passing stranger. It fascinated her, and Dezi seemed to register her fascination, occasionally slowing the car to a cruise.

The children seemed unaware that anything was wrong. When Dezi stopped at a red light, she watched a chubby girl wield a snaky water-spouting hose, sending a throng of shirtless kids flying into alleys and abandoned lots. On a sidewalk, a Puerto Rican–looking kid bounced a ball to a black kid, and the black kid caught the ball with one hand, taking a drag off a cigarette with the other.

"Here it is," Dezi announced, parking the car. "The famous Stanford Gardens."

She got out and shut the car door. The closest thing to a garden she saw were the geraniums a few people were trying to grow from windowsill mayonnaise jars. Dezi laughed at the look on her face and took her hand. "C'mon, Miss Tia, laugh sometime."

She unlatched her hand from his, pretending to attend to her scrape. "I wonder if it'll heal?" she said, knowing that it would, but needing something to say to account for her hand's removal.

"I'll take care a that." He put his hand around her shoulder and before she could think of a way to remove it, a group of kids appeared, wreathing about them.

A little boy about seven years old with smooth brown skin and hair as straight as an Indian was apparently the leader of the group. "Dez-zeeeee!" he singsonged, blocking their path. Dezi playfully tried to fake the boy out, but he would not let go of Tia, dragging her along. "Go away, Gerard. Can't you see I got a young lady here who ain't used to little hoodlums stinking up the way?"

All the children except the one named Gerard made twinkling voodoo motions with their fingers. "Oooooo! Dezi's got a new wo-maaaaan!"

The boy named Gerard flicked his palm open while his entourage clung to Dezi. They hugged his legs, yanked his arms, all the time squealing his name. Gerard's face turned serious while the others laughed and shouted. "Gimme some money," Gerard said, his palm still out, "the kind that folds."

"Nuh-uh," Dezi said. "Not today."

The other kids all began to plead with outstretched palms, explaining why they needed money.

"My tooth hurting me and I need some candy to make the pain go away."

"See that spot? See that spot on my arm? Doctor say that spot gone kill me. He say money make it go away, though."

Gerard kept his face wise and smileless, his hand outstretched.

"I'll tell," he said to Dezi, his eyes steady. "I *will* tell."

"These kids," Dezi said, shaking his head with mock weariness. He pulled out the folded, rubber-banded wad of money from his pocket and then tugged at some bills. The kids crowded around Dezi and Tia so closely she could smell their sticky kid fragrance. Dezi began pulling off five-dollar bills, and the kids' silence was so profound that for a moment the only sound she heard was the canned laughter from a faraway TV.

❧

D EZI PILOTED her through a maze of walkways and into his apartment. It was the first time she'd seen a place in which a man lived by himself. The carpet was a worn, nubby beige, the color carpet she'd expected all the Stanford Gardens apartments to have, but Dezi covered his with randomly placed sheepskin rugs—one under the glass coffee table, one leading to the small kitchen, one out in the area that passed for a hallway. Everything else was black acrylic made to look like lacquer, trimmed with thin gold accents. Everything was the same shiny black, the coffee table upon which sat a thriving philodendron, the stand that held his stereo system and television, the frame of Dezi's one print: an airbrushed night skyline that could have been any city, anywhere. The apartment was neat, the air weighted with coconut incense.

Tia could not shake the sight of that bundle of money. She'd seen it earlier that day, but now it set off alarms: it was at least twice more than what she'd seen on the collection plate at church. Once, when her aunt had fallen asleep, she'd watched a TV special called *Gangland Diaries*. It showed drug dealers making so much money and living so recklessly that some made up wills at the age of fifteen.

After Dezi had sat her down and gone into the bathroom to get alcohol for her wound, she stood up. He walked out carrying an alcohol-soaked cotton ball.

"Listen," she said, "I really should go. Really."

"No. I don't think you should." He took hold of her arm so that the cotton ball hovered over her scrape. "Atlanta's a dangerous city. This'll only sting for a second."

She didn't know him, and she'd gotten into his car as if it were nothing. She began to think of ways he might kill her, or more likely than not, according to the TV special, she'd become his enemy's hostage.

He pulled her even closer to him, the smell of his cologne overpowering the rubbing alcohol. "You don't trust me, do you?"

"I didn't say that."

In one quick motion, Dezi grazed the cotton ball along the scrape. She didn't yelp until she saw him grinning at her. "That didn't hurt," he said.

"It did! You were supposed to tell me when you did it."

Dezi kissed her cheek, and threw away the cotton ball as though the two actions held the same value. Though it was the first time any male had kissed her, she didn't feel the import of this until after it was done. She had always imagined that when someone kissed her, her eyes would be closed in anticipation, she would be waiting to receive the kiss, and her beloved would be waiting to give it—waiting, of course, for the proper moment. Dezi had taken something away from her when he kissed her, but she could not name it.

He cooked two slabs of steak while she waited on the couch. It was the first time in a long while that she'd stopped moving. Sitting Indian-style, she tried to imagine herself a yogi thinking back into all her past lives. She closed her eyes, but all she saw was the orange from the blood vessels of her eyelids. Dezi brought out two plates of steak, no vegetables. It was tough, chewy, and oversalted; his cooking philosophy was to add generous shakes of every spice he had available.

"So," Tia said, "your pockets seem pretty full. You must have a good job."

Dezi caught the accusation in her voice and smiled. "You see any banks 'round here? Where would I put my hard-earned dough?"

"The hard-earned dough you make doing what? Dealing drugs?"

Dezi shrank back as though stung, hands flying up in the air, offended. "Why black women do us this way? Why does every man with a roll gotta be a drug dealer?"

Tia cut a piece of steak and looked at him.

"Let me ask *you* a question. How'd you get here?"

"Bus."

He stopped cutting and forking the meat, utensils in his hands like crab claws. "I mean, what were your *circumstances*?"

"I'm doing a genealogy project," she said.

"You came from some country-bumpkin town *by yourself* to do a genealogy project?" He nodded, waiting for the real reason.

Tia hadn't wanted to tell him, she had been doing a good job talking tough, but the words came out by the gallon. She told him about church, about Marcelle and Sister Gwendolyn. She told him about the bus ride and not being able to find a place to stay, about sleeping in the woman's car, and getting chased. She told him about her mother, and finally asked, "Do you know a woman named Rosalyn Dunlovey?"

He looked up to the ceiling and then a wave a recognition crossed his face.

"Is she, like, sort a medium height? Long hair like yours? Pretty brown eyes?"

Tia put down her fork. "Where is she?"

Dezi laughed and waved his hand. "Naw. I don't know her."

She began to hit him, slapping at him wherever she could, but he caught her, hugging her so that her hands would stop hitting him. She wrestled with him, inflamed that he could keep her down without much effort. "Hey. Hey. Hey," he said. "I didn't mean to joke like that."

She had never hit anyone that way, but doing so made her feel closer to Dezi, as though they'd weathered some ordeal together.

He told her about Gerard. "His mama's an addict. A *real* addict. She suck your dick and shit." He looked at Tia, eyes apologizing for the language. He shook a Newport out of its package and lit it. "I give them kids money, and you know what? All them other kids buy candy and shit. They money gone"—he snapped his fingers—"just like that. Not Gerard. He take that money and get on the MARTA. He buy him some chocolate bars like schoolkids be selling and go to white neighborhoods. He puts on a little limp and gets some big TB-sounding coughs going and say he's selling for the Leukemia Foundation. Them white folks eat it up. Homeboy buys his own clothes, shoes. Not fancy ones. Just ones that fit."

"Sounds like he's a good kid."

"Hell yeah."

"Sounds like you're setting a good example for him."

He turned on the TV as if to tune out what she'd said. The TV movie was one in which a kid gets left home when his family goes on vacation. Burglars come after him, but he eludes them at every step. Dezi laughed the whole way through, sometimes actually slapping his knee. When it ended, he said, "Next time you run away, do like that white kid and unstring some pearls. Then when dudes be chasing after you, you can trip them up."

THE NEXT morning, before he left, Dezi told Tia that maybe she should go home. It baffled her; he'd seemed so intent on making her stay. He tried to give her money, but she refused. Dezi paused at the door's threshold, taking her hands in his, and seemed like he was going to tell her something, but didn't.

The previous night, Tia had slept on the couch, Dezi on the bed. She'd thought she'd woken once and seen him staring over her. The only light was that of streetlamps, filtered through the window blinds so that Dezi's face seemed to be caged. But in the dream, when she tried to speak, she couldn't say anything, and when she tried to move, she was unable to. She assumed it had been a dream, assumed that if it weren't a dream, he would still be standing over her come morning, but he wasn't.

After she showered, Tia took out her clarinet and began playing from *The Marriage of Figaro*. She loved fingering the succession of B-flat–C combinations that sounded like a tickle. The succession began to go up a half-scale that fluttered into a series of alternating D's and E's. Then the waterfall of the music began. The trumpets had the main part for a while, and she had never had a need to play it. In band, the clarinets sat back and played whole bars of *tut-tut-tut-tut* while the trumpets did their thing, then the flutes, then the baritones. Tia tried to play the trumpet part. She pressed variations of the silver side keys that looked like the lazy flats they played; she tested the round finger keys that circuited the tube's holes in halos of thin metal. Within an hour, she had figured out the trumpet part and played it, then replayed it. She went into the bathroom so that she could look in the mirror as she played, but she was so proud of herself, she couldn't get through three bars of music without seeing a goofy smile creep up around her mouthpiece.

She left the bathroom and was about to put the clarinet away when she saw a woman sitting on Dezi's sofa. She did not know how the woman got in, but there she was, swallowed up in the velour folds of the couch, shins spread like a colt's. She wore a purple fitted jacket with a tiny purple skirt, a set of keys fanned out against her thigh. Her hair fell about her shoulders in thick black waves, and her pockmarked face was covered in makeup a shade lighter than her neck. She looked up at Tia, not startled so much as studious, as though Tia were an enigmatic painting.

"Who are you?" Tia asked. She realized she was holding the clarinet like a spear.

"Who am I? Who the hell are *you*?"

Tia waited a while before answering. "I'm a friend of Dezi's. Are you a—customer?"

The woman pushed herself from the couch and stood up, walking into the kitchen. "Naw, I ain't no customer. What the hell make you think that?" Water ran from the faucet, the fridge opened, bottles and jugs and wrapped packages sounded as if they were being thrown onto the counter.

She came back into the living room, where Tia was still standing, still holding on to the clarinet. The woman had a good half of a bologna sandwich hanging from her mouth. Through the bread and meat she asked, "How'd you meet Dezi?"

Where one might have expected a blouse underneath the purple jacket was nothing but an expanse of chest and cleavage. Her earrings dangled, grazing her shoulders. She laid what was left of the sandwich on the arm of the couch and began to unbutton her jacket.

"I'm *hot*. You hot?" She undid all five buttons and took off her blazer as though Tia were merely a curious pet. She stood nonchalantly in a lacy purple bra, sighed, then picked up the sandwich again. During bites she muffled, "I don't even have to ask if you hot. Black folks always hot." She swallowed another bite of sandwich. "Plus you dressed like you fell off the Amish wagon."

Tia looked down at her blouse and skirt, but before she could even think of a response, the woman fanned herself with the sandwich hand and said, "Good God, I wish that boy'd get some AC up in here!" She stopped fanning and eating long enough to pick up Dezi's forgotten Newports. She peered down the hole ripped through the top, pried one out, then crumpled the empty pack in her fist.

"I met Dezi a few days ago when I was looking for a job. He said I could stay for a while."

"Ohhh ho." The woman smiled, lighting the cigarette. Two columns of smoke swirled from her nostrils. Her head bobbed up and down, amused.

"He didn't tell me he had a girlfriend."

The woman laughed, then pushed Tia's shoulder as though they were longtime friends. "Baby, you don't even know which end is up!" She laid the burning cigarette against the saucer of the coffee-table plant and steered Tia to the couch, sitting her down. She sat next to Tia and made a smiling pantomime of introduction, daintily offering a bejeweled hand. Tia shook it, sending the woman's bracelets rattling.

"My name is Marie. What's your name, Miss Lady?"

"Tia. Tia Townsend."

"All right, Miss Lady Tia. You didn't exactly answer my question, so let's start over. How did *you* meet *Dezi*?"

Tia blinked hard, trying to remember. Although it had only been two days ago, it seemed like much longer. Her head flooded with many lies she could have told, but the way the woman sat, in her purple bra, her eyes the sort even liars couldn't lie to, she blurted out the truth. "I ran away from home. And I didn't have a place to stay and he said I could stay with him. If he's your boyfriend or something, I didn't do anything. I swear—I mean, you're not supposed to *swear,* but I *promise* I wasn't trying to be his girlfriend or anything."

Marie picked up her cigarette and stared at the airbrushed skyline on the wall, then embarked on a long series of thoughtful puffs.

She quickly turned to Tia and said, "Wanna sandwich? I didn't even offer you no food, girl!"

Tia declined.

Marie put out the Newport in the plant's saucer where it sizzled in the water and died. "Well," Marie said, turning to Tia as though she was trying to make her understand something she should already know, "Dezi and I are business partners. And I don't push no drugs, either."

Tia nodded her head slowly, now comprehending, but to be sure, she used the delicate term she'd heard her great-aunt Roberta use. "Are you a lady of the evening?"

This sent Marie howling, her head shaking back and forth like women in church getting happy. "Girrrrl! I ain't heard that word since I was sporting pigtails in Savannah! Who taught you that!"

Tia said quietly, "I just learned it somewhere."

Marie kept laughing, finally ending it with the luxuriant sigh of one who's had a good time. "'Lady of the evening,'" she said in bright soprano. "You must a come a *long* ways from home."

BEFORE TIA left the apartment, she folded up the sheets and blankets she'd slept on and placed them in a soft cube on the couch. She left a note for Dezi saying that she thought it was time for her to go back home. She did not mention that she'd found out that he was not only a drug dealer, which was bad enough, but a pimp. She knew she was not going back home, but she had to tell him something to explain why she'd left. She thought about going back to the park, then going to the far south side of town where well-off black people lived. Surely someone there would take her in.

She sat in the park but hadn't the energy to play music for money.

She watched for what seemed like hours as the park groomers cut the lawn; in the wake of huge riding mowers, the grass stretched in a carpet of green, reminding her of the cemetery near her home in Montgomery. She looked down at her open clarinet case, the pieces of the instrument glinting limousine black in the sunlight. She was filled with a sickness and longing, wanting to hear the simple sound of air blown through a wooden tube. Her clarinet case and backpack were too cumbersome to carry around the city, and she tried to think of a place to store them while she searched for somewhere to sleep for the night.

Then she remembered the bus station lockers. She found out how to take the MARTA from Stanford Gardens to the bus station, and there they were in front of her, a row of lockers with combinations. She put her change into an empty locker and was about to lift her case when she saw the photocopied flyer on the next locker. "Missing," it read, and below the large lettering, despite the poor copy job, she could make out her own face, a picture of her from junior high, her smile forced from the school photographer.

"Tia!" a voice called.

Tia looked around the bus station, expecting to find her aunt Roberta, the pastor, and church members, standing in unison like a choir. And there would be Marcelle, feigning surprise as if she hadn't seen Tia since Sunday school.

But it was Dezi, leaning against the doorjamb of the video arcade, wearing a black nylon jogging suit, his gold cross on display. He ran toward her, out of breath, holding roses. "Hey," he panted. "Got your note but didn't think I'd find you."

She hadn't thought she'd ever see him again, and though she had felt nothing but anger for him that morning, now she felt the relief of seeing someone familiar.

Tia remembered when Marcelle and her mother had first come to Hope and Grace. Marcelle had sat next to Tia on her pew, as if to say, *We will be friends.* Back then, Tia wanted to be mad, to send a look that said, What makes you think I don't already have friends, but Tia already knew what her own face was saying: *Yes, we will be friends. Yes.*

Tia scanned the bus station. Everyone, it seemed, was too busy trying to catch their buses, trying to find the restrooms and pay phones and food, to notice the flyers with her face on it. She stared at Dezi blankly.

"I'm sorry," she said, "but I'm on my way home. Like you suggested." She hoped he wouldn't notice the open locker door, but then again, he might just think she was retrieving something. He didn't seem to notice the lockers, but he gestured toward her with the roses, and when she didn't move, threw his arms up in the air, a salesman hating to see goods go to waste. The roses jostled in their translucent plastic. They were typical roses, scattered with sprays of baby's breath, the roses themselves bright red, petal edges slightly wilted and wine-colored. He walked toward the door where taxis snailed up to the curb and waited. She wanted to tell Marcelle everything that had happened in the last few days, wanted to see Marcelle strain to hide her shock.

No one had ever given her flowers. At first, Tia walked slowly. Then, when the roses in Dezi's hand seemed within reach, she ran toward them.

O N   T H E car ride back to his place, she made Dezi pull over twice within the space of half an hour. Only when they neared his neighborhood did she tell him about meeting Marie.

"Me? A pimp?" he said, sounding genuinely surprised. "No. I mean. It's complicated with Marie, but I'm not pimping her."

"Why are you lying to me?" she asked. "You don't even know me and you're lying."

"Look. All I sell is some good herb and a maybe a little dope on the first of the month. But I don't sell pussy."

"O.K. So Marie is just *there*."

"I told you. It's complicated with her."

She was now entangled in something larger than herself. When she'd watched horror movies, it seemed easy enough to know when the victim should leave, run, hide. There were always shrieking violins and threatening, sawing cellos to alert you to danger. But here there were none, and she banged her head against the dash, as if trying to beat sense into it.

"Stop that," Dezi said. When she didn't, he put out a hand to cushion her forehead. "Stop it!" he said. "You got Tourette's or something?"

When they entered the Stanford Gardens lot, Dezi's car screeched into a parking space, the brakes slamming.

"Look," he said when they'd returned to his apartment. He turned off his pager. "I'ma only have time for you from now on."

Though he'd kissed her on the cheek the previous day, this time his lips pressed against hers and it took her a while to understand that she had to open her mouth to receive his tongue. His mouth smelled of smoke and Tic Tacs. He pushed his tongue over hers, and it seemed to be searching out the cavities of her teeth. The vinyl slick of his jogging suit rubbed against her blouse, and his hands shoved the cotton fabric up past her bra. Suddenly she remembered the bra she had on, an old one with tiny, inelegant sprouts of elastic popping from the straps.

She stopped him, pulling her blouse down, him pulling it up again. Against her skirt she felt what she knew was his erection, and the way the knowledge of this came at her was so undiluted that she wanted to yield to it. This, she thought, was why everyone talked about sex, why widows in church seemed to spin and whirl when given the chance, unraveling their skeins of frustrations and woes. Dezi's erection was as insistent as his tongue, and as they swam over one another on the couch, she knew that this was her chance, like birth, to be part of someone. Then it hit her with a sadness: if sex and birth meant being part of someone, then death meant you belonged to nobody at all.

She pulled down her blouse, but her skirt was bunched up around her waist. She smoothed it down and it fell with accordion-like wrinkles. Though she felt she had to worry about pregnancy, she remembered that her panties had never come off.

Dezi didn't speak, couldn't speak, it seemed, until she had gathered her backpack and clarinet case.

"Where you going?"

"To see Marie."

I T W A S after five o'clock when she gave up searching for Marie. She walked Dezi's neighborhood in widening circles. Though people knew of her, no one knew where she lived, or which places she frequented.

Tia ate a sit-down dinner at a real restaurant in an area called Little Five Points, and with tip paid fifteen dollars, leaving her with twelve. When she returned to Dezi's neighborhood, it was nearly night. The only prostitutes who were out were the transvestites, a different crop and greatly diminished from the beautiful ones she'd

seen the night before. These prostitutes made only the vaguest gesture in the direction of femininity—a dress on one, some lipstick on
another. Several of them still had mustaches, or, doubling as breasts,
two blown-up balloons, their green, red, and blue cleavage bloom-
ing from low-cut tops. It was one of these balloon-bosomed prostitutes who told her that Marie sometimes went to a bar called The
Palisades.

She'd never been inside a bar before, and this one looked like an
alley that someone had, over the course of years, walled and roofed
with stray bits of wood and plaster. Everyone stared at her as she
stood in the doorway. Marie turned around.

"Look what the cat drug in."

She didn't know what you were supposed to do in a bar, so she
stood in the doorway, unable to move for fear she'd do something
laughable. Marie got up from her stool with exaggerated peevish-
ness and pulled Tia to the bar counter. "Give my girl a drink." Then
Marie cut her eyes at Tia. "You probably never even had a drink.
Give homegirl here a lemonade."

"No," Tia said, "I want a *drink* drink."

The bartender raised his eyebrows, impressed. The men at the
bar raised their glasses. One of them said, "I'll buy the little lady
a drink."

Marie held a single palm. "Don't even try it. I'm the one doing the
buying if any buying's to be done."

"That'd be a first."

"Shady, give her one of your Bloody Marys. That'll put her off
drinking till kingdom come." The bartender—Shady—disobeyed,
making Tia something so fruity she thought he'd skipped the alcohol.

Marie turned serious. "Since I'm assuming that you don't go to bars regular, you must a come looking for me." She didn't say it friendly, like she'd been that morning. She looked down at the ice at the bottom of the glass, rearranging it with her straw. "Must need a place to stay."

"No," Tia said. "I don't."

"Don't be no fool, girlfriend." She met eyes with the bartender. "Gin and tonic."

"I just came to say I did something with Dezi."

Marie moved in closer. "You use protection?"

"I don't think it's what you think."

Marie dug into her purple purse and produced a handful of condoms. She pressed them in Tia's hand, under the bar, and squeezed Tia's hand tight, many times, as if trying to Morse code a message.

Tia put the condoms in her skirt pocket. "I'm just asking for your help. I mean, you're a—"

"A what?" Marie looked at her, daring her to say the word. "A whore?" Marie answered not bothering to lower her voice. The men at the bar looked at them. The bartender spray-gunned a drink, shaking his head. "Let me tell you something, *little girl*. I'm an independent. Damn straight. Not like these other girls." She gulped the gin, made a face as if she were about to belch, then swallowed it in triumph. "And I don't work *for* Dezi. We partners, me and him. Business partners. I stop off and get a nap or some food. If I need to spend the night, he lets me. Don't get me wrong, I *do* pay him. But sometimes I stop by his place just to shoot the breeze."

Tia looked at her. Perhaps Marie was drunk. She wanted to believe that Marie was drunk because it seemed as though Marie had turned on her. Obviously there was something more to Marie and Dezi's relationship than that. Perhaps they were a couple, in some weird form. She wanted to ask about it, if she could find the right words, but it didn't matter. Marie's unforgiving smile ended further discussion.

"But see," Marie said, her hands chopping the air in explanation, "I'm saving up. There's these condominiums they got over in Buckhead. I'm saving up so me and my baby girl can live there. These condos are slick. Pool, gardens. A little health club with shiatsu massage. *Shiatsu.*" Marie grinned uncontrollably at the word, then got serious again. "This here"—she gestured at her outfit and, it seemed, to the entire bar—"is part-time."

"You have a daughter?"

"Yeahhh," Marie said, her voice getting dreamy. "A daughter and a son. Boy lives with his father. Daughter's in day care."

"Sounds more like night care," one of the men said.

Marie looked hurt, though she acted as though she hadn't heard the man. Tia tried to make Marie feel better by sliding closer to her, trying to finish the fruity drink. "What's your husband like?"

"Oh, he ain't my husband. Not no more. Divorced. He's a good man, but he got issues." She rolled her eyes as though it was too much to go into.

"Like?"

"Like he like fucking other mens," the same man said. The men at the bar tittered and snickered like girls for a moment, then looked the other way to avoid Marie's wrath.

"Yes," Marie said defiantly. "All right, nosy butt. He do like 'fucking other mens,' to use your nasty terminology. But I'm O.K. with that, hear? That's his business." She flicked her hand as if the men were mere motes of dust. "Look," she said to Tia, "he takes care of his son, and that's *good*." Then she raised her voice, for the whole bar to hear, "More than I can say about a lot of Nee-groes up in this place."

"Your ex-husband friends with Dezi?"

"Hell, naw." Marie shook her head wearily, absently tugging at her hair. "Dezi, boy. He helped me through some times. Dezi *try* to pimp, a few years back. You should've seen his skinny butt out there. He just didn't have it."

Marie pushed her empty glass toward the bartender as if this were sad news. "He likes you, though. I can tell even though I ain't seen him with you. But don't fool around with that man. You what, eight? Nine years old?"

Tia wasn't going to dignify the joke, but then said, "Fourteen going on fifteen."

"How old you think Dezi is?"

Tia didn't bother answering, knowing that whatever she said would be wrong.

"Dezi's what age . . ." Marie looked at the martini glasses hanging from the ceiling, "Thirty-two. Thirty-two come November," she said almost wistfully. "Fourteen. Thirty-fuckin'-two." She weighed the different ages in her palms like a balance beam gone out of control.

Tia sighed. The alcohol, disguised with fruit juice, was starting to have an effect. Marie offered to walk her back, but Tia said no, she knew how to get there.

SHE RETURNED to the apartment complex, getting lost in the maze of identical concrete buildings. She saw a dim figure lurking behind one of the generic bushes, and felt her bladder contract and almost loosen with fear. It was Gerard. He tossed a ball, then dribbled it with amazing control.

Relieved that it was only him, she yelled, "It's too late for you to be up."

"Look, woman, I *live* here. I be up *all* hours."

"Well you shouldn't be."

"Damn, lady," Gerard said, "you must think you somebody's mama." The words were without malice and suddenly she wished she'd had brothers and sisters. Her mother seemed more impossible to her than ever. As she remembered the woman on the phone, the woman who should have been her mother, Gerard tossed the ball to her, surprising her, but she caught it just when she thought she couldn't. She threw it back to him.

"You need a little work," he said by way of farewell, dribbling his way to the neighboring complex.

Tia finally found the right door. It was unlocked.

"Where you been?" Dezi asked.

"I told you. I went to see Marie." She pushed her way past Dezi, into the apartment.

He closed the door, putting a gun on the table.

"What," Tia said, "are you doing with a gun?"

Dezi winced, annoyed. "What you think I'ma do? You don't got no key. *And* it's late. Gotta strap myself in case *someone else* come busting through."

"I could knock on the door, like a normal person. You could let me in, like a normal person. No gun involved."

"Girl, I don't even want to hear it. *Like a normal person,*" he mimicked, high and whiny.

Then it hit her. They were fighting, like lovers.

❧

SHE DID not stop him, and there was no ceremony. Her blouse was off, her skirt was in a heap on the floor, and he had undone his pants with a single hand.

He wiped the saliva from her mouth with the pads of his fingertips. It had been a long time since she'd felt anything smooth next to her skin, and now, so much of her skin was touched by skin not her own. He stroked a spot on the back of her neck, and it both frightened and mesmerized her, like when she'd once seen her own hand move, without her permission, into a candle flame. She knew what it was that lay on her thigh, and it moved of its own accord, like a water hose flicking out of control in the grass.

"Let me," he said.

His hands no longer felt smooth as they pushed against her, and she understood that he expected more than nakedness. She remembered overhearing girls in the junior high cafeteria talk about sex, about how men spurted sticky semen into women. They squealed with delight at the grossness of the word "semen," squirting mustard onto their corndogs with exaggerated gestures.

"I can't," she said, trying to sit up, but he was heavy and pressing.

His tongue flicked and circled against her neck. He said something, but she could not hear it. She squeezed her thighs together, but his hand found its way between them. She bolted upright, against his weight, covering herself in the blanket she'd folded just hours before. He stood up and sighed. Completely naked, his muscles looked embedded, sleek and round as cobblestones. His gold tooth glinted in the darkness.

"Shit!" he yelled. He stared down at his erection, holding it in disgust, and when it finally shrank, he whirled around and punched the framed skyline on the wall. The frame clattered against the top of the stereo, the glass shattering onto the sheepskin rug.

"It's Marie," she said. "I know about you two."

"Marie!" He thrust his head back, throat exposed like a sacrifice. He paced the living room before sitting on the couch beside her. He took one loud, impatient breath. "All right. What'd she tell you?"

Tia woke that evening and could not remember how she'd fallen asleep. Though the children no longer yelled and played outside, she thought she could hear echoes of them. Then, as the world began to come into focus, she heard the awkward dicing of Dezi making something in the kitchen. Liver and onions.

The smell of it filled her with homesickness. For one year that was her favorite meal, and whenever the topic of food came up her aunt Roberta didn't miss an opportunity to tell church members that most children hated liver, but it was Tia's favorite, and this was good because liver was cheap. The living room light had not been turned on, and in the evening darkness Tia could feel that she was still in her underwear, covered by the blanket. She touched the inside of her panties, which were sticky and wet.

She had felt this way before—listening to her aunt Roberta's snores, moving her hand between her thighs. It had been a mystery to her when she felt electric waves of peace and fear flow through her, the weightless moment before an elevator descends, when it feels like the bottom has dropped. When she drew back her hand it had always felt and smelled slick and wet, like the skim of water atop fresh potter's clay. But those nights in her bed seemed long ago. This was now, and she kept thinking "semen."

When she screamed, she could hear nothing else. Dezi came out of the kitchen and tried to put his hand over her mouth, but her cries ran over his fingers. She grabbed her clothes, swinging them at him.

"Tia!" He pinned her down.

"You did it to me!"

Her legs kicked, but she sank into the soft, endless maw of the couch as he held her down. She wrestled away from him, only for him to pin her down again, but she kicked and flailed the whole time, and finally her knee punched his groin. Dezi rolled off her and onto the floor with a low moan.

"No," he said, quietly, calmly. "No, I didn't do anything. Trust me. I didn't. "

She put on her skirt and her blouse, her clothes straying at haphazard angles. She swung the door open and fell; Dezi had her by the foot and yanked her into the apartment, Tia's chin dragging the doormat along with her.

"I want you to repeat after me—"

"I'm wet!" she sobbed, until she screeched at a new, high pitch, "YOU!"

"I didn't do anything!"

"I'm wet!"

"Tia, baby, I did not do *anything* inside you. You fell asleep and I was hungry. I made me some—"

But she shrieked, a woman in labor, then scalded with water. She screamed until she went hoarse and had to gulp air before she could scream again.

"Shut up!" he yelled.

She saw him cover his ears, but she couldn't stop, and so he dragged her along the shag of the carpet and sheepskin until her face felt the cold linoleum of the kitchen floor and she saw the endless, reeling flowers of the kitchen wallpaper. She gargled on her own spit, felt blood trill down her nostrils. He slapped her, as though reviving the dead. Her teeth locked, biting nothing, and her screams dead-ended into low grunts.

She could not remember getting up, her hand finding the knife on the counter. The smell of onions on the blade, pungent and insinuating.

There was no drama to his voice, just the word in its nudest form. "Don't."

S H E   R A N and no one followed, past the signless signs, past billboards, past the transvestite whores with the balloons for breasts. Then she ran up against a wall of soft purple and cocoa butter. Marie.

Marie adjusted herself from the run-in, eyelashes curtsying apologies to the man with whom she'd been speaking. The man sucked his teeth and ambled down the sidewalk.

Tia told her everything, pausing when any car drove past, thinking it Dezi's. She apologized to Marie for kissing him, told how she had felt herself, down there. How she believed he'd done something so horrible that she had cut him and slashed him, and how by the time he'd grabbed hold of the knife she had run out the door.

"Good Lord," Marie said. "You see him come after you?"

"No."

"Well, he will. If you cut him up, he *will* come after you." Marie wiped Tia's face and rocked her. "Come here," Marie said, and led her to an abandoned building that had neither doors nor windows.

"All right, Miss Lady," she said. She waved her cigarette in the air like a wand. "He ain't got no business with you anyway. You fourteen? Fifteen? That's statutory rape, right there. That's what that's called." At first she thought Marie was going to hide her there, but Marie knelt at Tia's feet, the heels of her thigh-high boots scratching on the fallen plaster. "Drop 'em."

"Drop what?"

"Your drawers, drop your drawers."

Tia backed away.

"Look girl, I'm just going to check on something, just to make sure. You should go to a clinic anyway for this, but they'll charge and I'm doing it for free."

She felt that she might cry, but instead she shimmied her panties down to her knees. Marie left her cigarette to balance on a stray block of wood, blew up a condom, worked her hand into it with difficulty. She peered up Tia's skirt. Then she prodded. By the streetlight shining through the squares where windows should have been, she looked at what was there, a thin slick of something. Then—Tia couldn't believe it—Marie tasted it.

"Nope," she said. "I think your juices just got to flowing. You ain't never got off on your own before?"

Got off?

Bleak, feeling the full extent of her ignorance pound on her chest like a gavel, Tia said yes. She pulled up her underwear.

Marie sighed then drew a long drag on the cigarette and kept going. "We sending you home. Yes sir. We can't have people like you running around here." She grabbed Tia by the arm, fingernails digging into Tia's flesh as she led her back to the street.

Outside she felt sick and cold despite the early autumn heat. The transvestites were gone, and only three women walked the stretch of sidewalk where Tia had found Marie.

"Lordamercy," Marie said, "I sho wouldn't want my baby girl out here in ten years. Look at this mess." Marie took Tia by the crook of the arm as if they were going on a stroll through the park. "Glad I won't be out here too much longer. Almost got my wad saved for the condo. Almost. Maybe another year."

Tia knew the only reason Marie was talking so much was to keep her company, but she couldn't bring herself to say anything. When silence grew upon silence, Marie stopped, rubbing Tia all over as if to warm her. "Snap out of it, girl. I'ma give you the name of a place you can go and get yourself checked out for real. I'll give you the number, but I'd rather get you on a bus back home. You want that, sugar doll? You wanna go home?"

"Yes," Tia said.

"Well, Marie will deliver."

Marie whistled, sharp and loud like a man. "Lydia! Lid-dee-ya! Get your ass over here!"

All Tia saw of the woman named Lydia was a metallic slip and red sneakers. Lydia waved her limp hand as if shooing away a fly.

"Ho, you best be moving your fat ass, I'm trying to get this church girl off and back to her peoples!"

Lydia walked with haunchy, bovine steps, taking nearly five minutes to make it down a single block. She looked bored, as though she'd only obeyed Marie out of curiosity.

"This poor child need to get her ass on a bus. She need some benjamins. What you got?"

Lydia made a face as if she'd been asked to hand over her liver. "She got a mouth and a pussy like everyone else on this corner. Make her *earn* her money."

"She's right," Tia said. "I can't take other people's money just because—"

"Give her twenty," Marie said. She unpried Tia's hand from her skirt pocket and made her hold it out as if begging for alms.

Lydia said no.

"*I'll* pay you back, ho. Now, hand it over."

While Lydia undid the Oriental topknot where she apparently kept her money, Marie called over two unsuspecting girls from across the street.

"Marie," Tia said, "I've got thirty-two dollars, I don't need any more."

But Marie inhaled grandly, and Tia understood that Marie liked doing this: bossing everyone around, demanding money from people unwilling to give it. For a moment, she felt a deep pity for the woman. She would have made a great executive, manager, fund-raiser, but here she was, on Northside Drive, walking the streets.

Then it occurred to her that if Marie and Dezi really were a couple, Marie was doing a good job of getting rid of her, making sure she had enough money to get on the bus home and stay there. Then she felt guilty about both thoughts, the former patronizing and the latter just plain catty.

Marie explained things to the two girls from across the street. One introduced herself as Shatrice, the other was Joan.

"We heard about your plight," Shatrice said, "and we'll do whatever we can to expedite your journey home."

"Thank you," Tia said.

"*Je vous en prie,*" Shatrice said.

"Uh-oh," Joan said.

A car screeched, found new direction, and started up again. A tan Celica, barreling down Northside. Finally Dezi careened into the corner and didn't bother to close the door after him. His cut had been wiped and cleaned, but fresh blood filled the gash, threatening to seep out. He was holding her clarinet case.

The other three girls moved a few paces back, close enough to watch everything, but far enough away to make a run for it.

"C'mon baby," he said, as if Marie were invisible, "I know you were just freaked out. I just want us to talk."

Marie stood in front of Tia. "She's going home."

"Come on, Tia."

"What did I *tell* you?" Marie said, eyes bugging out at him. "I said she's going H-O-M-E!"

He pointed at her with a bandaged finger. "I'm not talking to you!" He paused, deflating the anger from his voice. "Let's go," he said to Tia. "Your bag is back at the place. I got your flute right here."

"I should apologize to him," Tia said to Marie. "He didn't even—"

"Like hell you should!" she said, then yelled, "Cradle-robber!"

Dezi took a step toward them. "Marie, this ain't none of your business."

Marie stepped forward, meeting his challenge. "Lay the horn down. Put it on the curb and leave."

Dezi had to peer around Marie to make eye contact with Tia. "Come on," he said, beseeching. But when she stepped back, away from him, he bounced like a boxer, impatient and eager to get into the ring. His voice hit an angry clef. *"Come on."*

"Leave, Dezi," Marie said.

In an instant he lunged for Tia; she felt his hand grazing hers. But she pulled away. Marie swatted at him, then he and Marie actually seemed to be fighting, her limbs askew as he grappled her, her jacket bunching in the middle and her midriff exposed. She was spiking his foot with the heel of her boot and clawing his face. Then the girls were in on the action, their fingernails scratching the nylon of Dezi's jacket, and once, catching Marie in the eye.

Tia had begun backing away, but she could not stop watching.

"Come on!" Dezi said. Then he fell to the ground, looking as if he were trying to tear out his eyes. Someone had Maced him. Marie sat down on the curb, as though defeated.

The street girls pinned Dezi to the ground with their high heels and platforms, screaming all at once to Tia, "Run! Run! *Run!*"

People stuck their heads out of their doorways, straining to see what was happening. In the distance, a siren.

Tia grabbed her clarinet. She hugged Marie, who reached in her thigh-high boots and snatched out a thin fold of money. She pressed it all into Tia's hand. "Run, honey." Her voice was tired.

"I need your address. To pay you back."

"Run! You heard me!" Marie pushed her so hard she fell off the curb. "Run, honey. And don't let nobody lock you in no closet no more."

Tia stood up and brushed gravel and broken glass from her skirt. And she ran.

Geese

WHEN PEOPLE BACK HOME asked her why she was leaving Baltimore for Tokyo, Dina told them she was going to Japan in the hopes of making a pile of money, socking it away, then living somewhere cheap and tropical for a year. Back home, money was the only excuse for leaving, and it was barely excuse enough to fly thousands of miles to where people spoke no English.

"Ja*pan*!" Miss Gloria had said. Miss Gloria was her neighbor; a week before Dina left she sat out on the stoop and shared a pack of cigarettes with Miss Gloria. "Japan," Miss Gloria repeated, looking off into the distance, as though she might be able to see Honshu if she looked hard enough. Across the street sat the boarded-up row houses the city had promised to renovate. Dina tried to look past them, and habored the vague hope that if she came back to the neighborhood they'd get renovated, as the city had promised. "Well, you go 'head on," Miss Gloria said, trying to sound encouraging. "You go 'head on and *learn* that language. Find out what they saying about us over at Chong's." Chong's was the local take-out with the best moo goo gai pan around, but if someone attempted to clarify an order, or changed it, or even hesitated, the Chinese family got all huffed, yelling as fast and violent as kung fu itself.

"Chong's is Chinese, Miss Gloria."

"Same difference."

The plan was not well thought-out, she admitted that much. Or rather, it wasn't really a plan at all, but a feeling, a nebulous fluffy thing that had started in her chest, spread over her heart like a fog. It was sparked by movies in which she'd seen Japanese people bowing ceremoniously, torsos seesawing; her first Japanese meal, when she'd turned twenty, and how she'd marveled at the sashimi resting on its bed of rice, rice that lay on a lacquered dish the color of green tea. She grew enamored of the pen strokes of kanji, their black sabers clashing and warring with one another, occasionally settling peacefully into what looked like the outlines of a Buddhist temple, the cross sections of a cozy house. She did not want to say it, because it made no practical sense, but in the end she went to Japan for the delicate sake cups, resting in her hand like a blossom; she went to Japan for loveliness.

After searching for weeks for work in Tokyo, she finally landed a job at an amusement park. It was called Summerland, because, in Japan, anything vaguely amusing had an English name. It was in Akigawa, miles away from the real Tokyo, but each of her previous days of job hunting had sent her farther and farther away from the city. "Economic downturn," one Office Lady told her. The girl, with her exchange-student English and quick appraisal of Dina's frustration, seemed cut out for something better than a receptionist's job, but Dina understood that this, too, was part of the culture. A girl—woman—would work in an office as a glorified photocopier, and when she became Christmasu-keeki, meaning twenty-five years old, she was expected to resign quietly and start a family with a husband. With no reference to her race, only to her Americanness in general, the Office Lady had said, sadly, "Downturn means people want to hire Japanese. It's like, obligation." So when the people at Summerland offered her a job, she immediately accepted.

Her specific job was operator of the Dizzy Teacups ride, where, nestled in gigantic replicas of Victorian teacups, Japanese kids spun and arced and dipped before they were whisked back to cram school. Summerland, she discovered, was the great *gaijin* dumping ground, the one place where a non-Japanese foreigner was sure to land a job. It was at Summerland that she met Arillano Justinio Arroyo, with his perfectly round smiley-face head, his luxurious black hair, always parted in the middle, that fell on either side of his temples like an open book. Ari was her co-worker, which meant they would exchange mop duty whenever a kid vomited.

By summer's end, both she and Ari found themselves unamused and jobless. She decided that what she needed, before resuming her search for another job, was a vacation. At the time, it made a lot of sense. So she sold the return part of her round-trip ticket and spent her days on subways in search of all of Tokyo's corners: she visited Asakusa and gazed at the lit red lanterns of Sensoji Temple; she ate an outrageously expensive bento lunch under the Asahi brewery's giant sperm-shaped modernist sculpture. She even visited Akihabara, a section of Tokyo where whole blocks of stores sold nothing but electronics she couldn't afford. She spent an afternoon in the waterfront township of Odaiji, where women sunned themselves in bikinis during the lunch hour. But she loved Shinjuku the most, that garish part of Tokyo where pachinko parlors pushed against ugly gray earthquake-resistant buildings; where friendly, toothless vendors sold roasted *unagi,* even in rainy weather. Here, the twelve-floor department stores scintillated with slivers of primary colors, all the products shiny as toys. The subcity of Shinjuku always swooned, brighter than Vegas, lurid with sword-clashing kanji in neon. Skinny prostitutes in miniskirts swished by in pairs like schoolgirls, though their pouty red lips and permed hair betrayed them as they darted into doorways without signs and, seemingly, without actual doors.

At the end of each day, she took the subway, reboarding the Hibiya-sen *tokkyuu,* which would take her back to the *gaijin* hostel in Roppongi. She rented her room month to month, like the Australians, Germans, and Canadians and the occasional American. The only other blacks who lived in Japan were Africans: the Senegalese, with their blankets laid out in front of Masashi-Itsukaiichi station, selling bootleg Beatles albums and Tupperware; the Kenyans in Harajuku selling fierce tribal masks and tarry perfumed oils alongside Hello Kitty notebooks. The Japanese did not trust these black *gaijin,* these men who smiled with every tooth in their mouths and wore their cologne turned on high. And though the Japanese women stared at Dina with the same distrust, the business-suited *sararimen* who passed her in the subway stations would proposition her with English phrases they'd had *gaijin* teach them— "Verrry sexy," they'd say, looking around to make sure women and children hadn't overheard them. And even on the *tokkyuu* itself, where every passenger took a seat and immediately fell asleep, the emboldened men would raise their eyebrows in brushstrokes of innuendo and loudly whisper, "Verry chah-ming daaark-ku skin."

Ari found another job. Dina didn't. Her three-month visa had expired and the Japanese were too timid and suspicious to hire anyone on the sly. There were usually only two lines of work for American *gaijin*—teaching or modeling. Modeling was out—she was not the right race, much less the right blondness or legginess, and with an expired visa she got turned down for teaching and tutoring jobs. The men conducting the interviews knew her visa had expired, and that put a spin on things, the spin being that they expected her to sleep with them.

Dina had called Ari, wanting leads on jobs the English-language newspapers might not advertise. Ari agreed to met her at Swensen's, where he bought her a scoop of chocolate mint ice cream.

"I got offered a job at a pachinko parlor," he said. "I can't do it, but you should. They only offered me the job because they like to see other Asians clean their floors."

She didn't tell him that she didn't want to sweep floors, that too many Japanese had already seen American movies in which blacks were either criminals or custodians. So when they met again at Swensen's, Dina still had no job and couldn't make the rent at the foreign hostel. Nevertheless, she bought him a scoop of red bean ice cream with the last of her airplane money. She didn't have a job and he took pity on her, inviting her to live with him in his one-room flat. So she did.

A n d s o did Petra and Zoltan. Petra was five-foot-eleven and had once been a model. That ended when she fell down an escalator, dislocating a shoulder and wrecking her face. She'd had to pay for the reconstructive surgery out of her once sizable bank account and now had no money. And Petra did not want to go back to Moldova, *could* not go back to Moldova, it seemed, though Ari hadn't explained any of this when he brought Petra home. He introduced her to Dina as though they were neighbors who hadn't met, then hauled her belongings up the stairs. While Ari strained and grunted under the weight of her clothes trunks, Petra plopped down in a chair, the only place to sit besides the floor. Dina made tea for her, and though she and Ari had been running low on food, courtesy dictated that she bring out the box of cookies she'd been saving to share with Ari.

"I have threads in my face," Petra said through crunches of cookie. "Threads from the doctors. One whole year"—she held up a single aggressive finger—"I have threads. I am thinking that when threads bust out, va voom, I am having old face back. These doctors here"—Petra shook her head and narrowed her topaz eyes—"they can build a whole car, but cannot again build face? I go to America next. Say, 'Fix my face. Fix face *for actual.*' And they will *fix.*" She nodded once, like a genie, as though a single nod were enough to make it so. Afterward she made her way to the bathroom and sobbed.

Of course, Petra could no longer model; her face had been ripped into unequal quadrants like the sections of a TV dinner, and the stitches had been in long enough to leave fleshy, zipper-like scars in their place. The Japanese would not hire her either; they did not like to view affliction so front and center. In turn, Petra refused to work for them. Whenever Dina went to look for a job, Petra made it known that she did not plan on working for the Japanese: "*I* not work for them even if they *pay* me!"

Her boyfriend Zoltan came with the package. He arrived in toto a week after Petra, and though he tried to project the air of someone just visiting, he'd already tacked pictures from his bodybuilding days above the corner where they slept across from Ari and Dina.

Petra and Zoltan loved each other in that dangerous Eastern European way of hard, sobbing sex and furniture-pounding fights. Dina had been living with Ari for a month and Petra and Zoltan for only two weeks when the couple had their third major fight. Zoltan had become so enraged that he'd stuck his hand on the orange-hot burner of the electric range. Dina had been adding *edamame* to the *udon* Ari was reheating from his employee lunch when Zoltan pushed between the two, throwing the bubbling pot aside and pressing his hand onto the lit burner as easily and noiselessly as if it were a Bible on which he was taking an oath.

"Zoltan!" Dina screamed. Ari muttered a few baffled words of Tagalog. The seared flesh smelled surprisingly familiar, like dumplings, forgotten and burning at the bottom of a pot. The burner left a bull's-eye imprint on Zoltan's palm, each concentric circle sprouting blisters that pussed and bled. Petra wailed when she saw; it took her two weeping hours to scour his melted fingerprints from the burner.

And still, they loved. That same night they shook the bamboo shades with their passion. When they settled down, they baby-talked to each other in Moldovan and Hungarian, though the first time Dina heard them speak this way it sounded to her as if they were reciting different brands of vodka.

After the hand-on-the-range incident, Zoltan maundered about with the look of a beast in his lair. The pictures from his bodybuilding days that he tacked on the walls showed him brown, oiled, and bulging, each muscle delineated as though he were constructed of hundreds of bags of hard-packed sugar. Though he was still a big man, he was no longer glorious, and since they'd all been subsisting on crackers and ramen, Zoltan looked even more deflated. For some reason he had given up bodybuilding once he stepped off the plane at Narita, though he maintained that he was winning prizes right up until then. If he was pressed further than that about his past, Petra, invariably orbiting Zoltan like a satellite, would begin to cry.

Petra cried a lot. If Dina asked Petra about life in Moldova or about modeling in Ginza, she cried. If Dina so much as offered her a carrot, this, too, was cause for sorrow. Dina had given up trying to understand Petra. Or any of them, for that matter. Even Ari. Once she'd asked him why he did it, why he let them stay. Ari held out his hand and said, "See this? Five fingers. One hand." He then made a fist, signifying—she supposed—strength. She didn't exactly under-stand what he was driving at: none of them helped out in any real way, though she, unlike Petra and Zoltan, had at least attempted to find a job. He looked to her, fist still clenched; she nodded as though she understood, though she felt she never would. Things simply made all of them cry and sigh. Things dredged from the bottoms of their souls brought them pain at the strangest moments.

THEN SAYEED came to live with them. He had a smile like a sealed envelope, had a way of eating as though he were horny. She didn't know how Ari knew him, but one day, when Dina was prac-ticing writing kanji characters and Petra was knitting an afghan with Zoltan at her feet, Ari came home from work, Sayeed follow-ing on his heels.

"We don't have much," Ari apologized to Sayeed after the in-troductions. Then he glared at the mess of blankets on the floor, "and as you can see, we are many people, sleeping in a tiny, six-tatami room."

Sayeed didn't seem to mind. They all shared two cans of a Japanese soft drink, Pocari Sweat, taking tiny sips from their sake cups. They shared a box of white chocolate Pokki, and a sandwich from Ari's employee lunch. Sayeed stayed after the meal and passed around cigarettes that looked handmade, though they came from a box. He asked, occasionally gargling his words, what each of them did. Having no jobs, they told stories of their past: Petra told of Milan and the runways and dressing up for the opera at La Scala. But mostly she recalled what she ate: pan-seared foie gras with pickled apricot gribiche sauce; swordfish tangine served with stuffed cherries; gnocchi and lobster, swimming in brown butter.

"Of course," she said, pertly ashing her cigarette, "we had to throw it all up."

"Yes yes yes," Sayeed said, as though this news delighted him.

Zoltan talked of Hungary, and how he was a close relation of Nagy, the folk hero of the '56 revolution. He detailed his bodybuilding regime: how much he could bench-press, how much he could jerk, and what he would eat. Mainly they were heavy foods: soups with carp heads, bones, and fins; doughy breads cooked in rendered bacon fat; salads made of meat rather than lettuce. Some sounded downright inedible, but Zoltan recalled them as lovingly and wistfully as if they were dear departed relations.

Dina did not want to talk about food but found herself describing the salmon croquettes her mother made the week before she died. Vats of collards and kale, the small islands of grease floating atop the pot liquor, cornbread spotted with dashes of hot sauce. It was not the food she ate all the time, or even the kind she preferred, but it was the kind she wanted whenever she was sick or lonely; the kind of food that—when she got it—she stuffed in her mouth like a pacifier. Even recollecting food from the corner stores made her stomach constrict with pleasure and yearning: barbecue, Chong's take-out, peach cobbler. All of it delicious in a lardy, fatty, condiment-heavy way. Miasmas of it so strong that they pushed through the styrofoam boxes bagged in brown paper.

"Well," Ari said, when Dina finished speaking.

Since they had nothing else to eat, they smoked.

They waited to see what Sayeed would do, and as the hours passed, waited for him to leave. He never did. That night Ari gave him a blanket and Sayeed stretched out on a tatami, in the very middle of the room. Instead of pushing aside the low tea table, he simply arranged his blanket under it, and as he lay down, head under the tea table, he looked as though he had been trying to retrieve something from under it and had gotten stuck.

Over the next few days they found out that Sayeed had married a non-Moroccan woman instead of the woman he was arranged to marry. His family, her family, the whole country of Morocco, it seemed, disowned him. Then his wife left him. He had moved to Tokyo in the hope of opening a business, but the money that was supposed to have been sent to him was not sent.

"They know! They know!" he'd mutter while smoking or praying or boiling an egg. Dina assumed he meant that whoever was supposed to send Sayeed money knew about his non-Moroccan ex-wife, but she could never be sure. Whenever Sayeed mused over how life had gone wrong, how his wife had left him, how his family had refused to speak to him, he glared at Dina, as though she were responsible.

One night she awoke to find Sayeed panting over her, holding a knife at her throat. His chest was bare; his pajama bottoms glowed from the streetlights outside the window. Dina screamed, waking Petra, who turned on a light and promptly began to cry. Ari and Zoltan gradually turtled out of their sleep, saw Sayeed holding the knife at her throat, saw that she was still alive, and looked at her hopelessly, as though she were an actress failing to play her part and die on cue. When Zoltan saw that it had nothing to do with him, he went back to sleep. Sayeed rattled off accusingly at Dina in Arabic until Ari led him into the hallway.

She sat straight up in the one pair of jeans she hadn't sold and a nearly threadbare green bra. Ari came back, exhausted. She didn't know where Sayeed was, but she could hear Japanese voices in the hallway, their anger and complaints couched in vague, seemingly innocuous phrases. *They have a lot of people living there, don't they?* meant, *Those foreigners! Can't they be quiet and leave us in peace!* And *I wonder if Roppongi would offer them more opportunities* meant, *They should go to Roppongi where their own kind live!* Ari tried to slam the door shut, as if to defy the neighbors, as if to add a dramatic coda to the evening, but Zoltan had broken the door in one of his rages, and it barely closed at all.

"He probably won't do it again," he said.

"What! What do you mean by 'probably won't'?"

Zoltan sleepily yelled for her to shut up. Petra sat in her corner with a stray tear running in a rivulet along one of her scars.

Then Ari was suddenly beside Dina, talking to her in broken English she hadn't the energy to try to understand. He turned the light out, his arm around her neck. Soon they heard Petra and Zoltan going at it, panting and pounding at each other till it seemed as though they'd destroy the tatami under them.

Dina and Ari usually slept side by side, not touching, but that night he'd settled right beside her and put his arm around her neck. Ari smelled like fresh bread, and as she inhaled his scent it occurred to her that his arm around her neck was meant to calm her, to shut her up—nothing romantic. Nevertheless, she nudged him, ran her palm against his arm, the smoothest she ever remembered touching, the hairs like extensions of liquid skin. He politely rolled away. "You should wear more clothes."

She tugged the sheet away from him and said, "I can't take this."

She hated how they all had to sleep in the tiny, six-tatami room, how they slept so close to one another that in the dark Dina could tell who was who by smell alone. She hated how they never had enough to eat, and how Ari just kept inviting more people to stay. It should have been just he and she, but now there were three others, one of whom had just tried to kill her, and she swore she could not—would not—take it anymore.

"Can't take?" he asked, managing to yell without actually yelling. "Can't take, can't take!" he tried to mimic. He turned on the light as if to get a better look at her, as if he'd have to check to make sure it was the same woman he'd let sleep under his roof. "But you must!"

S H E   H A D   nowhere else to go. So she and Sayeed worked out a schedule—not a schedule exactly, but a way of doing things. If he returned from a day of looking for work, he might ask everyone how the day had gone. In that case, she would not answer, because she was to understand that he was not speaking to her. If she was in one corner of the room, he would go to another.

Sometimes she would take a crate and sit outside the stoopless apartment building and try to re-create the neighborhood feeling she'd had at home with Miss Gloria. The sun would shine hotly on the pavement, and the movement of people everywhere, busy and self-absorbed, would have to stand in for the human music of Baltimore. The corner grocery stores back home were comforting in their dinginess, packed high with candies in their rainbow-colored wrappings, menthols, tallboys and magnums, racks of chips and sodas, but best of all, homemade barbecue sandwiches, the triangled white bread sopping up the orange-red sauce like a sponge. Oh, how she missed it. The men who loitered outside playing their lottery numbers and giving advice to people too young to take it, the mothers who yelled viciously at their children one minute, only to hug and kiss them the next. How primping young boys played loud music to say the things they couldn't say. How they followed the unspoken rules of the neighborhood: Never advertise your poverty. Dress immaculately. Always smell good, not just clean.

For a few minutes, the daydream would work, even in Japan.

Once, when looking for a job in Shibuya, she eyed a cellophane Popsicle wrapper nestled up against a ginkgo. It was gaudily beautiful with its stripes of orange ooze from where a kid had licked it. Just when she felt a rush of homesickness, a Japanese streetworker, humbly brown from daily hours in the sun, conscientiously swept the little wrapper into his flip-top box, and it was gone.

THE DAY after Sayeed tried to kill her, she took the train to Roppongi, and though she had no money for train fare, she pounded on the window of the information booth, speaking wildly in English, peppering her rant with a few words of Japanese. She said the machine hadn't issued her a ticket. The Japanese girl at the information counter looked dumbly at the Plexiglas, repeating that the machine had *never* broken. They would not outwit her: Dina knew that the

Japanese did not like to cause scenes, nor be recipients of them. She pitched her voice loudly, until everyone in the station turned around. Finally, the information girl pressed a hidden button and let her through.

She did not want to go back to Roppongi, where she'd first lived, where she had unsuccessfully searched for jobs before, but Sayeed's knife convinced her to redouble her efforts. She hoped to get a job from Australians or Canadians who might overlook her lack of visa. She wished she'd taken the job at the pachinko parlor, but now it was gone; she hoped for a job doing anything—dishwasher, street cleaner, glass polisher, leaflet passer—but she did not get one.

THEY COULD not go starving, so they began to steal. While Ari was away at work, Zoltan swiped packaged steaks, Sayeed swiped fruit and bread and one time even couscous, opening the package and pouring every single grain into two pants pockets. Even though she never would have stolen anything in America, stealing in Japan gave Dina the same giddy, weightlessness that cursing in another language did. You did it because it was unimportant and foreign. She stole spaghetti, rice, fruit. Keebler cookies all the way from America. But Petra outdid them all. She went in with a sack rigged across her stomach, then stuffed a sweater in it to look as though she was pregnant, and began shopping. When the sack got full, she'd go to the bathroom, put on her sweater, and pay for a loaf of bread.

But Petra's trick didn't last long. She went to get Zoltan a watermelon for his birthday and the sack gave way. She gave birth to the watermelon, which split open wide and red, right in front of her.

The store manager, a nervous Japanese man in his forties, brought her to Zoltan, telling him, in smiling, broken English, to keep her at home.

Since then, the stores in the area became suspicious of foreigners, pregnant or otherwise. They'd all been caught. They'd all made mad dashes down the street, losing themselves in crowds and alleys. And they didn't even have the money to get on the train to steal food elsewhere. It was impossible to jump the turnstiles—they were all electronic. Eventually they got to a point where they never left their one-room flat, knowing that they would see people selling food, stores selling food, people eating food, people whose faces reminded them of food.

And then they simply gave up. Some alloy of disgust and indifference checked the most human instinct, propelling them into a stagnant one-room dementia. It was a secret they shared: there were two types of hunger—one in which you would do anything for food, the other in which you could not bring yourself to complete the smallest task for it.

A R I C A M E home from work and declared that they must all go to the park. They looked at him uncomprehendingly. Sayeed went to his corner of the room and said, under his breath, "They know." Zoltan stood there, looking as though he had somewhere to go but had forgotten where. Petra bit her fingernails, her sunset-blond hair in unwashed clumps, framing her scars.

"Why the park?" Dina asked.

"Look," he said, reaching into his backpack to show them a block of cheese that was hardened on the ends, some paprika, a box of crackers, a plum. Dina remembered that all that was left in the refrigerator were two grapefruits. She salivated when her gaze settled on the bunch of bananas on the countertop. These he did not take.

"Let's go," he said.

Sayeed rose from where he'd been sitting on the tatami; Zoltan grabbed Petra's arm and led her toward the door. Once they'd gathered at the doorway, they looked at one another in silence, as if they had nothing further to say. Ari did not bother to lock the door.

T H E Y   S A T in Shakuji-koen Park, dazed with the sunlight, surrounded by an autumn of yellow ginkgo trees. For the most part, the sky was gray, shot through with fibrous clouds. The Japanese families sat like cookies arranged on a plate. The son of the family closest to them was as bronzed as Dina, a holdover tan from the summer. He bit into the kind of neat, crustless sandwiches Dina had seen mothers unwrap at Summerland. The girl was singing while her mother was talking to another mother, who agreed, *"Ne, ne, ne!"* as she bounced a swaddled baby on her hip. The father dozed off on a blanket of red and white squares.

The boy nibbled at his sandwich as the five of them watched. When the boy saw the foreigners staring at him, at his sandwich, he ran to his sister and pointed. Five *gaijin,* all together, sitting Buddha-like. The boy looked as though he wanted to come right up and ask them questions in the monosyllabic English he had learned from older boys who had spoken to *gaijin* before. Do you have tails? If so, would you kindly show them to me and my sister? Do you come out at night and suck blood? He would look at Dina and ask if the color rubbed off. He wanted to ask them these questions and more, if his limited English permitted, but the girl had enough shyness for the both of them, and held him back, a frightened smile on her face.

Ari took out the crackers, the cheese with the hard ends, the paprika, the salt, and the plum.

"I lost my job," he said.

Quietly, shamefully, they mustered out their *Sorry*s. She'd expected him to lash out, tell all of them to leave, but he didn't.

"I'll pay you back," Dina said, "every penny."

"You mean yen," Ari said.

They ate the crackers with sliced plum and cheese on top. Then Petra spoke.

"I do not like cheese," she said. Everyone looked at her, her pouting lips and unblinking eyes. Zoltan clenched her arm. Petra had taken her slices of cheese off her sandwiches and Zoltan grabbed the slices with one fist and thrust them at her. They fell humbly into the folds of her shirt.

"You don't have to eat them," Ari said. But Petra knew she had to eat the cheese, that the cheese mattered. She ate it and looked as if she might cry, but didn't. They sat for a while. The food melted in Dina's stomach just as the sunset melted, their synchronized fading seeming to make the whole world go dimmer and volumeless. Then she felt a sharp pain, as though the corners of the crackers had gone down her throat unchewed. None of them spoke, and that seemed to make the pain in her stomach worse. They watched the people and the lake and the sun, now only a thread of light.

"Look," Sayeed said.

Geese. Stretching their necks, paying no mind to humans. Zoltan bolted upright from where he lay and ran after them. For a few moments, the geese flew hysterically, but then landed yards away from him, waddling toward escape, all the while snapping up bits of crackers the Japanese had thrown just for them. When Zoltan started the chase anew, Dina realized he was not after the crackers but the geese themselves. She imagined Zoltan grabbing one of the thin, long necks, breaking it with a deft turn of wrist. And what would all the Japanese, quietly sitting in the park, make of it all? She skipped over that scene, speeding ahead to the apartment, everyone happily defeathering the bird, feathers lifting and floating then descending on their futons and blankets, the down like snow, the underfeathers like ash. They'd land on Petra's trunks, empty now that all her clothes had been sold, and they'd land on the tea table at which they used to eat. They would make a game of adjusting the oven dials, then wait out the hours as the roasted gamy smell of the goose made them stagger and salivate. And there would be a wishbone, but it wouldn't matter, because they'd all have the same wish.

Zoltan ran as haphazard as a child chasing after them, and when he seemed within grasp of a few tailfeathers, the geese flew off for good. When he returned, he dusted off the blanket before sitting down, as though nothing had happened.

All Japanese eyes were on them, and it was the first time Dina thought she had actually felt embarrassment in the true Japanese sense. Everyone was looking at them, and she'd never felt more foreign, more *gaijin*. Someone laughed. At first she thought it was Sayeed, his high-pitched laughter that made you happy. Then Dina saw that it was one of the Japanese picnickers. Families clapped, one after the other, cautious, tentative, like the first heavy rains on a rooftop, then suddenly everyone was clapping. Applause and even whistles, all for Zoltan, as though he had meant to entertain them. Ari made a motion for them to stop, but they continued for what seemed like minutes, as if demanding an encore. They did not stop, even when Zoltan nuzzled his head into Petra's gray corduroy shirt so no one could see him weep.

I T W A S a week after they saw the geese that Ari sliced up the grapefruit and banana into six pieces each. Dina watched them eat. Sayeed, his face dim as a brown fist, took his banana slice and put it underneath his tongue. He would transfer the warm disk of banana from side to side in his mouth until, it seemed, it had grown so soft that he swallowed it like liquid. He nibbled away at half a wedge of the grapefruit, tearing the fibers from fruit to skin with his bitten-down lips. He popped what was left of his grapefruit into his mouth like a piece of chewing gum.

Petra let her slices sit for a while and finally chewed the banana, looking off from the side of her eye as if someone had a gun pointed to her head. She wrapped up her grapefruit slice in a bit of leftover Saran Wrap and went to her corner to lie down.

Zoltan rubbed his eyes, put the banana slice on the flat side of the grapefruit and swallowed them both whole, grapefruit peel and all.

Ari ate his slices with delicate motions, and after he'd finished, smiled like a Buddha.

Dina ate her fruit the way she thought any straightforward, normal American would. She bit into it. One more piece sat on the plate.

"Anybody want that?" Dina asked. No one said anything. She looked around to make sure. No one had changed. She ate the last piece, wiped the grapefruit juice from around the corners of her mouth, looked at the semicircle of foreign faces around her, and knew she had done the wrong thing.

She needed to go to Shinjuku. Once again, she claimed the turnstile wouldn't issue her a ticket, and although the girl at the counter didn't look convinced, she gave Dina a ticket. When she got to Shinjuku, it was going on noon. *Sararimen* hurled by, smiling with their colleagues, bowing for their bosses to enter doors first. Mothers shopped, factory workers sighed, shopworkers chattered with other shopworkers. The secretaries and receptionists—the "Office Ladies"—all freshened their lipstick and straightened their hairbows. The women in the miniskirts rushed past as though late.

She stood in the Shinjuku station, though she hadn't ridden the train to get there. She read an old magazine she'd brought along. Finally, a *sarariman* approached her.

"Verrrry sexy."

H E P A I D for the love motel with a wad of yen. "CAN RENT ROOM BY OUR!" screamed a red-lettered sign on the counter. Dina ascended the dark winding staircase, the *sarariman* following. The room had only a bed and a nightstand, though these simple furnishings now seemed like luxuries. He watched her undress and felt her skin only after she'd taken everything off. He rubbed it as if he were trying to find something underneath.

The inside of her closed eyelids were orange from a slit of sunlight that had strayed into the room. The *sarariman* shook her. She opened her eyes. He raised his eyebrows, looking from Dina to the nightstand. The nightstand had a coin-operated machine attached.

"Sex toy?" he asked, in English.

"No," she said, in Japanese.

The motel room sheets were perfect and crisp, reminding her of sheets from home. She touched the *sarariman*'s freshly cut Asian hair, each shaft sheathed in a sheer liquid of subway sweat. The ends of the shortest hairs felt like the tips of lit, hissing firecrackers.

He was apologetic about the short length of time. "No problem," she told him in Japanese.

SHE LEFT with a wad of yen. While riding the *tokkyuu* she watched life pass, alert employees returning to work, uniformed school children on a field trip. It all passed by—buildings, signs, throngs of people everywhere. When the train ran alongside a park, yellow ginkgo leaves waved excited farewells as the train blazed past them. Fall had set in, and no one was picnicking, but there were geese. At first they honked and waddled as she'd seen them a week ago when Zoltan had chased them, but then, as the train passed, agitating them, they rose, as though connected to a single string. Soon the geese were flying in formation, like planes she had once seen in a schoolbook about Japan.

The book told of kamikaze pilots, flying off to their suicide missions. How each scrap-metal plane and each rickety engine could barely stand the pressures of altitude, how each plane was allotted just enough fuel for its one-way trip. The pilots had made a pledge to the emperor, and they'd kept their promises. She remembered how she'd marveled when she'd read it, amazed that anyone would do such a thing; how—in the all-knowing arrogance of youth—she'd been certain that given the same circumstances, she would have done something different.

Doris Is Coming

❧

DORIS YATES STOOD in the empty sanctuary and wondered if the world would really end in a matter of hours. It was New Year's Eve, 1961, and beyond the pebbled amber church windows the world seemed normal enough; the bushy teaberry and arum pressed their drupes against the windowpanes as if begging to be let in, the speeding Buicks and Fords on Montgomery Road sounded like an ocean. Farther out in the world other Negro youths sneaked out of their homes and schoolrooms to sit stoically at the Woolworth's while whites poured catsup on them. King and Kennedy were transmitted onto the television screens of Stutz's Fine Appliances and Televisions. Whenever she went there, Doris would sit with old Stutz while he smoked and complained: "No news of

Lithuania!" he'd say with a disgust one would have expected to settle into resignation since there never was—and never would be—
any news about Lithuania. Just as she thought that the world might
end that very night, sunlight illumined the windows, clear as shel-
lac, bright as if trying to wake her. She remembered the bottle of
furniture oil at her feet and the rag in her hand and began to polish
the pulpit.

Cleaning the church was her mother's job, but that day, the day
the world would end, it was hers. Her mother cleaned house for the
Bermans, the one Jewish family in Hurstbourne Estates. Doris's father picked up her mother just outside the neighborhood because
the Bermans' neighbors had complained that the muffler of Edgar
Yates's old Hupmobile made too much noise. This meant Doris's
mother Bernice had to walk nearly a mile to meet Doris's father, and
was too tired to clean the church besides.

"They sure can cut a penny seventy-two ways," Doris's father
would say whenever the Bermans were mentioned. It was his belief
that all Jews were frugal to a fault, but Doris's mother would correct
him. "It's not the men that's like that, it's the women." Once, when
this exchange was playing out, Doris had said, "Can't be all that
stingy. It was a Jew man who gave Dr. King all that money." She
waited, not knowing whether she would get swatted for talking.
Bernice and Edgar Yates were firm believers that their seven children should be seen, not heard. Doris was lucky that time; all her
mother did was make a sound not unlike the steamy *psst* of the iron
she was wielding and say, "Proves my point. It's not the men, it's
the women."

Nevertheless, the furniture polish she stroked onto the pulpit was
donated by Mrs. Berman and the rag she held had once been little
Danny Berman's shirt. As Doris wiped down the pulpit, she thought

of the Jewish boys from up North getting on that bus in Anniston, taking a beating with the rest of the Negro students. She'd seen it all with her family on TV, from the store window of Stutz's. It was important, historic, she felt, but underneath the obvious importance there had been something noble and dangerous about it all. She'd called the NAACP once, to see how old one had to be to join a sit-in, but when she couldn't get through and the operator asked if she'd like to try again, her suspicions were confirmed that all those Movement organizations were monitored. Once she'd even asked Reverend Sykes if she could go to a march, just one, but the answer had been no, that Saints didn't go to marches. Then he quoted the scripture that says, "One cannot be of two masters, serving God and mammon both."

She could hear the main church door open and felt a rush of cold air, the jangle of keys being laid upon wood. The service wouldn't begin for another two hours or so, and she felt cheated that her quiet time was being disturbed. At first she thought it was her mother, then, for a brief moment, Reverend Sykes. When Sister Bertha Watkins appeared at the far end of the aisle, she tried to hide her disappointment.

Sister Bertha unbuttoned her coat, inhaling grandly, the way she did before she began her long testimonies. "Well, are you ready?"

"Almost, ma'am. I'm doing the dusting and polishing before sweep and mop."

"No," Sister Bertha smiled. "Not 'Are you finished?' *Are you ready?* For the Rapture?"

ACCORDING TO the Pentecostal Assemblies of the World, an organization comprising the Kentucky–Tennessee–Ohio tristate area, the countdown to the end of the world began in 1948. That year marked the founding of Israel as a nation, and the countdown to the arrival of the Second Coming of Christ. A preacher from Tennessee had put the first Rapture at '55, seven years after Israeli nationhood, and when the Rapture had not occurred, the Pentecostal Assemblies of the World recalculated, slating the Second Coming for the last day of 1961.

On New Year's Eve, after she'd cleaned the church, Doris took her seat at her usual pew with the other girls her age. Girls who spent much of the service wondering whether Reverend Sykes conked his hair or if it was naturally wavy like that; why he hadn't found a wife yet and which of them would make likely candidates. They passed around notes that got torn up and stuffed into an innocent Bible; they repressed their laughter so that it would sound like a cough.

The service began like most, with testimonies, though tonight there were more people than usual. Doris listened to Brother Dorchester testify that he'd heard birds chirping about the end of the world. Sister Betty Forrester stood and said, "May the Lord take me tonight, because I *sho* don't want to go to work tomorrow!"

When Reverend Sykes rose, everyone gave a great shout, but he sent them a serious look, placing his folded hands on the podium.

"Bear with me, Saints. It's New Year's Eve, and while the world out there jukes around, I want to talk about another holiday. I want to talk about Thanksgiving. Now, y'all may be thinking, 'Why is Reverend Franklin Sykes talking about Thanksgiving? Don't he know he a few months too late? Don't he know he a little behind? Don't he know that our Lord and Christ and Savior Jesus is coming tonight? Don't he know *anything*?'"

"Yes y' do," a Sister in the back of the church piped up.

Reverend Sykes smiled. He could look thirty or forty or fifty, depending on how he smiled and for whom. "Like I've told y'all before, I'm just a country boy. And in the country when *Daddy* wanted to get some meat on the table by *Christmas,* he knew how to get it. You see, 'fore Thanksgiving came *around,* we'd go out and catch us a turkey. Now you can train a horse to bite on the bit. Train the ox to go the straight *and narrow* way. But Saints! You can*not* train *no turkeys*! Even the chickens will come when you feed them, and in time, lay their eggs in the nest. All the other birds—the *gooses* and the *sparrows* and the *chickadees*—will go *south* when the winter comes. And the Lord shows them the way to go north in the spring."

"Amen," a few women called out. Doris also said, "Amen," though a bit late, wondering where he was heading with it all.

"When the raaaain comes pouring *down*—they won't try to run and hide. No, Saints! They don't heed the Lord's call like the other animals. All the turkey wants to do is follow all the *other* turkeys! They get so *tangled up* in one another, that they will *push* the weak ones on the bottom, but guess what? *All* the turkeys gonna drown! That's right. Don't be a gaggle of turkeys, Saints! Because when the *raaain* comes—!" He walked back to the pulpit and closed his Bible as if that was all he needed to say.

"Preach it, Brother!"

People were up on their feet, shouting, for they now knew the turkeys were all the sinners of the world and the rain was the Rapture that would surely occur that night. They danced and shouted in the aisles like never before. Doris stood as well, looking to see if her mother had arrived, when she spotted a white lady, standing, her hands swaying in time with everyone else's. She definitely wasn't one of the white Pentecostal women who occasionally visited colored churches. This lady had auburn hair, in deep waves that grazed her shoulders like a forties film star's, whereas saved white women were forbidden to cut their waist-length hair, the straggly ends like dripping seaweed. Those women wore ruffles and brooches from the turn of the century, but this lady was dressed in a smart, expensive-looking suit. Then it hit Doris—the white lady wasn't a lady at all, but a girl. Olivia Berman, Mrs. Berman's daughter. Beside Olivia was Doris's mother, who, despite the commotion, was completely silent. Why was Olivia Berman, a Jewish girl, here?

Everyone else was so caught up that no one noticed that Doris's mother wasn't, but Doris could not concentrate. If Jesus had come at that very second she would have been left behind because she wasn't thinking of Him.

IT WAS nearly one o'clock in the morning and 1962 when they quit their shouting and settled into prayer. Jesus hadn't come, and the children—up past their bedtimes—began to grumble and yawn. When the last hymn had been sung, the last prayer spoken, and the last "Amen" said, Doris found herself outside, buoyed by the night air, scrambling to find the rest of her family. It wasn't hard with a white girl around. The rest of the congregation swirled around them, looking at them but saying nothing. There was no ignoring Olivia: her whiteness, her strangely erect posture, her red hair, the abrupt way she had of tossing her head like a horse resisting a rein.

Outside, everything was extremely as it had been. Jesus had not arrived, but Doris wished He had, if only to keep everyone speculating why Doris and her mother had brought a white girl to church.

"You remember Olivia," her mother said after the service. "She'll be going to Central." Her voice was changed, all the music gone out of it and replaced with the strange, overenunciated syllables she used talking to white folks or imitating them. Bernice Yates usually bade each and every Saint a good night, but that night she looked only at Doris and Olivia.

Before Doris could remember to be polite, she said, "Why are you going to public school? What happened?"

Her mother shot her a look. "Nothing *happened.*"

"It's okay, Bernice," Olivia said, lightly touching Doris's mother's shoulder.

Doris cringed. Not even her father called Doris's mother by her first name. Only Mrs. Berman—who paid her mother a paycheck—could call her Bernice.

If Olivia caught the ice in Doris's eyes, she didn't let on. "You see, Doris, I got kicked out. I'm in need of some saving myself, that's why I came here tonight."

Doris's mother laughed, high and irregular. "Miss Olivia loves to kid around."

"I changed my name, Bernice. Livia. Not *O*-livia. And I'm not kidding around. I came to find out all about Christian salvation."

Doris watched as her mother looked at Olivia. It was hard to tell whether Olivia was making fun of them. Though Saints were gladdened when anyone became interested in the Holiness Church, this was too much. Jews were Jews, and that was that.

Doris remembered how she'd always thought of how lucky the Jews were: Reverend Sykes had said that whether or not they believed in Jesus, they wouldn't go to hell like other nonbelievers, because they were Chosen. That would mean heaven would be stocked with nobody but Pentecostals and Jews. Doris thought how strange it would be, getting whisked away to heaven only to find things much the way they were when she used to help her mother clean at the Bermans': Mrs. Berman with her pincurls whorled about her head like frosting on a cake, little Al and Danny Berman playing the violin, eyes rolling to the ceiling at Stravinsky's beautiful, boring music. She remembered when Al and Danny quit the scherzo they'd been practicing and started up "Take Me Out to the Ball Game," sawing on their expensive violins as if they were country fiddles. Mr. Berman had let out a primitive yell, thudding something to the ground, the only time Doris had seen him mad.

Olivia Berman offered to drive them home. Doris's mother said that with her daughters Etta Josephine and Doris now there, the car would be too full, and implored Miss Olivia to go ahead home. Doris's mother insisted that no, it was not too far for them to walk. That they'd been doing it for years.

S H E   W A S the only Negro student in the class, the only Negro in all her classes. And though Mr. Fott, her Honors History teacher, rarely called on her, she was fine with it. She was relieved that he graded fairly, though sometimes he'd comment on her essays with a dark, runic hand: *Do you mean Leo XIII believed the state must remain subord. to the interests of the indiv. composing it? Despite his antipathy of laissez-faire policies?* At least he didn't speak to her the way Mrs. Prendergast always did, slowly, loudly, as if Doris were deaf.

On the first day Olivia came to Mr. Fott's class, she wore earrings like tiny chandeliers and a pillbox hat, like Jackie Kennedy, though no one wore hats to school. She entered minutes after the bell had rung, and though Mr. Fott made efforts to flag her down, chide her for tardiness, introduce her to the class, she rushed straight to where Doris was seated and cried, *"Doris!"* Doris made no move to get up, but Olivia descended upon her in an embrace, then turned to the

218

class in mock sheepishness, as if she could not help her display of emotion. "Doris and I haven't seen each other in *forever*."

That, of course, was a lie; they'd just seen each other three days ago. But before that night at church, Doris hadn't seen Olivia in years. For the longest time Doris could have sworn she'd heard her mother saying something about Olivia going to a girls' boarding school. But that turned out not to be true: two or three years ago, at supper, when Etta Josephine had asked about her, Doris's mother had said, "You know what? I don't know where they keep that girl? But you know how white folks is. Got family living on the other side of the planet. Hop on one a them airplanes like they going to the corner store." Then she lowered her voice to a gossipy whisper. "But you know what? Now that you mention it, I do believe she's in the sanatorium." Doris hadn't believed it at the time, and had gradually forgotten about her.

"Miss . . ." Fott glanced down at his roll book. ". . . Berman, is it?"

"Why, yes. It is."

"Miss Berman, please be seated. For the record, miss, this class starts on time."

"WHO DOES that Mr. Fott think he is, Doris? I mean, what's his problem?"

Outside school only a few of the yellow buses had pulled into the lot. Doris had been waiting for hers when Olivia—Livia—had spotted her. Livia stared, mutely insistent that Doris answer.

"He thinks he's the teacher, Livia," Doris finally said, "a man to be respected." She hugged her coat tight around her, praying for her bus to pull into its space and save her. She wished her old friend Helen was around so that she wouldn't be such a target for Livia, but now that Helen was in all-colored classes and Doris was in white ones, she rarely saw Helen. "All those white folks make me nervous," Helen had once said when she'd walked Doris to English. It hadn't occurred to Doris to *be* nervous, but now she was more annoyed than nervous; annoyed that this girl would use her mother's first name, annoyed that this girl would come to her church, her school. "Your mother never talks about you," Doris said, suddenly angry. "And where've you been all these years? Where'd you come from anyway?"

Livia took a cigarette from a silver case that looked as thin as a card, then lit it. She inhaled, nostrils dilating, eyes rolling in ecstasy. "I came from walking to and fro upon the earth. And up and down on it." She looked askance at Doris, as if to see whether Doris recognized that she was quoting from the Book of Job: Satan's answer to God's question, *Whence comest thou?*

"Don't use Bible verses that way," Doris said, then added, "and don't talk to me in class." She immediately regretted the words: her mother would slap her if she found out Doris had insulted the daughter of her only employer.

Livia looked at her, surprised. "Don't talk to you? I was doing you a favor. I mean, who *does* talk to you, Doris? Who? Name one person."

"I don't need anyone to talk to. Especially not white people. I talk to my family. I talk to the pastor."

"Reverend Sykes," Livia said thoughtfully, as though it were the title of a poem. She exhaled, and the smoke mazed ghostly around her face, then lifted like a veil above her pillbox hat. "Yes, Reverend Sykes. I don't think Reverend Sykes lets you do the things you want."

"Love not the world, neither the things that are in the world," Doris said. But the retort sounded hollow: she could not help but remember how Reverend Sykes had disapproved of her going to sit-ins, and wondered what Livia knew about Reverend Sykes besides what she'd seen that night at church. And why had Livia come to church at all? Doris decided that she said things purely to shock, said things so that people like Doris's mother could say nothing in return while Livia sat back in smug satisfaction, observing what she'd wrought.

Doris's bus had arrived, and though she tried to think of the worst thing she could say to Livia before parting, all she could manage was, "And I hate your hat."

WHEN SHE got home it was dark. The boys were running about the house and Etta Josephine had not come back from her job shucking walnuts. But she knew her father must be home; she could hear him hammering away. Her father was trying to build a third bedroom where their back porch had been, but the partition made from blankets never kept out the draft. She turned on the kitchen stove to warm the house and start dinner, wondering why her father had picked winter, of all times, to tear down two major walls of the house. The *pock, pock* sound of nails being hammered into place had somehow grown spooky, as though some force were chipping its way into the house and would eventually take them all whether they invited it in or not.

She dialed the living room radio to its highest volume so she could hear it in the kitchen, over her father's pounding and sawing. She'd finished mixing the meal and egg yolk for the cornbread and had begun frying chicken when the white radio announcer delivered news about the Albany Movement in Georgia; how the colored leaders of that area had petitioned for sewage, paved roads, and a moratorium on the stoning of Negro ministers' houses. It was suspected that the colored citizens of Albany would protest once again if their grievances weren't met, the announcer said. Then the announcer finished on a note of his own that made Doris so mad she forgot to pay attention to what she was doing and burned her hand on the skillet. *When,* he implored, *will the tumult end?*

DORIS HAD excused herself after dinner, saying she needed to gather leaves for her biology-class leaf collection. And though she knew she was headed to Stutz's, she hadn't exactly told a lie. She *did* need to collect leaves for Mrs. Prendergast's class, though they weren't due until the end of spring.

"Dorrie!" Mr. Stutz said when she entered his store that night. "It's Dori-ka!" He took a break from smoking hi cigarette to cough, loud and insistent.

She'd supposed that Dori-ka was some Lithuanian diminutive, but she'd never asked him. She liked that she had another name, in some other language, and didn't want to ruin the mystery of it by finding out what it meant.

"Hello, Mr. Stutz. How's your wife and family?"

Stutz made a face and waved his hand. "Want, want, want. They all want. I tell them, in Lithuania, you are freezing. Here, in America, your brain is frying!"

He laughed at his own joke, though Doris didn't know what was so funny. She didn't always understand him, but she liked his accent. And he seemed lonely. Sometimes, when he stood among his televisions and appliances, he looked like the only person in a graveyard, so she tried to laugh when he laughed.

"Game show is not on, Dorrie. But come. Take chair."

She sat on the stool next to him, and for a while they did not speak. They watched *Marshal Dillon,* Stutz smoking his cigarette peacefully. Then they sat through *The Lloyd Bridges Show,* and when it was over, Stutz said, "Ah. He should not try that show. He was better in *Sea Hunt.*"

Doris had not been able to enjoy either of the programs: she could not forget the radio broadcast she'd heard earlier, how the announcer seemed to loathe the colored people of Albany when all they'd wanted was to march for decent sewage disposal without being stoned for it. She thought of what Livia had said about Reverend Sykes not letting her do what she wanted, then looked at Mr. Stutz and announced, "I'm going to go to a sit-in."

He looked at her, puzzled. "Oho! First I am thinking, She is already *sitting,* she is already *in* store." He shook his head then raised a single finger. "You mean like TV."

"Yes," she said. "But they're not just on TV. They do it for real."

"I know that they are *real,*" he said, as if she'd insulted his intelligence. "But I think: Good maybe for others. Not so good for Dorrie."

She leapt from the stool on which she'd been sitting. "What do you mean 'not so good'? You think I should just walk around and not care that I have to use a separate everything! That my father shouldn't be able to vote!"

"Dorrie *not yell at Stutz!*"

She sighed her apology, and after a few deep breaths, he seemed to accept it.

"I not say it *baaad,*" he said, trying to reconcile. "But Dori-ka is *nice girl—*"

How could Stutz not understand? She was about to object, but he placed a stern hand on her arm to keep her from interrupting him.

"Nice girl. I like Dori-ka. I don't want people to put *Senf* and catsup all over Dori-ka like they do on TV."

Whenever he and Doris had watched news footage of the sit-ins in Greensboro, they'd seen whites as young as the Negro students squirting mustard and catsup all over the protesters. It had amazed her that the students could sit so still, taking it, occasionally wiping themselves off, but never shouting or hitting.

"And Dori-ka," he said, "I am businessman. I think of things from business perspective. If you do what they say called 'integrate,' what will everyone here do?" He waved his hand beyond the window, to where Amos Henry cut meat in his butcher shop, where Mozelle Gordon ran the little store that sold sundries. And there, also in his gesture, was Thomasina Edison, who did everyone's hair, her hot comb heating in its little pod, waiting to do its Saturday-night miracles. "All these business," Stutz said, "all of them Negroid. All," he said, placing his hand on his heart, "but Stutz."

"Now, when someone need hairs cut, they go over *there*. When they need meat cut in half, they go over *there*." He pointed out the window as though outside lay the seven wonders of the world. "When you 'integrate,' I predict, everyone will go to white, none to black. Why? Because white America will build big palace. They will say, 'Why go to Negroid store? Little-bitty tchotchke store? We have everything here!'" Then, with a flourish of his hand, he said, "No more Negroid store. Poof. All gone."

She didn't think that would happen. Couldn't imagine anything like it. But even though Stutz didn't really understand, she felt something like affection for him. When the *Red Skelton Show* theme music began playing, she knew it was time to leave. She stood in front of him, and though both made as if to hug each other, they didn't.

৸

A WEEK later, after Wednesday-night Bible study, Doris decided to ask for a meeting with Reverend Sykes. Her mother would take at least half an hour to make her rounds, hugging and God-blessing everyone in sight, and her brothers could spend all night outside playing stickball in their winter coats.

"Of course, Doris," Reverend Sykes said when she asked to speak with him. "It's been a while since we had one of our talks." He gathered his Bible notes from the pulpit and led her to his office: a hymnbook closet that had been only half cleared of books. He gestured for her to take the seat opposite his and made a little laugh. "Remember when you read some book about digestion, then asked why stomach acid didn't kill Jonah when he was in the belly of the whale?" He smiled, remembering.

It was true. Doris used to want to know why it was fair for David to have Bathsheba's husband killed, just because he wanted to marry her himself; why Jacob got to have Esau's birthright, when Esau's only fault—as far as Doris could see—was that he was hairy.

"This isn't a question," Doris said, "though it involves a Bible story. It's more of a theory."

Reverend Sykes made a mock-impressed face at the word "theory."

"Well, I was thinking about how Jesus turned two fish and five loaves of bread into enough to feed five thousand people, showing how when you feed a physical hunger, folks are more receptive to hearing a message that'll then feed their spiritual hunger."

"Amen," Reverend Sykes said, nodding. "Couldn't a said it better myself. A spiritual hunger that needs to be fed by the Word of God."

"But Reverend Sykes," Doris said, "what if a thousand had to eat their bread and fish in the valley, while the rest got to eat theirs up on the hill? That's what's happening now. We colored have to eat our fish and bread in the valley. The white folks get to eat theirs up on the hill."

He rubbed his eyes with his fingertips. "Well, it seems like you've got a decision to make, Doris. Do you wanna starve, but keep your house with a hilltop view? Or do you wanna live in the valley with a full belly? Hmm? And what's so wrong with the valley, Doris? The Lord says, 'Consider the lilies of the field, how they toil not, neither do they spin . . .'"

"But Reverend Sykes," she said, voice quavering, "what if the valley is flooded? And why should you have to choose?" She was already near tears, and if she continued in this vein, whatever she said would surely start her crying.

"Doris," he said. He reached across the desk and placed her hands in his, holding them solemnly. "This is about those marches and sit-ins, isn't it? Now I know there's *Dr. King* out there," he said, making the name sound like a fad, "calling himself *preaching*. But do you want to be with all those girls and boys who'd go to jail in a second? Not even caring how much their mamas and daddies have to pay to get 'em out. Do you want that?"

The answer seemed to be no, but it got caught in her throat, like a hummingbird. She finally said, "They're only asking to be treated equal with white folks. Like how God would treat them. That's why the other churches support the sit-ins."

Reverend Sykes let go of her hands and kicked his feet up on the desk. "And these *other* churches. I suppose they're Baptist and A.M.E.? Now, them folks think you can sin on Saturday night and sing hungover with the choir Sunday morning. Did you see that mother of that unsaved family that came in on New Year's? That woman! Coming to church in a red dress, of all things."

Doris hadn't noticed any such woman, she'd been so surprised to see Olivia in the pews. But she looked hard at the Reverend and said, "Yes. I remember. The night the Lord was supposed to come."

"TODAY," Livia said, "you'll be sick." This was the Tuesday after Doris had spoken with Reverend Sykes. After Mr. Fott's class, Livia took Doris by the crook of her elbow, steering her away from third-period French.

Livia played hooky all the time, and though Doris knew this was what Livia had in mind, knew it was wrong, there was something thrilling about riding in a car with someone besides her parents, going someplace she knew would not be church.

"I can't," Doris said, though she knew she would.

"Alice is already waiting in the car." Alice, another girl in History class, spoke to Livia because speaking to Livia always got you noticed. Alice had begun to dress like Livia, one time even wearing a pillbox hat to class.

Livia drove a turquoise-and-white Mercury Park Lane, a far cry from Doris's father's Hupmobile. They saw *Splendor in the Grass* at the Vogue, Livia sitting in the colored balcony with Doris. Finally Alice came up, too. It was the second movie Doris had seen since her family had joined the church. The first had been a French movie she saw for extra credit, the one time she'd gone against the church's teachings without confessing what she'd done.

They drove from St. Matthews to Germantown, covering the city. When they got to Newburg, Alice let out a long sigh. "I bought my dress for the Winter Dance," she said, turning to Livia. "It's a long satin sheath with roses on either side of the straps. The straps are that minty green color everyone's wearing, but the rest is one long flesh-colored sheath. Mama would die if she saw it, but what's bought is bought."

"Flesh colored?" Doris said.

"I know! Scandalous!"

"You mean, the color of your flesh?" Doris said.

"Well, who else's would it be?" Alice looked to Livia as if searching for a sane opinion.

"You mean *your* flesh color. And Livia's and Mr. Fott's. Not mine."

Alice stared at Doris. "For the love of heaven, it's just a word."

Livia said, "But why use the word if it's not accurate? It's simply not the color of everyone's flesh."

"Well, how should I say it? What should I say when describing it? Say, 'Oh, I bought a dress the color of everybody else's skin except Doris's'?"

"I'm not the only one."

"I could say it was a flesh-colored dress and everyone would know what I was talking about. Everyone would know exactly what I was talking about."

"I'm sure they would, Alice," Livia said. She laughed, high and free. "*Everyone* would."

Alice pinched her fingers together, as though holding a grain of salt. "It's those little things, Doris. Why do your people concentrate on all those little, itty-bitty things?"

WHY SHOULD she care about what Alice said? That phrase. "Your people." Livia had kicked Alice out of the car right there on

Newburg Road, where cabs didn't come and buses were scarce. It was a hard thing to do—kick someone out of a car—and Livia had had to open the passenger side door, drag Alice out against her will, tug and tug until Alice, unwilling to make too much of a scene, finally stayed put on the sidewalk. Her face scrunched up mean and hateful, as if she was too proud to cry, though obviously she wanted to. Livia looked disappointed that Doris wouldn't help kick Alice out, but Doris hopped into the front seat where Alice had sat just the same.

"That's better, now, isn't it," Livia had said, as if she'd done it all for Doris, but Doris didn't speak to her the whole way home. Alice had annoyed her, offended her, but she didn't see any sense in doing anything about it. Acknowledging too much just made it hurt worse. Livia's self-satisfaction and self-righteousness felt just as bad as Alice's thoughtlessness. When Livia drove Doris to the West End part of town where Doris lived, she seemed to delight in seeing so many Negro faces.

During supper, Doris hardly said anything, and no one seemed to notice. Charleroy and Edgar talked excitedly about stickball, about grade-school gossip, about their teacher's bosom until, finally, their mother told them to hush.

I T   W A S   the family's habit to walk after supper, a leisurely stroll that made them feel wealthy. Once they got to Stutz's Fine Appliances, they'd stop and survey the fifteen or so TVs on display as if they were finicky purchasers looking for the exact one that would suit their needs. In the beginning, Doris's mother would make noises of approval or disapproval of the various models, and her father would crane his neck to examine the side finish and sturdiness of the cabinets. They had all played along when they'd started going to Stutz's so long ago, though they all knew that they didn't have the money and wouldn't for a long time. As far as Doris knew, she had been the only one to actually go inside and talk to the old man.

They stood outside of Stutz's swaddled in coats and watched Lucy and Ethel and Fred beg Ricky to let them on his show. Lucy, ridiculous in a ballerina costume, Ethel in a cha-cha dress, and pudgy Fred in the same dress but wearing a Shirley Temple wig.

Old man Stutz came outside, hobbling. "Hello, friends. Hello, Dorrie."

They looked at Doris, and a chill went through her as if she didn't have a coat on at all. Never before when she and her family visited at night had Stutz been there, only his son, the one he called Lazybones, who never made an effort to go out and greet window shoppers.

"Hello, Mr. Stutz. Mr. Stutz, this is my family." She went through the introductions, and her parents fell silent. The boys pinched each other and tried not to laugh.

"All the answers," Stutz said, wagging and pointing to Doris with a little too much exuberance. "She knows all the answers to all the game shows! You want to buy?" He gestured extravagantly at the television they'd been watching.

Her mother laughed as she had at Livia. Nervous, uncertain. "Well, mister, we'd like to. We're working on it."

"Work on it, work on it!" Stutz said, smiling broadly and bobbing his head.

When they left to walk back home her mother said, "That little Russian man sure is funny-looking."

"Woman, you always got to talk 'bout how someone look," her

father said. "Someone nose always too big or too little. Or they teeth missing. Or they breath stank."

"Can't help it if he's funny-looking."

"Lord made him that way. He Russian."

"Rich as he is, he can do something to his face. Keep it from being so funny-looking."

"He's Lithuanian," Doris said, "not Russian."

And little Edgar, popping her on the thigh, said, "Who asked you?"

A FEW weeks after the car ride and movie, Livia did not show up for class. Doris assumed she was playing hooky, but then two days passed, then three; still no Livia. Finally she went to Livia's home-room teacher to check whether Livia had been in school at all. She'd been marked present that day, and though Doris looked for her, she couldn't find her. She was not in Fott's class, hadn't stopped by to lean up against Doris's locker and dole out pithy bon mots.

As soon as the last bell rang, Doris searched the front of the school, and when she did not find Livia there, she walked to the stu-dent parking lot. There, the white kids stared at her the way de-partment store clerks stared at her family when they went to try on clothes. They stared, then looked away as if they hadn't seen any-thing at all.

Doris ran toward the gym, remembering how the smokers al-ways hovered near it. Doris was out of breath, but Livia didn't seem to notice or care. She stood there and smiled as though awaiting in-troductions at a cocktail party.

"Doris," she said.

"Where've you been?" She wanted Livia to say, *To and fro upon the earth and walking up and down on it.* That was always Livia's answer. *Say it,* Doris willed. *Say it.* She'd missed those lines from Job, missed Livia more than she thought she would. *Say it.*

"I've been around," Livia said. She sounded drunk. "Around and around."

"*Around?* What about school? What about—" She caught herself before she could say, *What about me?*

"I hate to say it, Doris, but my time here is limited."

Doris thought death, sickness. Livia going insane like Natalie Wood in *Splendor in the Grass*; she imagined Livia laid up with satin sheets like Greta Garbo in *Camille,* the movie she'd seen for extra credit for French class.

"*No,*" Livia said, reading her mind. "Nothing serious. I'm going to school up North. I can't stand it down here anymore. You shouldn't either."

She didn't know what Livia could mean by that: Where would she go? What choice did she have? And had she known things to be any other way? Only rich folks like the Bermans could afford to go wherever they wanted.

"My mother said you were in the sanatorium," Doris said. "Was that where you were before? Is that where you're going?" She checked Livia's face for some crumb of emotion.

Livia smiled brightly, as if Doris never ceased to amaze her, then drew Doris up in a hug. "Oh, Doris," she said. "Don't you know that the real crazy people are the ones who do the same thing over and over again? Expecting a different result every time?"

O N T H E school bus all the Negro kids talked like a party, relieved to be going home. When they spoke to her, it was either a question about Holy Rollers or a question about what whites did in class, how they acted and how they treated her.

"Do they throw things at you?" one boy asked.

"Naw," a girl answered in her stead. "She'd beat 'em up like Joe Louis."

She got off right before Stutz's. None of the televisions were on window display. Without the televisions, the windows were dustier than she'd remembered. It seemed as though someone had stolen them all, but there was no broken glass. She cleared the film of dust off the window and peered in. In the rear of the dark store, televisions sat mutely on the floor like obedient children. Someone was moving around inside. The figure took a large box down from the counter and set it on the floor. He remained hunched over it for a long time, heaving, as if to gather strength for the next one. When the figure finally stood, she saw that it was old man Stutz himself.

She tapped on the window, saw him frown, then, recognizing her, smile with all his wrinkles. He invited her in with a grand sweep of his arm, like a baseball player winding up to pitch. "Come in, come in," he said, though the glass was so thick she could only see him mouthing the words. She threw her hands up. "How? The door is locked?" He frowned. Then, understanding, unlocked the door.

"Mr. Stutz." She started to take off her coat, out of habit, but the store was so cold she kept it on. "How are you?"

He wiped his forehead with his handkerchief, folded it in fourths, then eighths, then put it in his pocket. He rubbed his huge eyelids. "Oh, not so good, Dorrie. Moving out. Almost two weeks now, you haven't heard?"

She tried to remember the last time she'd seen him. Perhaps a month ago. "No. I guess I haven't been by in a while."

"This is the problem. You see it? This is the very problem. People come by. They watch. Laugh at Lucy. Ha ha ha, look at Lucy, love Lucy." He made a crazy face, though whether it was supposed to be Lucy or Ricky, Doris could not tell. Then Stutz's face went from crazy to somber. "The people, they love Lucy, they go home. No one buys. No sales, no money. No money, no Stutz." He threw up his hands like a magician making himself disappear. "No Stutz," he said again. He ambled over to the nearest chair, brought out a second one for Doris. She sat, watching him settle into his. He coughed for a long time, then brought out his handkerchief and pressed it against his lips. "And other things," he said, "but I don't want to offend."

Her skin prickled. "What other things?"

"The neighborhood."

"They're good people."

"Yes," Stutz said sadly, his eyes wise and sclerotic, "Good people." He swept his hand toward the barren store window. "This neighborhood. Good people, yes, but what's-their-name, right here on Fourth Street. Chickens in the yard. Scratch, scratch scratch. Cockadoodledoo. Lithuania in America. And those boys, playing baseball in the middle of the street. Do cars want to stop and buy from Stutz if they will get a crack on their windshield? I don't think so." Stutz shook his head in a slow, ancient way. "Good people. Yes. But."

It was true. Sister Forrester still kept chickens in her yard, and her brothers' friend Juny Monroe got every boy a mile around to play stickball in the street. The games lasted for hours. She could understand how, surrounded by televisions all day, one would be able to see that the rest of the world was different from Fourth Street, prettier, more certain, full of laughter and dresses and men who wore hats not only when they went to church but when they went to work in offices and banks too.

Old Stutz seemed to see something in Doris's eye and said, "Aha! But as they say, there is a silver lining. A smart girl you are, Dorrie. You go learn, come back, make better. You see. I planned it all out for you. Just do."

"It's not that easy."

He waved his hand. "Easy? Easy? I come from Lithuania. I leave my wife and my Lazybones son behind. I work. I send money. They come. Now my wife watches television and points. She wants a fur. Okey, dokey. I say, 'I go to the wood and catch you a fur.' She says, No no no no, and slams all the doors."

She wanted to say, *But you're white.* She wanted to say, *In another generation, your Lazybones son will change his name from "Stutz" to "Stuart" or "Star" and the rest of America will have forgotten where you came from.* But she couldn't say it. He coughed and this time unfolded the handkerchief and spat into it, so instead she said, "And I suppose you had to walk to school, twenty miles, uphill, in the snow."

His face brightened, surprised. "Aha! I see you are familiar with Lithuania!"

SHE WALKED from Stutz's and up along Fourth Street. When she got to Claremont, the street where she lived, she kept going, past Walnut and Chestnut and all the other streets named after trees. She hit the little business district, which was still lit for New Year's, the big incandescent bulbs on wires like buds growing from vines, entwining the trees and lighting the shop façades. When she walked farther, she felt, for the first time, some purpose other than solitude motivating her. She rushed, and did not know why, until she found it. Clovee's Five and Dime. As soon as she saw it, she knew what she was doing.

It was warm inside, and she made her way to the soda fountain, even warmer from the grill's heat. A white man stood at the ice cream machine and whirred a shake. Two white men sat at the counter and talked in low, serious tones, occasionally sucking up clots of shake through a straw.

There was one waitress, hip propped against the side of the counter, wiping the countertop with a rag that had seen cleaner days. Without looking up she said, "Sorry. We don't serve colored people."

"Good," Doris said. "I don't eat them." She remembered Helen telling her that this was the line someone had used during a sit-in, and Doris was glad to have a chance to use it.

The waitress frowned, confused, but when she finally got it, she laughed. "Seriously, though," the waitress said, turning solemn, "I can't serve you."

The two men talking looked over at her and shook their heads. They began talking again, occasionally looking over at Doris to see if she'd left.

"What if I stay?"

The waitress looked to the man making the shake, eyes pleading for help. "I don't know. I don't know. I just don't make the rules and I feel sorry for you, but I don't make 'em."

The man walked over with a shake and gave it to the waitress, who bent the straw toward herself and began to drink it. "Look," the man said to Doris, "I wouldn't sit here. I wouldn't do that."

"You wouldn't?"

"I wouldn't if I were you."

She sat. Shaking, she brought out her World History book. She'd made a book cover for it with a paper bag, and she was glad she'd done it because she was sweating so much it would have slipped from her hands otherwise. She set it on the counter, opened it, as if she did this every day at this very shop, and tried to read about the Hapsburgs, but couldn't.

It occurred to her that other students who did sit-ins were all smarter than she; they'd banded together, and had surely told others of their whereabouts, whereas she had foolishly come to Clovee's all by herself. She stared at her book and didn't dare look up, but from the corner of her eye she noticed when the two white men who'd been talking got up and left.

The man at the ice cream machine made himself some coffee and beckoned the waitress to him. When he whispered something to her, she swatted him with the rag, laughing.

Once Doris felt the numbness settle in her, she felt she could do it. She tried at the Hapsburgs again.

The waitress said, "Student? High school?"

"Yes, ma'am. Central."

"My daughter's over at Iroquois."

"We played them last Friday." Doris didn't know what the scores were, didn't care, but had heard about the game over the intercom.

"Well." The waitress started wiping the counter again, going over the same spots.

When Doris closed her book, about to leave, she said, "I just want you to know I'm leaving now. Not because you're making me or because I feel intimidated or anything. I just have to get home now."

The waitress looked at her.

"Next time I'll want some food, all right?"

"We can't do that, but here's half my shake. You can have it. I'm done."

The shake she handed over had a lipstick ring around the straw, and a little spittle. Doris knew she wouldn't drink it, but she took it anyway. "Thanks, ma'am."

OUTSIDE Clovee's Five and Dime, the world was cold around her, moving toward dark, but not dark yet, as if the darkness were being adjusted with a volume dial. Whoever was adjusting the dial was doing it slowly, consistently, with infinite patience. She walked back home and knew it would be too late for dinner, and the boys would be screaming and her father wanting his daily beer, and her mother worried sick. She knew that she should hurry, but she couldn't. She had to stop and look. The sky had just turned her favorite shade of barely lit blue, the kind that came to windows when you couldn't get back to sleep but couldn't quite pry yourself awake.